Carolyn G. Hart

Design for Murder

WHEELER
PUBLISHING, INC.
ROCKLAND, MA

★ AN AMERICAN COMPANY ★

Published in Large Print by arrangement with The Bantam Dell
Publishing Group, a division of Random House, Inc., in the United States
and Canada

Wheeler Large Print Book Series.

Set in 16 pt Plantin.

Library of Congress Cataloging-in-Publication Data

Hart , Carolyn G.
    Design for murder / Carolyn G. Hart.
        p. (large print) cm.(Wheeler large print book series)
    ISBN 1-58724-112-9 (softcover)
    1. Darling, Annie Laurance (Fictitious character)—Fiction. 2. Darling,
Max (Fictitious character)—Fiction. 3. Booksellers and bookselling—
Fiction. 4. Women detectives—Fiction. 5. South Carolina—Fiction.
6. Large type books. I. Title. II. Series

[PS3558.A676 D47   2001]
813'.54—dc21
                                                          2001040845
                                                                CIP

For Phil, Philip, and Sarah,
with all my love

1

THE TYPIST NODDED.

It was finished, as neat a design for murder as could be envisioned. Murder with malice. To be enjoyed by a select group. Well, wasn't it deserved?

For an instant, the writer hesitated. Was public humiliation deserved? There was no question as to the answer. And perhaps the effect would be to break the pattern of silken domination, to end the ruthless manipulation masked by charm.

A gloved hand gently loosened the last sheet from the typewriter. It was an agreeable irony that the plan should be typed on the old machine that sat in the corner of the director's office of the Chastain Historical Preservation Society. Should these pages ever be linked to this particular typewriter, it would reveal only that the manuscript had been produced on a machine easily accessible to the cream of Chastain's social hierarchy.

When the pages were neatly folded and placed in the waiting envelope, the writer read the cover letter again, then painstakingly traced a signature. It took only a moment to slip the letter inside and seal the envelope. Everything was in readiness. As soon as the mystery expert was officially hired, the letter could be mailed.

The writer looked up at a wall calendar which pictured the Prichard House, one of Chastain's oldest and loveliest antebellum mansions. A crimson circle marked April 7.

2

IDELL GORDON TUGGED restlessly at her sheets. She should have gone to the dentist. Well, too late now. The upper-right back molar throbbed. She kept her eyes squeezed shut, hoping for the blessed release of sleep. But sleep wouldn't come. Finally, wearily, she struggled upright and levered her ungainly body to the edge of the bed, peering at the luminous dial on the bedstand. Almost three o'clock. Swinging her legs over the side, she slipped into her scuffed pink satin houseshoes. Oh, her jaw, her jaw. She padded across the room to her bath and reached up for the brown plastic vial of Valium tablets. One of them might help her sleep. She filled a bathroom cup with water and swallowed the tiny pill, then suppressed a groan. It would take a while for the drug to help. She almost walked to her easy chair, but she knew she would feel better if she kept moving. She crossed the room, dodging the potted plants and the rocking chair and the rickety maple whatnot, and opened the French window to step out onto the second-floor balcony. The soft night air swept over her, soothing and calming. It was almost warm enough to walk out in her nightdress, though it was only mid-March, but she grabbed up a shawl that she'd thrown over her rocking chair earlier that evening. The moonlight speckled the grounds below, hiding the burgeoning weeds in the beds along this side of the Inn. She sighed. Her back always hurt when she hoed, but she couldn't afford to hire a gardener this spring. Occupancy of the Inn had been down, and it was going to be touch and go on the bills. A little flicker of panic moved in her chest. What was she going to do if the Inn failed? It would be jammed for the house-and-garden tours in April, but that wouldn't make up for empty rooms later in the summer. She paced up and down on the balcony, gingerly holding her jaw and trying not to whimper, and careful, too, to step quietly so as not to arouse any of the sleeping guests. Then, sharp and harsh as a peacock's cry, the gate to the grounds of the Historical Preservation Society squeaked open. Idell recognized the sound at once. She'd known it for years, the sound of the gate that marked the boundary between her Inn and the Society grounds. But why would the gate be opening? And at this hour? She bent to peer over the railing. How curious! How strange! She would have to ask—fiery hot pain lanced her jaw. She gave a soft moan and turned to go back inside.

3

CORINNE PRICHARD WEBSTER stood in front of the ormolu-framed mirror. Despite the dusky, aged glass, her reflection glistened as brightly as crystal. She always enjoyed her morning encounter with her own image. Beauty was her handmaiden and had always been so. She felt confident that to men she represented the unattainable goal of perfection. Once, when she'd asked Tim if he'd like to paint her, he had been silent for a long time, then he'd said, even if grudgingly, "You're like the first streak of rose at sunrise." Tim was almost as poetic as he was artistic. It sickened her to realize that he'd been beguiled by Sybil, who was no better than a slut for all the glory of her old name and her wealth. Well, they needn't think she would let Tim take his paintings from the museum. After all she'd done for him, he must realize that it was his duty to stay in Chastain. Her mouth thinned with determination, then curved in a humorless smile. They thought it was settled, but he couldn't very well have a show in New York without any paintings—and the paintings belonged to the Prichard Museum.

She lifted a slender white hand to touch the

tightness between her eyes, and the tiny wrinkles disappeared. She stared at her face appraisingly. Her eyes were still as vividly blue as always, her skin as smooth and soft as a young girl's. She felt a flash of satisfaction. She did so despise women who let themselves go. Lucy's face popped into her thoughts. Skin like leather from too many hours in her wretched garden and no more imagination in fashion than one might expect from a librarian. Boring, that was how Lucy dressed, although she could look quite nice when she chose. On Sundays, for example, she always wore a well-cut silk dress and a hat and gloves. Corinne shook her head. Hat and gloves. Almost no one wore them nowadays—except Lucy. It certainly dated her. Corinne looked at her reflection in continuing satisfaction. No one could say that about her. She was always *au courant,* and no one thought she was as old as Lucy, either. It was certainly a good thing she'd been firm years ago. It wouldn't have done for Cameron to marry Lucy and make her a Prichard, not a girl whose father ran a clothing store. The Prichards had never been small shop-keepers. The Prichards owned plantations and, long ago, sailing ships and warehouses.

Her eyes narrowed, and she no longer looked at her reflection so she didn't see the transformation. At one instant, the mirrored face was soft and beguiling, almost as beautiful with its classic bones, silver-blonde hair, and Mediterranean blue eyes as on her wedding day at nineteen almost forty years before.

Then, as Corinne Prichard Webster thought about her niece, Gail, and the manner in which she was behaving, throwing herself at a totally unsuitable man, the face hardened and looked all of its fifty-nine years, the eyes cold and hard, the mouth thin, determined, and cruel.

The phone rang.

Corinne didn't move to answer it, but she looked across her bedroom, past the silken canopied bed and the Queen Anne dresser to the compass rose desk which sat in an alcove, the blue velvet curtains unopened yet to the morning. The white and gold telephone, a French reproduction, rang again. Corinne waited, certain she knew the caller.

A gentle knock sounded at her bedroom door, then Marybelle stepped inside.

"The call is for you, ma'am. Mr. Roscoe Merrill."

Corinne nodded. "I will answer it, Marybelle."

As the maid softly closed the heavy door, Corinne moved to the telephone. Picking up the receiver, she lifted her chin. If Roscoe Merrill had been in the room, he would have recognized that stance. It was Corinne at her most imperious.

"Yes, Roscoe." She listened, then said impatiently, "The private man reveals the public man." He spoke again, but Corinne was shaking her head. She interrupted sharply, "It won't do any good for you to take that tone with me. I will do what I feel is right. You should have considered the consequences of your actions. I certainly feel that Jessica has every right to know." At his angry response, she depressed the cradle. Her face was implacable as she replaced the receiver.

The green and pink porcelain clock on the mantel delicately chimed the quarter hour. Vexed, Corinne shook her head. She was running late this morning, and there was much she had to do. There was that matter of the clinic and John Sanford's foolish plan to expand it. That would draw more country people into Chastain, overburdening the hospital with the kind of people who couldn't pay. John must be made to see that he was out of line. Corinne yanked on the bell pull. She would have time for Marybelle to draw her bath, then she must hurry. So many things to attend to. That silly mystery program, for one. She felt a surge of irritation. Such a cheap idea. For once she agreed with Dora, but it had been obvious that the Board was going to approve Roscoe's stupid proposal. She'd voted yes, even though she was seething inside. After all, she couldn't let it appear that the Board was taking such a major step without her approval. At least, as president, she'd retained control of hiring the mystery expert. That was another reason to make Roscoe pay for his actions, which she certainly intended to do. There was a proper way to act and an improper way. That reminded her of Gail. She would talk to Gail without delay. Corinne sighed, overburdened. There were so many demands on her time and energy. Then she straightened and looked toward the dusky mirror, her face again soft and unlined. After all, she was Corinne Prichard Webster. People depended upon her, so many of them. What would they do without her?

4

"I WANT ALL OF them. Every last one of them."

The penetrating voice grated on Annie Laurence's ear drum. Her hand tightened on the receiver, but she kept her reply light and cheerful. Think of it this way, she lectured herself, every demand by Mrs. Brawley translated into a cordial hum on the cash register.

"I don't believe they've all been reprinted yet. But I'll be glad to order them as they're scheduled."

"Hildegarde Withers is *wonderful*! It's a crime they've been out of print all these years." The tone was accusing.

Annie didn't quite see it as a capital offense, but she murmured agreement. "Don't worry, Mrs. Brawley, I'll order them for you. And, if you like, I can round up all the Stuart Palmer titles second-hand—"

"I want *new* books."

"Oh, certainly. By all means. Now, I have your number. I'll let you know as soon as the first title arrives."

It took several seconds more to end the conversation. Mrs. Brawley's singleminded pursuit of a goal ranked high on any all-time list, neck-and-neck with Carrie Nation, Johnny Appleseed, and Zsa Zsa Gabor.

Once free of the phone, Annie returned to a jollier pastime, reading mystery reviews in *Publishers Weekly*. The latest Robert Barnard sounded marvelous. And there was a new book by Sister Carol Anne O'Marie. She would—

The front doorbell sang. Annie dropped the magazine on the wicker table, pushed up from her favorite rattan easy chair, the one with the softest red and yellow cushions, brushed by a flourishing Whitmani fern, and stepped into the broad central corridor of Death on Demand. She hurried past the angled gum shelving with the various mystery categories toward the front desk and the rather stunning woman who was surveying the interior of the bookstore as if it were a Peruvian slum.

Annie's smile tightened. You don't have to *like* customers, she reminded herself, although, as a general rule, she did. Mystery readers, as a class, were bright, well-informed, and articulate. This well-preserved blonde was a stranger to her. Maybe she'd just moved to Broward's Rock. She certainly looked prosperous enough to afford the island's casual but expensive lifestyle. Annie swiftly appraised the elegant cream suede suit, the crimson silk tie, the brown alligator pumps and handbag, and a wedding ring that glittered like the Waldorf chandelier.

"Good morning. May I help you?"

Deeply blue eyes flicked disdainfully from Edgar's sleek feathers to a splashily bright poster affixed to the True Crime section, which advertised the latest book on the luckless headmistress with the unfortunate love life. Carnelian lips thinned in disgust.

Annie could feel a rush of heat to the back of her neck. Steady, she thought, foreseeing lurid headlines. MYSTERY SHOP OWNER BLUDGEONS OBNOXIOUS CUSTOMER.

"I'm looking for a Miss Annie Laurance." The tone indicated the same eagerness that might be experienced upon searching for a boa constrictor.

"I'm Annie Laurance." And to hell with you, lady.

"Oh." Frosty eyes scanned her. The artfully darkened blonde brows drew down in a delicate frown. "You're very young."

Tempted to respond with a combative, "So?," Annie evinced exemplary restraint, and merely said again, a little more insistently, "May I help you?"

"I'm Corinne Prichard Webster."

Annie waited.

"From Chastain."

"Chastain. That's not far from Beaufort. I understand it's a lovely old town."

"You've never been to Chastain?" Incredulity lifted the well-modulated voice.

"Not yet," Annie admitted, her smile now unforced.

"Oh, well. I don't know what to say."

Annie was beginning to feel trapped in a surrealistic conversation. It was time to hack her way out of this encounter. Maybe this expensive blonde was a nut. "Are you looking for a particular book?"

"A book. A mystery? Oh, heavens, no. I don't read them." Her moral superiority was clearly established.

"This is a mystery bookstore."

"Yes, I know. I'm here on behalf of the Chastain Historical Preservation Society. One of our Board members, Roscoe Merrill, recommended you."

Merrill. Merrill. Then she remembered him, a stocky lawyer with a shiny bald head and humorless brown eyes. But he liked Rumpole, so there had to be a spark of humanity beneath that pinstriped exterior. What on earth, she wondered, had Merrill recommended her for?

Mrs. Webster didn't seem cheered by the recommendation. "Are you familiar with the annual house-and-garden tours in Chastain?" She looked at Annie doubtfully.

Recalling the chaste gray and pink poster she'd seen in the hallway of the Broward's Rock Public Library, Annie nodded.

"It has been suggested—" The smooth voice thinned just a trifle, and Annie detected a ripple of irritation. "The Board decided that we could enhance the success of our annual house-and-garden tours if we offered a further enticement." She enunciated each word as if she were sucking a lemon.

The Board of the Chastain Historical Preservation Society must be hard up for support if it'd sent an emissary all the way to an off-lying island. Annie was looking forward to an unctuous refusal to harbor promotional material, something on the lines of, "This is a mystery bookstore, and we only offer information of interest to mystery readers," when the magic words "some kind of mystery program" registered.

"Mystery program?"

"Yes. Now, of course, if you don't feel that you can handle an assignment of this nature, it would be understandable. After all, you certainly are very young, and there isn't much time to develop it. We would need to have the scripts, if that's how it's done, by next Thursday. If you feel the time is insufficient, I will explain to the Board and perhaps another year—"

"Mystery program?" A happy surge of adrenaline tingled from her ears to her toes. "You mean, figure out the plot and create the clues and run the whole thing? Oh, God, I'd kill to do it!"

When the door finally closed behind Corinne Webster's trim figure, Annie unclenched her hands and felt the tightness ease from her neck and shoulders. What a poisonous creature! A Gila monster would have a certain charm in comparison. But the chance to run her very own mystery nights program was too exciting to lose, so she'd ignored the Board president's clear distaste for the entire idea. Something funny there. Obviously, the little tyrant had been maneuvered into approving the Mystery Nights. Be interesting to meet the other Board members. Well, she'd have her chance on Thursday when she presented them with her wonderful Mystery Nights program. And she could thank Roscoe Merrill for suggesting her for the job. Annie felt utterly confident that she would indeed create a super-duper mystery. How could she miss? She'd read every mystery from *Les Miserables* to *Death From a Top Hat*. Her mind teemed with ideas—a mannequin which turns into a body, babies switched at birth, letters hidden in the attic. Grinning, she reached for the phone and called Ingrid to see if she could work full-time for the next few weeks. Then, she hurried down the aisle to make a fresh pot of Kona coffee. The better to think with.

Ingrid arrived before the brew was finished. Annie filled mugs for both of them, and Ingrid settled in behind the front desk, emitting enthusiastic coos as Annie described her new project.

"The House-and-Garden tours start Monday, April 7. I'm going to put on a mystery program the first four nights, and end up with a Denouement Ball on Friday night. And they're going to pay me $1,000!"

Ingrid applauded.

Delighted with herself and the prospect, Annie freshened her mug and wandered happily among the shelves. There were so many *interesting* ways to commit murder. Douglas Clark used castor-oil beans in *Premedicated*

Murder. V. C. Clinton-Baddeley took honors for originality when he created a poison of ant's brew in *Death's Bright Dart.* H. F. Heard opted for a swarm of deadly bees in *A Taste of Honey,* and Elspeth Huxley aimed a poison-tipped stick in *The African Poison Murders.*

And think of the fascinating variety among victims: a charming, likable woman with good intentions in Dorothy Simpson's *Last Seen Alive,* the narcissistic coed in Jane Langton's *Emily Dickinson Is Dead,* an arrogant braggart who made the fatal mistake of collecting killers in Agatha Christie's *Cards on the Table,* a woman who married too many times in Raymond Chandler's *The Long Goodbye,* and the socially impeccable Cogswells in Virginia Rich's *The Baked Bean Supper Murders.*

Where to begin? With victim or detective? Margaret Truman recommends starting with the victim, and Robert B. Parker insists the point of mystery fiction is the detective, not detection.

Should her mystery take advantage of its setting in one of South Carolina's oldest coastal towns, as Leslie Ford milked the atmosphere for every last drop of Spanish moss in *Murder with Southern Hospitality*? Or should she appeal to the mystery addict's interest in faraway places, as Mary Stewart did in *My Brother Michael* and James McClure in *The Steam Pig*?

She bent to straighten the row of Ruth Rendell titles. Now those kinds of stories wouldn't do at all for this genteel group. No,

better something more on the order of Mary
Roberts Rinehart or Louisa Revell. Or perhaps—The bell above the door rang. She
stepped into the central aisle, looked toward
the front, and saw Max peering at her determinedly from the doorway. Ingrid beamed at
Max, then shot her a shamefaced glance.
Ingrid was the most wonderful employee in
this or any other bookstore, but she was
clearly on his side now.

The newcomer grinned at Ingrid, but his
eyes were on Annie.

She waved her hand at him. "Come on in.
The floor isn't mined." He was obviously
girding for battle, still confident that he
would prevail. Dammit, she loved him, the silly
ass, but she wasn't going to be swayed.

He still stood, half in and half out of Death
on Demand, and she thought about Calvin
Gates's first encounter with Mr. Moto in
Mr. Moto Is So Sorry, the two at cross purposes,
Calvin tenaciously pursuing his destiny, and
Mr. Moto intent upon his own ends. Even the
enormous stuffed raven beside the door
seemed to be looking at Max sympatheti-
cally. Was everybody, dead birds included, on
Max's side? And Agatha, of course, was
moving languidly toward him. Where was
her sense of loyalty? Didn't she know who her
mistress was? But the small, silky-furred
black cat was already twined gracefully around
his leg. Absently, he reached down to pet
her, then cleared his throat decisively.

She hurried to forestall him. She wasn't up
to another discussion today. Besides, even

though they were at odds, Max would be delighted at her good fortune.

"Guess what? I get to plan my own murders. For money! And I can't decide between cyanide or electrocution or maybe defenestration. But don't you think cyanide in champagne has a lovely ring?"

"In a glass or bottle?" he inquired mildly. He finally came all the way inside. Ingrid patted his arm as he passed her and was rewarded with his sexy grin. Annie struggled to concentrate on her immediate task, but she felt the old familiar thrill, the unmistakable tingly delight at his presence. He looked freshly scrubbed, as if he'd just stepped from a shower and into his crisp white shirt and gray poplin slacks. Was there a hint of dampness in his thick blond hair? For a moment, she thought about Max in his shower, the water slapping against his tanned, muscled chest, then she firmly brought her mind to heel.

"What's the difference?"

"Cyanide in a bottle, if mixed in a punch, could fell hundreds. Are you and Ingrid planning a reception for the store?"

"I prefer to entertain my customers, not kill them," she retorted. She glanced around. Actually, the increase in customers at Death on Demand this spring had been phenomenal— and she didn't believe it had anything to do with her notoriety as half of the team which solved the first murders in modern times on Broward's Rock. At least not much. They came because they wanted to see the shop.

Some wanted books. After all, she carried the best selection of mystery and suspense novels this side of Atlanta. Some were readers who relished matching the painted scenes on the back wall to favorite books. Local artists vied for the right to paint new scenes every month, and the contest successfully lured patrons in month after month. And, of course, all the area mystery writers liked to come, too, though they'd been a little slow to return after last fall's excitement. Hopefully, everyone was starting to forget about the murder in the shop.

"I guess I'd better put the cyanide in a glass."

He moved so close she had trouble concentrating on her topic.

Casually, she stepped back a pace, then realized she was wedged between Max and the romantic suspense section.

"Whose? Anybody I know? I thought I was the only person you were mad at right now." He managed to look both injured and appealing. Dammit, why did he have to remind her of a Brittany spaniel? What was there about Max that she found so irresistible? Well, she was going to avoid any further discussion of their dilemma, no matter how pathetic he managed to look. It was a pose, of course. He was a bullheaded, insensitive, money-flaunting brute.

"Come on and have some coffee," she said brusquely, wriggling past him into the aisle and leading the way to the back of the shop. Behind the coffee bar, several hundred white mugs sat on shelving. Each mug carried the name of a book which had earned recognition as an all-time great in mystery fiction. She poured Max a fresh cup and refilled hers. Max lifted his mug and sniffed it suspiciously.

"What's wrong?" she asked.

"Just making sure the cyanide hasn't popped from the champagne to the coffee."

She laughed. "I'm not that mad at you. I'm thinking about cyanide for the Chastain Mystery Nights." She described Mrs. Webster's visit. "Although it's going to be a royal pain to work with Her Highness."

Max took time to see which famous mystery title was written in red script on his white mug *(The Lone Wolf)*. He raised an eyebrow quizzically.

She hastened to reassure him. "Nothing profound is intended. My mugs are not fortune cookies." And she waggled her own, which carried the legend, *The Beast Must Die*.

He lounged comfortably against the bar, drank some coffee, and sighed.

It was wonderful the way good coffee could improve his disposition. She must remember that for future mornings together—if those mornings ever materialized. The prospect didn't look so good at the moment.

"So you're being unleashed to develop a murder program. Do they have any realization they may have uncapped a bloodthirsty genie from a bottle?"

She felt a surge of relief. She had successfully deflected him from the purpose of his visit. With luck, she could keep the conversation on cyanide and murder and away from the dangerous topic of September.

She put her mug on the yellow formica top of the coffee bar and smiled at him rapturously. "It's going to be so much fun. Max, do you want to help?" she asked eagerly. "No kidding. We can do it together." She ignored the quick gleam in his eye. "I mean, like Frances and Richard Lockridge. Or the Gordons. Or Per Wahloo and Maj Sjowall." She bent over the bar, fished out a notebook and flipped it open, then scrounged vainly in the pocket of her white slacks for a pen. Max obligingly handed her one. "Look, what do you think? Should we do a locked-room mystery like John Dickson Carr's *The Hollow Man* or Clayton Rawson's *The Footprints On the Ceiling*? Maybe we should consider psychological suspense like Helen McCloy's *The Slayer and the Slain* or Charlotte Armstrong's *Mischief.* Or an academic murder, like Amanda Cross's *Death in a Tenured Position* or Gwendolyn Butler's *Coffin in Oxford.* And there're always sporting murders. Let's see, it was archery in *Death at St. Asprey's School* by Leo Bruce, bullfighting in *Puzzle for Pilgrims* by Patrick Quentin, running in *Dead Heat* by Linda Barnes, basketball in *The Giant Kill* by Kin Platt, golf in—"

"Annie. Annie. ANNIE!"

She paused, images still flashing in her brain like neon on a rainy Saturday night.

"Quiet now. Take a deep breath."

Obediently, she breathed. Then she shook her head impatiently. "I'm not choking."

"I thought you were hyperventilating. Take it easy. Approach it logically." His voice was low, deep, soothing, and extraordinarily irritating.

"I am fine, thank you. It's just that there are so many wonderful possibilities—"

Max was trying hard not to laugh. He set his mug down and reached out to ruffle her hair. "Annie, love, I do enjoy you so."

She looked at him skeptically. "Are you making fun of me?"

"I'd never do that," he said virtuously, but the corner of his mouth twitched suspiciously.

They both laughed, and she realized this was the happiest she'd been in weeks, immersed in mysteries and laughing companionably with Max. Agatha leaped gracefully up to the bar to join in the merriment. Annie stroked her and felt ridiculously happy. It was almost as if she and Max hadn't quarreled. Well, it wasn't exactly a quarrel. But it was a disagreement. In spades. This moment forcibly reminded her in what direction happiness lay. But she had to retain her independence.

Oblivious to her unspoken soliloquy, Max reached for the notebook and took his pen.

"Okay. First things first. Who will play the role of the suspects?"

She understood at once. "Oh, sure. That limits some of the possibilities." Her mind ran over and discarded murder in the Himalayas, on a submarine, or while deep-sea fishing. "The roles will be played by members of the Historical Preservation Society."

He quirked an expressive eyebrow. "If they are anything like the women in my grandmother's bridge club..."

"Allowing for cultural distinctions between Connecticut and South Carolina, I would imagine they are soulmates."

Devilment glinting in his dark blue eyes, Max leaned forward. "Hey, I've got a great idea. Make the victim a Hollywood producer in 1926 and have the suspects be a bunch of young starlets. Oh wow, can you see these old ladies in vamp clothes and beads and bangles..." He melted in laughter.

She laughed, too, then mused, "Actually, I can see casting that horrid Mrs. Webster as an aging star, who everybody hates. Maybe an old folks' home for retired actors and actresses, and she has a chance for a big role, and all the other old-lady stars are jealous and one of them spikes her bedtime toddy with cyanide."

He shook his head, half in awe, half in despair. "You do have a fertile mind, love, but let's skirt any possibility of slander. Your Mrs. Webster probably wouldn't like that role at all."

His caution surprised her. Max could act like a lawyer most unexpectedly. But how marvelous that he wasn't predictable. Now, what was she doing mooning on about Max? The mystery was the thing.

"She's not my Mrs. Webster. But, you're probably right. I'd better not use her as the victim." Absently, her face scrunched in thought, she stood on tiptoe and stretched.

Her mind worked better when her muscles were loose. "Okay, we're going to build a story that centers around upper-class, middle-aged suspects."

He poised the pen over the notebook. "How do we go about it?"

"Just like Agatha Christie did. We *think*." She ran her hand excitedly through her short blonde hair. "Did I ever tell you my favorite Christie story?" She charged ahead: "One day when walking in her garden with a friend, Christie abruptly announced her book was finished. This excited her companion, who had always wanted to read one of Agatha's books before it was published. The friend asked for permission to read the manuscript. Dame Agatha looked very surprised, then responded, 'Oh, I haven't *written* it yet.'"

"Oh, that's great."

"So we have to do the same. We have to figure everything out." Her eyes narrowed in concentration.

He tapped the paper with the pen. "How do we do it?"

"Here's what we need," she explained confidently. "Victim. Five suspects. Motives. Alibis. Clues." She traced the outline of the title on her cup. "I mean *real* clues, like half of a torn letter, a smudged postmark, cigarette butts, a box of insecticide. I'll scatter clues around the crime scene for the detectives to find."

"Who's the victim?" He scratched at his thick blonde hair with the stub end of the pen.

She pressed her fingers against her temples

for a long moment, then nodded. "How about a bank president? Think of the lust, greed, and general hatred that can swirl around a bank president." She pictured Roscoe Merrill's shiny bald head. Any prosperous lawyer could look like a bank president.

"Dark secrets in the hallways of high finance," Max intoned.

"We'll call the bank president Thompson Hatfield—and we'll use Kansas as a setting. Agricultural banks are nosediving all over the place in the Middle West. Now, here's what happens," and she leaned close to Max. They were elbow to elbow as he wrote furiously to keep up with her bullet-fast pronouncements. "Motives *abound*. His wife's in love with another man, he's about to foreclose on a huge ranch run by his brother-in-law, his stepson's been embezzling, the vice president of the bank wants his job, he's going to fire the PR director, and he's the only man who won't agree to merging with another town bank to save it from going under."

"And somebody slips cyanide into his coffee thermos," Max suggested. "See, there's your cyanide."

Clues to be found at the murder scene: The name of his wife's lover written in his appointment book, the torn foreclosure notice for his brother-in-law's ranch, a key chain belonging to the vice president who wants his job, a gun registered in the name of the PR director, a Stetson hat that belongs to the president of the rival, failing bank, and a strand of hair belonging to his wife. (She is a redhead.)

23

"Well, now that that's settled," Max began, and once again he had that determined, bull-headed *September* look in his dark blue eyes.

She threw herself into the breach. "Oh, no, we've just started. We have to figure out the information to give to the suspects."

The phone rang at the front desk, but Annie knew Ingrid would answer it.

"Let's see, we'd better draw up a timetable, then we'll decide who was where and—"

"Max," Ingrid's voice warbled cheerfully. "It's for you."

He reached for the extension behind the coffee bar. "Hi, Barbie. Sure, I'm free. I'll be right back." He hung up and whistled. "Barbie said this guy's waiting to see me, and he's talking a thousand-dollar retainer."

Annie was tickled. Max actually sounded interested. It wouldn't be the money, of course, but the chance to have a job. Perhaps he was reforming. Max excited at the prospect of work!

He paused at the front door and called back meaningfully, "I'll be back in a little while. We've got to talk."

She stood by the coffee bar, her arms folded. Ingrid, her springy gray hair in tight curls from a new permanent, bobbed down the center aisle like a curious but ladylike bird. She had decided opinions on Annie and Max's disagreement, but she practiced her own brand of tact. After she poured both Annie and herself fresh coffee, she said, "Sounded like you were having fun for a while."

"Yeah." She refused to meet Ingrid's eyes.

Ingrid gently touched her arm and once again backed into her subject. "You know the old saying about pride. Well, pride is a mighty cold bedfellow. And people, if you hurt them too much, you can lose their friendship. And that would be a shame."

Annie felt a sick ache in her heart. Lose Max? It seemed such a small thing, really, to want to plan the wedding her own way. A simple, small ceremony here on the island, paid for by her. But Max was obstinately insisting on a magnificent, grandiose, *immense* wedding in his hometown, at his expense.

She took a gulp of the hot coffee. "I'd better see if that delivery's come," and she carried her coffee mug past the scattered tables to the storeroom.

"Call me if you need any help," Ingrid offered, before turning up the central aisle to the cash desk. Annie knew she was offering more than assistance with unloading boxes, and she was torn between affection and irritation. Darn it, did *everybody* think Max was right—except her? She put her coffee on the worktable and attacked the unopened carton of used books, bought from a collector in California. Wrestling the box open, she started pulling out the wads of crumpled newspaper. The top volume, well-wrapped in plastic, was an autographed first-edition copy of *The Thirty-Nine Steps.* It was a wonderful find, but she didn't enjoy the usual flip-flop of pleasure. Instead, she slapped the cardboard carton shut, retrieved her coffee mug, and wandered back out into the bookstore. She'd not thought in terms of *losing* Max. Why, any fool could see how much fun they had together.

Even the excitement of working on the upcoming Mystery Nights waned as she considered Ingrid's unsettling but well-meant warning. Restlessly, she paced into the American Cozy area, full of rattan chairs, wicker tables, and tangly ferns in raffia baskets. But the mingled smell of recently watered greenery and both musty and new books lacked its usual charm. Absently she noticed that Agatha had been chewing again on the fern closest to the Christie shelves. On a normal day, she would steal a half hour at least to look at her newest acquisitions, and perhaps succumb to the temptation to forget all duties, pressing or otherwise, and just curl up with one. Only yesterday she'd received a mystery she'd been seeking for years, Sax Rohmer's *Fire-Tongue*. This was the famous book that he started without a solution, couldn't solve himself, and finally had to ask his friend Harry Houdini to solve for him.

But not today. *Fire-Tongue* could wait until she'd completed the Mystery Night scripts—and stopped brooding about Max.

Come on, Annie, she instructed herself sternly, don't be a gothic wimp. Everything would be all right with Max. She felt a flood of good cheer, with just a faint undercurrent of apprehension. Okay, she'd get back to work on her very own murder. Humming "Happy Days Are Here Again," she returned to the coffee bar, put down her mug, and reached for the notebook. Now, what would

cast members need to know about their characters to portray them successfully? She
leaned against the bar and stared upward, and
her eyes paused on the watercolors pinned to
the back wall. By golly, these were a triumph.

In the first watercolor, a large, slope-shoul-
dered man in a gray suit knelt beside a long,
thin body in a black overcoat. The kneeling
figure, with the face of a blond Satan, gripped
a flaming cigarette lighter in his left hand. The
flame flickered close to an open, immobile eye.
His empty bloodstained right hand was raised.
A football-shaped parcel wrapped in brown
paper lay beside the body.

In the second picture, the strong-jawed,
brown-eyed private detective in a wet trench-
coat clutched his dripping hat in one hand and
looked impassively at the young, slim, naked
woman sitting stiffly, in the pose of an Egyptian
goddess, in a highbacked teakwood chair.
Her eyes were opened wide in a witless stare.
Her mouth was agape, her small, pointed
white teeth as shiny as porcelain. Long jade
earrings dangled from her delicate ears. A
corpse lay face up on the floor near a tripod
camera. He wore Chinese slippers, black
satin pajama pants, and his embroidered
Chinese coat seeped blood from three wounds.
Strips of Chinese embroidery and Chinese and
Japanese prints in wood-grained frames decorated the brown plaster walls of the low-
beamed room.

Annie's eyes narrowed thoughtfully. Maybe
they were too easy.

In the third sketch, a body lay sprawled on

the floor of a cabana overlooking surging ocean waters, a single crimson bullet wound in the head. A husky, dark-haired man with a scraped and bruised face and weary gray-blue eyes looked questioningly at his friend in the doorway and the .32 target pistol in his hand.

In the fourth painting, a yellow jeep with a front-end blade accelerated directly at the big, aging jock standing by an open pit in a subtropical pasture. Visible in the pit was the glossy, red-brown body of a dead horse. The driver of the jeep was shirtless, a mat of black hair on his tanned, muscular chest. He wore a white canvas cap and oval aviator's sunglasses. His quarry, crouched by the pit, ready to spring out of the jeep's charge, had light eyes and dark hair. He wore boat pants, sandals, and a faded white shirt. A vulture hovered overhead in the yellowish sky.

In the final painting, an athletic, savvy-looking man stood poised in the archway of the living room of an old apartment, a gun in his hand. Velveteen hangings covered the walls. Skulls flanked an altar. A naked girl, her body painted with cabalistic and astrological signs, was tied to a cross, which hung from the ceiling. The cult's almost naked priest, wearing only a hood, stood near the cross, brandishing a stubby stick.

The old-familiar thrills coursed through her. Mysteries, the stuff of life. She bent over the bar and began to write, as fast as her hand could fly. By golly, this was going to be a won-

28

derful mystery. And all her own. She whistled cheerfully as she worked. The Mystery Nights would be a smash and everything, of course, would ultimately come right between her and Max. He would see reason and agree to her plan for the wedding.

As Annie would later say, had she but known....

5

MAX HELD A FRESHLY sharpened No. 2 pencil between his index fingers, but he didn't write a word. The yellow legal pad lying in solitary splendor on his leather blotter was blank. Nor did he offer refreshments to his prospective client, though he knew good, strong coffee pilfered from Death on Demand steamed in his stainless steel Krups coffee thermos. Max felt neither receptive, sociable, nor agreeable. Max didn't like Harley Edward Jenkins III.

Harley Edward Jenkins III sat in the red leather chair as if he owned it, Max, and the island. Only the latter was partially true, since he did control forty percent of the stock in Halcyon Development Inc., the real estate investment holding company which had created the luxury homes and condominiums on Broward's Rock.

"So get on it today." Jenkins started to rise, which wasn't especially easy for someone of his bulk. He bulged, despite the deceptive embrace of an artfully tailored navy blue Oxford suit.

Max held up his hand. "Just a minute."

A frown creased Jenkins's porcine face, and he pursed his fat lips impatiently.

"I want to be certain I understand you."

Jenkins jerked his head in acknowledgment and balanced on the edge of the chair. Max thought he resembled a rhino in a hurry to get out on the savannah and gore some fresh meat.

"You're in a business deal," Max summed up. "You want to buy some land cheap. The guy who owns it is running around on his wife. You want me to follow him, get some choice pictures, and hand them over to you. Right?"

Jenkins wet his thick lips. "I don't quite like the way you put that, Darling. Let's say I merely wish to improve my position in negotiations, gain some leverage."

Max slapped the pencil crisply on his desk and leaned forward. "I've got some advice for you, Jenkins."

The businessman's red-veined face turned a mottled purple.

"Why don't you go after money the old-fashioned way, Jenkins? Why don't you *earn* it?"

He was grinning as the door to his office quivered on its hinges as Jenkins, livid with fury, slammed it shut.

He couldn't wait to tell Annie about this encounter, even if he did owe a little to Smith

Barney for his bon mot. He wished he'd had a camera to capture the shock on that sorry bastard's face.

Then he sighed. Dammit, he hadn't had a job for three weeks. Not that it mattered financially, of course. It's not as if he'd ever have trouble paying the rent. But Annie did like for him to be busy. That girl must have been frightened by a Puritan spirit in her cradle.

Actually, he felt that his office was an artistic creation able to stand on its own merit without any need for utilitarian justification. He looked around in satisfaction. The room was large. An elegant rose-and-cream Persian rug stretched in front of the Italian Renaissance desk. Annie's tart observation had been that the desk deserved at least a cardinal's red robe for its owner. Glass-covered bookcases, filled with statute books and annotated treatises, lined one wall, though he made it very clear to clients that he was not practicing law. In fact, clients were usually more than a little puzzled as to his exact role, which suited him fine, since he had decided upon reflection that he didn't care to be bothered to take either the South Carolina bar or to obtain a private investigator's license. In his view, it was cruel and unusual punishment to require anyone to take more than one bar exam. He had manfully (if that weren't sexist) passed the New York bar. As for a private investigator's license, the sovereign state of South Carolina required either two years of work in an existing licensed agency or two years as a law enforcement officer before one could be obtained. Hence, his office window bore the legend, CONFIDENTIAL COMMISSIONS.

As he had earnestly explained to a skeptical Annie, it was his aim to help his fellow man (or woman), and to that end he was willing to undertake any mission which was both legal and challenging. After all, he didn't have to be either a lawyer or a private detective to ask questions and solve problems. A discreet but inviting ad ran in the Personals Column of both the *Island Herald* and the *Chastain Courier:*

> *"Troubled, puzzled, curious? Whatever your problem, contact CONFIDENTIAL COMMISSIONS, 321-1321, 11 Seaview, Broward's Rock."*

At this very moment, however, he was glumly debating why he ever thought this was going to be fun. And the one thing he was absolutely, positively, without question convinced of was that anything in which he engaged be first and foremost fun.

That did not include skulking about with a camera in hopes of obtaining blackmail material. Still, he wished it had been a legitimate case.

He reached out and picked up a silver photograph frame from the corner of his massive desk. He held it up to the light, and Annie smiled at him.

Wonderful, marvelous Annie with her short

blonde hair streaked with gold, her serious, steady gray eyes, and her gentle, kissable mouth—the most exasperating, mule-headed, aggravating female he'd ever encountered. By God, didn't every woman want her wedding to be special? And wasn't that what he was offering? Hadn't his mother been at her most charming and least flamboyant when he and Annie visited her in Connecticut at Christmas? And Mother, with three superbly married daughters, had buckets of experience in planning weddings and would be delighted to help.

The trouble with Annie—one of the troubles with Annie, he corrected himself sourly—was her stiff-necked pride which confused money with independence. What he needed to do was to make it clear to her that money, when you had it, must never be master. The best way to keep money in line was to treat it as disposable and spend it. This theorem was Darling's Law of Finance, quite on a par and in happy contrast (at least in intent) to Veblen's Principle of Conspicuous Consumption. Veblen had no sense of humor. He took money very seriously indeed. As did Annie.

What to do about Annie?

Max folded himself comfortably into his well-padded, high-backed swivel chair, which could be tilted almost horizontal and contained a vibrator and heating element. He flipped two switches and relaxed as the chair lowered and began to purr. Propping his Cordovan loafers on the gleaming desk top, he regarded the portrait. Time for an end-around run. When opposition held the middle ground, the smart general foxed his way to an unprotected flank in the manner of Leonidas Witherall, the erudite sleuth created by Phoebe Atwood Taylor writing as Alice Tilton. He shook himself. There he went again. Obviously, he was beyond help. Annie's approach to life had infiltrated his mind.

Max thought cheerfully for a moment about unprotected flanks, then concentrated.

If he couldn't persuade Annie of the merits of a grand wedding, which were undeniable, then he must beguile her. How best to do that?

She could not be bribed, heaven forfend, but perhaps she could be inveigled. What could he do that would persuade Annie that he, Max, was the world's most wonderful man, and should, of course and as a matter of justice, be deferred to? He spent several delightful seconds imagining Annie in a posture of deference.

She loved surprises.

His eyes narrowed, his face furrowed in thought. Surprises—the shop—Agatha—

Raising the picture high, he let out a whoop. Of course! Why hadn't it occurred to him sooner? He flipped the chair's switch. Upright, he plopped the picture next to the phone, yanked up the receiver, and punched a button. "Barbie, dial international information, then get Sotheby's on the line."

The object of this deliberation was at that moment braking as she coasted onto the ferry. Hers was the first car aboard. Stumpy Ben Parotti waved to her from the cabin. As the ferry lurched away from the dock, Annie pulled on her cherry-red cable-knit cardigan and got out of her aging blue Volvo to stand next to the railing. The cool April air was perfumed with fish, saltwater, and tar. She breathed deeply. Broward's Rock was the best place in the world to live, an unspoiled island with civilization's amenities. Pity those poor deprived millions who called someplace else home. Leaning on the metal railing, she shaded her eyes from the noon sun and looked across the softly green waters of Port Royal Sound at the mainland, then fished a thin book from her pocket. The guidebook, which had been published by the Chastain Historical Preservation Society, contained a succinct but detailed history of Chastain, its most famous houses and people.

She smiled a little at the history's opening sentence:

Chastain was never the center of commerce and art that was Charleston or even the shipping haven that was Beaufort.

The writer apparently harbored a sense of inferiority. Had no one ever suggested accentuating the positive?

She continued reading:

Nor can Chastain rival Charleston (founded in 1670 at its earliest site) or Beaufort (founded in 1710) in age, but Chastain, first settled in 1730, proudly claims its place in the sun as the favorite coastal hideaway of South Carolina's lowland plantation owners, who sought its healthful breezes during the deadly fever months of May through October, and in so doing built and maintained some of the loveliest antebellum mansions extant. Chastainians then and now feel themselves blessed above all others in the gentility, beauty, and grace of their city, secure on its bluffs above the Broad River.

Chastain was first settled by Reginald Cantey Chastain, who received a grant from King George the year after the Province was returned to the King by the Lord Proprietors, Carolina's first rulers. Chastain's prosperity was great in these early years as she offered a safe port, stable government, and only occasional harassment from the Indians. During the Revolutionary War, when Charleston and the surrounding countryside suffered greatly, Chastain was little touched. What seemed great misfortune when the city fell to the British early in the war turned out to be her greatest fortune, as she was spared fighting and destruction. Indeed, Chastain was apparently favored by Heaven. During the War Between the States, she was early occupied by Federal troops, and therefore escaped the horror of Sherman's torch, although her loyal sons and daughters found it painful to endure the sequestering of their enemies within their homes. However, this indignity was ultimately to preserve for the glory of the present the grandeur of yesterday. Some of the oldest homes in South Carolina survive in Chastain, including the famed Prichard, Chastain, McIlwain and Benton houses.

The horn alongside the cabin gave three toots, Parotti's signal that landfall neared.

Slipping behind the wheel, she dropped the guidebook on the seat. Sea gulls moved in a rush of wings from their pilings as the ferry thumped against the buffering rubber tires, and Parotti lowered the ramp. First on was first off, so she quickly put the Volvo in gear and bumped onto the dock, then negotiated the ruts in the lane for a half mile and turned right onto the blacktop. A weathered sign announced: *Chastain 13 miles.*

She drove with the window down, enjoying the clear, fresh air with its underlying sourness of marsh and bay water leavened by fragrant Carolina jessamine and pine resin. The greening marsh grass announced the coming of spring. Pale green duckweed scummed the roadside waters, and fiddler crabs swarmed over the mudbanks. Tall sea pines crowded the shoulders of the road. Pine pollen coated the road and the shoulders and everything else in the lowlands with a fine lemony dusting from the yellow-purple spring flowers. As she neared Chastain, a stand of enormous live oaks screened a plantation home from view. Only glimpses of tall red-brick chimneys revealed its presence. Delicate swaths of Spanish moss hung from the low, spreading limbs.

Her first view of Chastain was unprepossessing, a fast-food hamburger joint, three derelict wooden houses, a jumble of trailer homes. She judged these with a jaundiced West Texas eye—one good wind would level them flatter than squashed pop cans. By the second

Kentucky Fried Chicken, she spotted a plaque announcing the Chastain Historical Area, with an arrow to the right. Stuck behind a smoke-belching chicken truck, she chafed at the slowness of the traffic and kept a wary eye peeled for the eccentric driving common to small towns (mid-block stops, unheralded turns, and blithe disregard for stop signs).

She turned on Mead Drive, followed it to Montgomery, found another plaque and finally reached Ephraim Street, which ran along the high bluff. A half dozen lovely old homes sat on large lots to her left. The river, sparkling like beaten Mexican silver, slipped seaward to her right.

She drove to the end of Ephraim Street and parked in a neat graveled lot on the point, appropriately named Lookout Point. She locked the car, being sure to scoop up the guidebook with its map of the historic homes, her camera, and an extra roll of film. She paused to admire a flock of stately brown pelicans diving toward the river and a luncheon snack of mullet, then turned to survey the street. Just opposite rose a squat, buff-colored, square building which housed the Chastain Historical Preservation Society. From her guidebook, Annie knew the building was originally a tabby fort built in 1790 when the country raged to join with the French against England and other European powers as the French battled to protect their Revolution. However, Jacobism languished when the French Revolution banished Lafayette. She imagined for a moment the bustle and effort that had resulted in the fort, the grounds churned by wagon wheels, and the smell of lime and crushed, burned oyster shell hanging in the air. Now a smooth carpet of grass lapped against flowing banks of brilliantly red and yellow azaleas. A brick wall separated the Society grounds from Swamp Fox Inn, which boasted that Lafayette had slept there during his triumphal tour of the South in 1825, an old man remembering the glories of his youth, still tall, lame in one foot, but with electric, crackling black eyes and a gentleman's charm of manner. The three-story frame Inn was an amalgamation of additions. Its center had been built in 1789.

She studied it with interest. Mrs. Webster had explained that the Inn was providing a room for the mystery expert in return for promotional mention in the House and Garden Week brochures. Annie had called that morning to reserve an adjoining room for Max, her helper, as she explained to the innkeeper. She sighed as she noted the paint peeling from the second and third story pillars, the untrimmed live oak trees, which threatened to poke holes in the weathered exterior, and the unkempt stretch of lawn visible through the sagging wooden fence.

Although nice surprises certainly could arrive in plain packages, it was her experience that poorly maintained motels, hotels, and inns featured hard beds, lousy food, and were either too hot or too cold. And she knew how fastidious Max could be. He was every bit as particular as Koko, the kingly Siamese in *The Cat Who Could Read Backwards.* Her heart sank. Oh well, it would be good for Max to traffic with hoi polloi. She pictured him arising from a lumpy bed and stepping into a lukewarm shower. Grinning, she crossed the street, her goal the famous Prichard House which would be the site of the Murder Nights entertainment. She was ready to survey the setting and figure out the practical elements. Where should the corpse be found? Where would the suspects be placed? And the Investigation Center? What clues should she strew at the Scene of the Crime?

Fortunately for her sanity and the logistics of the week, the three featured homes were all here on Ephraim Street, right in a row. As she understood it, ticket holders would first tour the ground floor rooms in the three featured houses, then gather on the lawn of the Prichard House for a buffet dinner to be followed by the coup de grace, the Mystery Program.

She stopped in front of the wrought iron fence to look at the Benton House. A two-story frame built in 1798, it glistened with recently applied white paint and looked as crisp as Tom Wolfe in a fresh white suit. Double porticoes flanked three sides, supported by simple Ionic columns. Black shutters framed the windows. Stubby palmetto palms were spaced every ten feet along the fence, but the magnificence here was in the grounds. Annie's eyes widened. *SOUTHERN LIVING* should see *this* garden. Lady Banksia, yellow jessamine, honeysuckle, pittisporum, a long shimmering arc of wisteria across the back of the deep lot, dogwood so brilliantly, pristinely white that it glittered in the sunlight, and azaleas—single blossoms, double blossoms, hose-in-hose blooms, in vivid splashes of color that included salmon, pink, orange-red, yellow, purple, and white.

Although an occasional car had passed as she made her way slowly from the Lookout Point bench past the Society Building and the Inn to this first historic home, Annie soon realized this part of Chastain didn't exactly teem with activity. The Benton House reflected back the early afternoon sunlight. The venetian blinds were closed, and the many windows offered no hint of its interior. Just then a middle-aged man came briskly around the corner of the house, pushing a wheelbarrow. He looked like a competent, no-nonsense gardener. If he were in charge of this garden, he deserved kudos indeed.

She propped her purse and the guidebook against the base of the fence. Removing her camera from its case, she held it up and took a series of shots. Returning the camera to its case, she picked up her belongings and continued down the sidewalk to the entrance to the grounds of Prichard House.

Each house along Ephraim Street sat far back on a large lot. This provided a great deal of space for the gardens and, the guidebook informed, accounted for the plantation-like appearance of many of the older homes.

SKETCH OF HISTORIC AREA

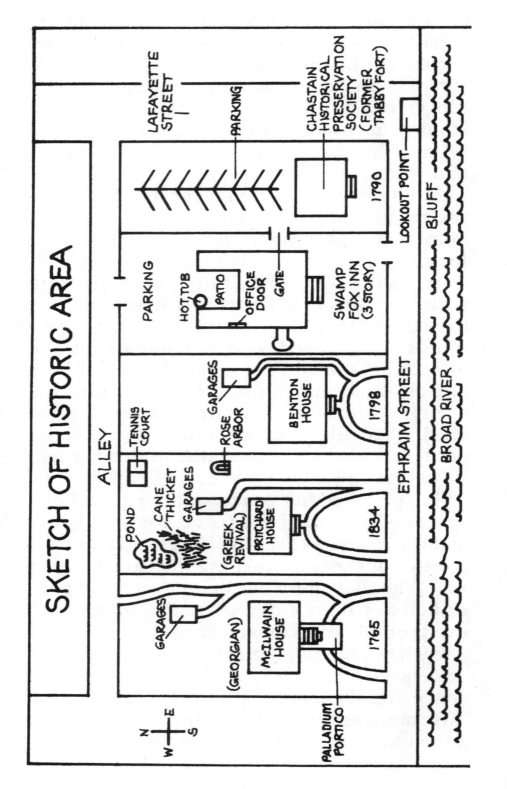

LAFAYETTE STREET

PARKING

CHASTAIN HISTORICAL PRESERVATION SOCIETY (FORMER TABBY FORT)

1790

LOOKOUT POINT

BLUFF

ALLEY

PARKING

HOT TUB

PATIO

OFFICE DOOR

GATE

SWAMP FOX INN (3 STORY)

TENNIS COURT

GARAGES

ROSE ARBOR

BENTON HOUSE

1798

POND

CANE THICKET

GARAGES

(GREEK REVIVAL)

PRITCHARD HOUSE

1834

EPHRAIM STREET

BROAD RIVER

GARAGES

(GEORGIAN)

McILWAIN HOUSE

1765

PALLADIUM PORTICO

N E S W

When Annie saw the Prichard House, she realized it fitted Mrs. Webster *perfectly*. There was nothing casual, downhome, or unpretentious about the Prichard House. It was a two-story, brick, Greek Revival mansion, with six immense octagonal columns supporting the double porticos. Pale pink plaster coated the exterior walls. A five-foot-high decorated parapet topped the second portico and four massive octagonal chimneys thrust up from the roof. Shining marble steps led up to the main entrance. Enormous and ancient live oak trees, festooned with long, silky strands of Spanish moss, dominated the front lawn. Most of the action would take place here. There could be few lovelier homes in all the South. Prichard House was, as Mrs. Webster had advised and Annie had nodded gravely, the jewel in Chastain's architectural crown.

The Prichard House garden featured a natural woodland with live oaks, mimosa, and magnolias interspersed with wildflowers and colorful banks of azaleas and yellow jessamine. Far to the back of the property, a tall stand of cane guarded a pond, providing only a tantalizing glimpse of dark water.

It was so imposing that she felt a twinge of hesitation in poking her camera through the wrought iron fence to take photographs. Thanks heavens, with the lovely speed of a .35 mm., it only took a few seconds.

The third historic home rivaled the Prichard House in beauty. McIlwain House was a lovely Georgian mansion, two stories, again on a high foundation, with a delicate extended front portico with slender columns supporting the second story partial verandah. Formal gardens ruled here, beds of roses flanked by dogwood, crepe myrtle, and azaleas.

Once again, she shot a series of pictures, then, returning to her vantage point in front of the Prichard fence, she made a rough sketch of the Historic Area.

Dropping the drawing into her purse, Annie pushed through a gate to the oyster-shell path that led to the grand entrance of Prichard House. She walked slowly, appreciating the soft crackle of the shells beneath her feet, the mixture of scents, jessamine, honeysuckle, and wisteria, and the silky freshness of the afternoon air. There was going to be plenty of room. She could order tents put up, three of them in a row, on the wide expanse of lawn embraced by the circular drive. What she needed now was to determine The Scene of the Crime, but she could only accomplish that by nosing around the gardens, and she had no intention of trespassing in these sacred precincts without permission. She wondered if Mrs. Webster would be surprised at her prompt appearance. Hired in the morning, at work by afternoon. Well, it should only endear her to the Board president.

It was a long walk to the shining marble steps. She was midway up when a car churned up the oyster-shell drive, spewing a plume of gray dust. Annie glanced toward the sound and glimpsed the face of a pale girl whose pretty face was contorted by fury. Then the gray Continental and its driver were beyond the house and only the cloud of oyster-shell dust hung in the air.

Annie's insatiable curiosity was piqued. Obviously, the girl must belong in this magnificent house. Only an inhabitant would have the effrontery to drive like that on grounds such as these. Who was she and why was she so angry? And on such a beautiful day.

Mounting the steps, she rang the front door bell and, faintly, deep within the house, heard a somber peal.

The gleaming white double doors rose nine feet tall. They opened in a moment, and a middle-aged woman in a maid's uniform nodded politely at her.

"Yes, Miss?"

"I'm Annie Laurance, and I'm helping Mrs. Webster with plans for the—"

A reverberating crash sounded from the back of the shining hall.

Startled, the maid swung around.

The driver of the car burst into the main hall. She was tall and willowy, with strikingly lovely auburn hair which she wore in an old-fashioned chignon. Her face was delicately boned and slender; her pale blue eyes were enormous. She would qualify as a beauty except that her face was white and pinched, the lips quivering in distress.

She ignored Annie. Perhaps, in her anger, she didn't even see her. She spoke to the maid, her voice shaking with fury.

"Where is Corinne?"

6

S UNLIGHT FLOODED THE old and elegant hallway from the open doorway to the left. Tall double doors were open, revealing a drawing room decorated in muted blues and grays. Annie, standing frozen at the entrance, glimpsed an English Sheraton cabinet filled with leather-bound books, a decorated Adam mantelpiece with bronze candelabra, silk-upholstered sofas and chairs, and pieces of Meissen and Sevres china. Matching double doors opened to the right into the dining room, which had walls of Williamsburg green. Silk damask curtains, a lighter green patterned in yellow, hung from the tall windows.

French wallpaper from the 1820s decorated the hallway, and sunlight spilled in a warm golden pool across the wide-planked floor. The young woman was as clearly limned as if by a spotlight, her spectacular auburn hair glistening like the flank of a sundrenched Kentucky colt, her delicate, anguished face a study in anger. And something more. Heartbreak?

It seemed so unlikely a place for drama. Or melodrama. The long hallway was immaculate, the floor glistening. A French Empire card table with dolphin feet sat beneath an ornate Chippendale mirror with a gilt eagle at its apex. A smell of potpourri, crushed roses and ginger, mingled with the homelier odors of freshly baked bread and floor wax. And the girl seemed an unlikely candidate for passion, with her patrician face and tasteful yet understated dress, a crisp white cotton cambric blouse with a high neck, front tucks, and long sleeves, and a mid-calf length cotton skirt with an aquamarine stripe. But her face was twisted with emotion, and her breathing was ragged.

"Where is she, Marybelle?" she demanded hoarsely.

"Miss Gail—" The older woman, clearly upset, reached out a hand. She was in her early fifties, attractive in her highly starched pale brown cotton dress with white ribbing at the collars and cuffs.

A soft, cultivated voice sliced through the emotion-charged atmosphere as cleanly as a surgeon's knife.

"Gail, you forget yourself."

They all looked up, like obedient marionettes, at Corinne Prichard Webster. She stood at the landing of the stairway, one hand lightly touching the mahogany handrail, her face composed, her lips parted in a Mona Lisa half-smile. The Palladian window behind her provided a dramatic frame for her cool loveliness. Her silver-blonde hair was softly waved, her face smooth and unlined, her cream suede suit the last word in elegance. She was beautiful, and she knew it. She wore that knowledge as a knight might flaunt a royal coat of arms.

"Miss Laurance, how nice of you to call. I want you to meet my niece, Gail Prichard." Her blue eyes blazed a warning at Gail.

The girl turned reluctantly toward Annie. She still breathed unevenly, with the half hiccups that signaled extreme stress. Her eyes slowly focused.

Annie watched innate good manners and long adherence to social norms struggle with emotions too deep to be ignored.

Corinne reached the foot of the stairs, and nodded toward the maid. "Thank you, Marybelle."

The maid pulled her pitying eyes away from the girl and turned away silently, her rubber-soled shoes squeaking a little against the highly polished wood floor.

Trying to spare the girl, Annie rushed into speech. She would have recited "Thanatopsis" to distract the blonde viper from Gail Prichard.

"I wondered if I might look over the gardens, Mrs. Webster. For the Murder Nights. If it's all right, I'll take some pictures, too."

"Of course, Miss Laurance. You are welcome to poke into every nook and cranny. We want you to feel very much at home while you work on the festival program. But we must observe the amenities before business. Gail, this is Miss Annie Laurance, who has so kindly consented to help us publicize the spring house-and-garden tours."

It was worse than watching a butterfly squirm to its demise against the hurtful intrusion of a pin. Watching Corinne Webster force her niece to make the proper response, no matter what private agony the girl was enduring, was as ugly a demonstration of raw power as Annie had ever witnessed. It put her right on a par with Mrs. Boynton in Agatha Christie's *Appointment with Death*.

Gail swallowed jerkily. She managed to hold out her hand and speak. "Miss Laurance—I'm glad—to meet you."

As Annie touched that slim, shaking hand, she felt a white hot bubble of anger. If Max were here, he would recognize the signs. He knew her, knew that she could erupt, and the devil take the hindmost, when she was pushed too far. This vicious, golden woman was coming perilously close to pushing Annie Laurance too far. Who the bloody hell did Mrs. Sainted Webster think she was to subject her to this paralyzing scene? At that moment, she would have been delighted to be teetering on a hanging bridge over a Borneo chasm, if a magic carpet could have whisked her there.

With a Herculean effort, she held onto her temper and began to back toward the door. "I won't trespass on your time. Thank you so much." She groped behind her for the hamhock-sized silver handle.

"Of course you aren't intruding." Corinne lifted a perfectly manicured hand, the nails sleek and blood red, and gestured toward the drawing room. An enormous purplish blue sapphire in an antique gold setting flashed like a Hessian's dress uniform. "You must have tea with us. I insist. I know Gail will enjoy telling you about the work she has done in planning the programs this year at the Prichard Museum."

Gail's face was the color of gray Sheetrock. Her anguished blue eyes looked like smears of rain-puddled ink.

Corinne smiled blandly at her niece.

A poison-ring tipped into Chablis would be far too good for Corinne Webster. That being out of the question and beyond her purview, Annie's immediate goal was to remove herself from the poisonous presence of Corinne Prichard Webster without succumbing to the temptation to tell the woman just how beastly she was. Her hand found the doorknob and turned it.

"Thanks so much, but I'm due back at the island for tea shortly." She tried to sound as if afternoon tea were an activity in which she unfailingly engaged, and her social calendar was filled *weeks* in advance. "I'll just take a few shots and be on my way." She waggled the camera at them, stepped out onto the front piazza, pulled the door shut, then turned and plunged down the gleaming marble steps as if pursued by the hounds of hell.

She didn't look back until she'd crunched down an oyster-shell path and ducked behind a line of palmetto palms. Her chest heaving with exertion, she skidded to a stop by a wooden bench and paused to listen.

A lawnmower whirred in the distance. Nearer at hand, a blower tidied fallen pine needles into flower beds. She peered around the splintery gray trunk of the palm at the front door of the Prichard House. It didn't open.

She had escaped without exploding.

And she had held her breath, too. She let it out with a rush and, for an instant, an infinitesimal space of time, wondered if she'd overreacted. No, Mrs. Webster rated on a scale with pirahnas, cobras, and Moriarty. Definitely not a choice for gentlewoman of the year. What a pleasure it would have been to let her have it.

That poor girl. Funny. She thought of her as a girl, though she must be about Annie's own age. But there was something young and vulnerable about Gail Prichard. What could have happened to upset her so dreadfully? What had Corinne Webster done? For it came down to that, without doubt.

But it wasn't any business of hers.

Her business was to create a successful mystery program, and she wasn't going to accomplish that by standing flat-footed staring at a door that remained closed. Good. She didn't want it to open. She wanted to mark the entire episode closed.

The temptation to march right back up those marble steps, punch the doorbell, and tell Mrs. Corinne Prichard Webster to stick it was almost overwhelming. To hell with the thousand-dollar fee. To hell with the Chastain Historical Preservation Society.

But she had given her word. If she didn't provide the script for the Murder Nights, the Chastain Historical Preservation Society would be left dangling in the wind, as they said in Texas. She felt, too, that she owed a good job to the faceless individuals who made up the membership of the Society. Mrs. Webster may be president, but surely the Society consisted of other and, more than likely, worthier Chastainians. Besides, Mrs. Webster clearly was lukewarm about the mystery program. By God, she was going to have one—and a blood-curdlingly marvelous one—like it or not.

Duty wrestled hotblooded temptation. Duty won.

She turned away from the mansion to study the geography of the garden. A long sweep of springy green lawn was embraced by the circular drive. There was certainly room for three tents, as much to mark various activities as to provide shelter. And no one would even admit to the *possibility* of rain. The mystery would begin promptly at seven P.M. with the introduction of the suspects and an explication of their relationship to the victim. The mystery buffs would be divided into ten teams, each with a maximum of ten members. After electing a Detective Captain, the teams would, one at a time, be taken to The Scene of the Crime, where they would be instructed to follow good police procedure, i.e., prepare a detailed sketch of the premises, careful not to disturb any evidence, and list all possible clues. The teams would then repair to the tents. The first tent would house Police Headquarters. There team members could study the medical examiner's report on the victim, the laboratory analysis of physical evidence, and obtain copies of statements which had been given to the police by the suspects. The second tent would provide areas for the interrogation of each suspect by the teams. In the third tent would be tables where teams could huddle to discuss the progress of their investigations.

Ducking beneath the low limbs of a gnarled live oak, she paced out the position of the tents. Then she scuffed a mark in the grayish dirt with her sandal. This would be a good place for the Death on Demand table. She could picture the table now, heaped with bookstore mementos, including blood-red, stiletto-shaped bookmarks, a stock of t-shirts with the store name, or pictures of favorite mystery sleuths, such as Hercule Poirot, Miss Marple, Sherlock Holmes, or Nero Wolfe, or slogans, such as I'D RATHER BE DETECTING, CRIME DOESN'T PAY ENOUGH, or POISON IN A PINCH.

Her irritation began to fade. She always enjoyed planning new and novel ways of spreading the good word about Death on Demand. And just think, most of the people signed up for the Mystery Nights must be mystery lovers. Why else would they come? She brushed away their interest in old houses and lovely gardens. These were *crime* enthusiasts, ready to swap knowledgeable tidbits about their favorites, ranging from *Bleak House* to *Home Sweet Homicide*.

And she had just had the marketing idea of the century. The watercolors! They were the first things everybody checked out at the store. The competition to be the first to name author and title was fierce. What would it cost to have the watercolors run off as posters and offer them for sale, too?

Whipping out a notepad from her purse, she scrawled a reminder to check the cost and confer with Drew Bartlett, this month's artist.

"Genius," she murmured to herself complacently. "Sheer genius."

Okay. Practical matters. Order the tents, tables, chairs. Make up instruction sheets for the teams.

The teams would be racing against the clock in their investigations. As soon as a team was certain it knew the murderer's identity, the Team Captain would write this information, along with the incriminating evidence they had detected, put the information in an envelope, seal it, and turn it in to Annie, who would initial it and stamp the time on the outside of the envelope. At the climax of the grand Denouement Ball Friday evening on the tennis court of Prichard House, the winning team would be announced. The winner would be the team which discovered the murderer in the shortest time, no matter which evening the team competed. A team which turned in its correct answer at 9:03 P.M. Wednesday would defeat a team which handed in the correct answer at 9:15 Monday night.

Now, where to put the body.

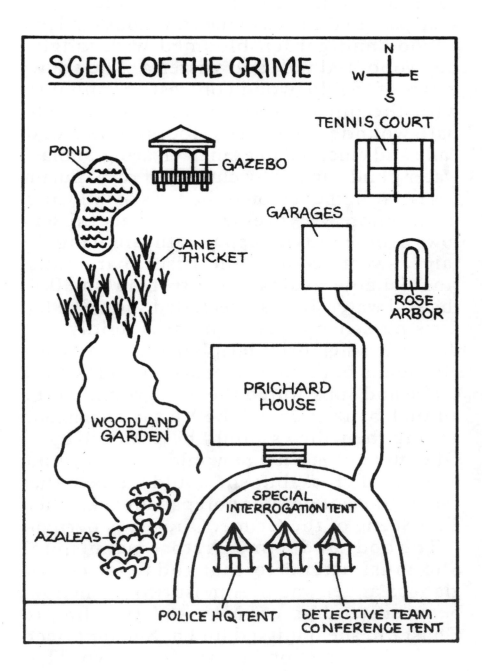

SCENE OF THE CRIME

N
W — E
S

POND

GAZEBO

TENNIS COURT

GARAGES

CANE THICKET

ROSE ARBOR

PRICHARD HOUSE

WOODLAND GARDEN

SPECIAL INTERROGATION TENT

AZALEAS

POLICE HQ TENT

DETECTIVE TEAM CONFERENCE TENT

She looked again at the smooth lawn, bounded by beds of lavender-pink and rose-red azaleas, then paced along a wide oyster-shell path to the back of the enormous lot. Here a woodland garden bloomed with tangled dogwood, redbud, and wisteria. The snowy white of the dogwood contrasted brilliantly with the purplish red of the redbud. The path wound past a twelve-foot tall thicket of cane and emerged in a small clearing. A black water pond, ringed by clumps of royal purple irises, lay in the sculpted shadows of immense, dark, knobby cypresses and graceful willows. Annie took a deep breath, enjoying the faint, sweet scent of the irises, barely distinguishable against the stronger smell of the still water. It was a secluded spot. She felt a rising sense of excitement. Rapidly, she discarded her original plan for Thompson Hatfield's body to be discovered in his bank office and substituted the background of the annual bank picnic. The Victorian gazebo among the willows would be a superb spot. Of course, this change would entail a whole new set of clues, but she could manage that easily. She got out her notepad and sketched The Scene of the Crime. Oh, it was perfect.

The body. A dummy? A store mannequin? She must attend to that today, also. She glanced at her watch. Almost two. Somehow, between fending off Max and traveling to Chastain, she'd missed lunch. She'd noticed a chili dog stand on her way into town. That would do nicely. But first, she'd drop by the Historical Preservation Society and leave some information to be stapled to the brochures. Mrs. Webster was clearly uninterested in promoting the Mystery Nights program, but she needn't think Annie Laurance was going to be fobbed off or ignored.

She was feeling fairly combative as she pushed through the massive wooden door of the old fort.

Two-foot-thick walls, inset windows, low ceilings, and forty-watt bulbs in wall sconces recreated the dungeon-like atmosphere the place must have had almost two hundred years before. The musty smell from long years of dust hung in the damp air. A wooden rack filled with pamphlets and brochures ran along the brick wall to her left.

"Good morning." An elderly woman with the soft, slurred speech of a native South Carolinian smiled and looked up at Annie with interest. She had masses of faded blonde curls and wore a shapeless baby-blue polyester dress and matching beaded earrings, but her heavy face radiated good humor and an unquenchable enthusiasm. She sat behind a mahogany Chippendale writing table. Both she and the old Remington on a typing stand behind her looked incongruously modern.

"I'm Annie Laurance, and Mrs. Webster has hired me to plan a Mystery Night program for—"

"The house-and-garden tours. Oh, I do feel this is going to be so thrilling. And such a wonderful idea. I think it was Mr. Merrill who thought it up. He and his wife went to a Murder Weekend in Atlanta last year and just had a wonderful time." She heaved herself up and came around the desk. "I'm Louisa Binning, the secretary. What can I do to help?"

What a difference in blondes, a gorgeous viper and a frumpy delight. Annie began to nurture kindly feelings for the Chastain Historical Preservation Society as Louisa, who turned out to be not only chatty but efficient, loaded her down with brochures, provided the names of caterers and equipment rental companies, swiftly took down the details of the Mystery Nights program, and promised production, "Oh, by next Monday at the latest," of a promotional blurb to be included in the previously printed House and Garden tour brochures.

"As for the body," she riffled through a stack of papers on the writing table and handed Annie a Red Cross brochure, "you can stop on your way out of town and talk to Edith Ferrier, one of our very nicest Board members. I'll call ahead for you. I just know she'll be glad to help out."

Adding the brochure to her stack of pamphlets, she said gratefully, "Mrs. Binning, I can't thank you enough for all your help."

"Oh, I love doing it. And it's my job." She beamed. "Now, about the slip-ins for the tour brochures. We can manage one color on our mimeograph machine. Do you think a dagger dripping blood?"

"Fantastic," Annie crowed.

"Disgusting," a voice hissed from the cavernous dimness of a bricked archway behind the secretary.

Annie jumped, but mellow Louisa merely turned her head and said, "Oh, there you are, Miss Dora. Come meet our young mystery expert, Annie Laurance. Miss Laurance, this is Miss Dora Brevard, who is the mainstay of the Society. No one knows more about Chastain and its history than Miss Dora."

A tiny figure, more like a gnome than a woman, poked out of the shadow. Shaggy silver hair framed an ancient face, the skin crumpled in cross-hatched lines. But the deep-set eyes, dark as raisins, peered out with ferocious intelligence. Dora Brevard wore a heavy black silk dress that rustled around her high-topped leather shoes and a rakishly tilted cloth hat with a purple feather. She gripped an ebony cane in one withered hand, but she moved with surprising speed, thumping across the stone floor to look up with keen suspicion at Annie.

"The goal of the Society is to preserve the heritage of Chastain." She tapped the cane to the stone for emphasis. Her voice had a crackly, dry quality like the rustle of old paper. "Adding these Mystery Nights," the words sounded like an epithet, "can do nothing but detract from our mission."

The secretary interceded quickly. "Now, Miss Dora, this young lady has come here today to get materials about Chastain. She's *very* interested in our history. And she wants to help us raise as much money as we can."

"Desecration," the old lady muttered. "That's what it is. All these people tramping through our houses—"

Louisa patted the bony shoulder soothingly. "Tourists come because they want to understand the past."

The old lady shrugged away the secretary's hand. Her beady eyes glittered with anger. "Cheap, that's what the world is today. Everything tawdry and false. And I won't stand for it here in Chastain. Do you hear?" She thudded the cane against the floor. Then, in a swift and disturbing about-face, the wizened features reformed in a cunning smile. "So you're interested in our history, are you, young woman. That's as it should be. And I'll see that you aren't filled with jiggery and pokery. You can walk me home, and I'll tell you about Chastain. Here now, you can carry my bag for me," and she thrust a crocheted receptacle into Annie's hands. It was surprisingly heavy. She glanced down and saw it was crammed to the brim with books, papers, and photostats.

"Records." Miss Dora stabbed a gnarled finger at the bag. "Deeds, land grants, birth and death certificates, and wills. That's the heart of the matter, wills." She cackled and darted toward the heavy door, the cane a staccato accompaniment. "Come along now. I don't waste time."

Annie glanced helplessly toward the secretary, who said meaningfully, "Miss Dora is Secretary to the Board."

"Secretary," Annie repeated blankly. "But I thought you—"

"Oh, I just work here. Miss Dora is *permanent* secretary to the Board."

And Annie was employed by the Board. She got the message, hefted the bag, and followed the tip-tap of the cane.

Out on the sidewalk, Miss Dora paused long enough to dart a malevolent glance down Ephraim Street. "I suppose Louisa gave you the brochure that describes the houses on the tour?"

"Oh yes, I have all the material on those houses." Annie was surprised to find her hands sweating. She found Miss Dora unsettling, to say the least. There was too much force and intelligence in those piercing brown eyes to dismiss her as merely dotty. It would be easy to imagine her as a Salem witch or Florentine poisoner.

"It's poorly phrased," the old woman snorted, "but accurate. So we'll walk up Lafayette." One hand tapped the cane and the other gripped Annie's elbow like a marsh hawk clutching a juicy rodent. The raspy voice swept ahead relentlessly, unfolding the pageant of the past. Annie, despite her wariness, was caught up by the vividness and pungency of the old lady's descriptions, and, unexpectedly, she glimpsed visions of long ago: The huge grave they dug for the yellow-fever victims. The glorious night when General Washington came for a ball. "That was in the Smiley house. It stood on the bluff over there where the fire station is." The devastating fire of 1756, which started on the docks, a careless match thrown into bales of cotton. "A new bride ordered the slaves to dip all her tablecloths and linens in the river and cover the roof, so the Mainey house was saved." The duels, the horse races, the elegant and civilized parties. The long, heartbreaking Federal occupation, and the grim days that followed the War when the homes of most old Chastain families were sold for taxes.

Miss Dora paraded Annie up and down Federal Street. "The first Episcopal Church stood just there. The present St. Michael's and All Angels was established in 1760, after the fire." She dismissed the stuccoed business buildings erected in the late 1800s as uninteresting, but grudgingly admired the Prichard Museum. "Built in 1843 by the Chastain Thursday Night Society. Men have always loved gaming." She bracketed the word, "Men," much as Miss Silver did when discussing the eating and drinking habits of the male species. But she wasn't as genial as Miss Silver, by a long shot. Then, the indefatigable Miss Dora led her back to Ephraim Street and they followed the curve of the River past Lookout Point. More lovely old homes fronted the bluff. "They built them on high foundations of tabby, that's the cement made from burning oyster shells to make a lime, then mixing it with crushed shells and sand. Two-story homes with front and side piazzas to catch the prevailing breezes from the southeast. It was hot in the summertime, mind you, but the open central hallways made the rooms as cool and fresh as the little airconditioned boxes they build today. There's the Cannehill house, eight fireplaces and a fine double verandah. Early 1800s. That's the Hapworth House, built in 1850, belonged to a doctor, sold for taxes after the War. A Board member, also a doctor, lives there today." Then the old lady, her wrinkled face twisted in a fierce scowl, paused to lean against her stick and glare at a magnificent Greek Revival mansion with a portico that rivaled the Prichard House in grandeur. A quartet of huge Ionic columns rose two stories and supported a gleaming white pediment. A luxurious, classic yellow Bentley lounged in the drive, the kind of automobile that proclaims its owner's wealth and cockiness.

"What a lovely home. And what a magnificent car," Annie said admiringly.

"She defiles her heritage," the raspy voice intoned.

Startled, Annie looked down at her tiny, black-clad companion.

"No better than a common whore, and I don't care if her name is Chastain."

"Really?"

The black eyes darted up at Annie, who hastened to explain, "I mean, really a descendant of the original Chastain?" She doubted if she could count high enough to figure out how many generations that spanned.

"Evil. That's what Sybil is. A Jezebel. It was a grave mistake when the Board made her a member, despite her lineage." Then, again disconcertingly, the rat's nest of wrinkles smoothed into a high, mirthless cackle. "But she makes them sit up and take notice. Especially Corinne." Her voice dropped to a subterranean hiss as she spoke the name, and hatred eddied in the perfumed air.

Miss Dora's house was two past the Chastain mansion. She snatched her carry-all from Annie at the gate. "Now, this mystery you're planning. Tell me about it."

Quickly, Annie sketched the saga of the banker.

Miss Dora bent her head forward, her reptilian eyes squinted in thought. When Annie finished, she jiggled her head and the straight silvery hair undulated under her hat like wisps of cirrus clouds. "Businesslike," she muttered. "But boring. Not like Peter Dickinson." Then she opened the gate and thumped up the walk, without a backward glance.

Annie stared after her. She couldn't decide whether to laugh or be angry. But, as she slowly retraced her path to Lookout Point and her parked car, she decided the old devil would certainly add some spice to her assignment.

And maybe she had something there. Boring. Maybe she should give the mystery program a whole new look, come up with some juicier characters, more original motives. But first things first. It was time to see about the body. Back in her Volvo, she consulted a street map of Chastain, which looked somewhat as though a child had taken pick-up sticks and flung them across the page. She had a little trouble finding the Red Cross office, which was tucked back on a side street between a French bakery and a U-Haul lot. She parked outside the bakery and virtuously resisted the temptation to succumb to an éclair stop. Business first. The door to the Red Cross office opened into a boxey room that smelled of yeast from next door and of ink and slick paper from the pamphlets stacked on a cardtable.

Three women were at work in the room. Annie had no trouble singling out the honcho. She smiled impartially at all three, but dismissed the overweight receptionist and frizzy haired typist from her thoughts and focused on the gaunt-faced woman with golden hoop earrings, deep-set green eyes, and red-gold hair piled atop her head in copious curls, moving to greet her.

"I'm Annie Laurance. I'm hoping you can help with some plans for the house-and-garden week."

"Certainly, certainly. I'm Edith Ferrier." She spoke in a hurried staccato. "Louisa called and explained about your needs. She thought our CPR doll might suit," and she pointed across the room at the five-foot-tall rubber doll lounging in a wicker chair next to an old-fashioned bottled water cooler.

"Oh, she'll be perfect. Though I might have to come up with a new mystery. I'd planned on a male murderee, but I can always think up a murder with a female victim."

The pleasantry slid right by Mrs. Ferrier, who peered at Annie intently. "Now, it's important that Rhoda—that's what we call her—Resuscitation Rhoda—not be treated roughly. It would be very expensive to replace her."

"We'll take excellent care of her," Annie promised quickly. "She'll be behind police tape marking the scene of the crime, so no one will touch her."

"That's all right then." Her head jerked back, and Annie recognized the sharp, unconscious reflex of a nervous habit. This taut redhead was strung tighter than a violin string.

"I'll run by and pick her up the morning of the seventh."

At the door, she thanked Edith Ferrier again. "It's really a great piece of luck that you are both the Red Cross coordinator and a member of the Historical Preservation Board."

"I'm busy. Very busy." There wasn't a glint of humor in her face.

"Mrs. Webster is going to be pleased that it's all worked out."

A short, taut pause, then, again, that quick, involuntary movement. "Yes, I suppose Corinne will be pleased. Things always do seem to work out when she is in charge."

They parted in a friendly fashion, Annie turning for a last wave as she climbed into the Volvo, but the smile slipped from her face as she turned the corner. She prided herself on sporting a fine set of antenna, guaranteed to sniff out subtle nuances in behavior and attitude. That instant's pause after her mention of Corinne—Annie's antenna quivered to attention. So here was someone else who didn't care at all for Corinne Webster. But what else was new? Miss Dora didn't like her. Mrs. Ferrier didn't like her. And she had yet to meet the evil Sybil, who apparently didn't like her either.

She pulled into the parking lot of the chili

dog stand. As she ordered, a cool breeze rustled the fronds of a nearby palmetto palm. A black cloud slid over the face of the sun, and it was suddenly cool. Although she wasn't susceptible to omens, if she were a gothic heroine, she would be looking over her shoulder. Instead, she munched on the dog and studied her list, checking off the notation: *Arrange for body.*

7

I T WAS A NIGHT THE angels made, just enough offshore breeze to caress and refresh, a hint of coming summer in the warmth captured by the wooden slats of the deck chair, the languorous wash of water against the pilings, the faint strains of "Some Enchanted Evening," and the nearness of Max.

Undoubtedly, a moment of human perfection, fleeting, impermanent, and precious.

And Annie almost succumbed. It was delightful to share a deck chair with Max and feel the warm weight of his arm around her shoulders, and know that in an instant or two, she could half-turn, raise her face, and his lips would meet hers.

She almost succumbed, but her mind still worked. For weeks now, she and Max had been butting heads about September, but ever since he had picked her up at seven, all the way through the magnificent Beef Wellingtons at the Island Hills Clubhouse cypress-paneled dining room, up to and including their hand-in-hand stroll along the harbor front, he had made no mention at all of the wedding.

Instead, he had smiled cherubically and acted as though they were in harmony on all planes.

Annie turned her head.

Max turned his.

Eyeball to eyeball, she demanded, "Why are you being so agreeable?" It was the same tone an American negotiator might use upon receiving the latest Soviet arms proposal in Geneva.

"Annie, that is unworthy of you."

His injured tone confirmed her suspicions. He was up to something.

She sat up, removing her face from such dangerous proximity to his. "All right, what's going on?"

"What do you mean?" He was as bland as cottage cheese. "I'm spending a very pleasant evening with my girl. Dinner. After-dinner drinks. A stroll along the harbor. And looking forward to what was once called a romantic interlude. You. Me. One deck chair and—" His hand tugged her closer, his face bent nearer.

She placed her hands on his chest. "Wait a minute. You've been hounding me for weeks to agree to a spectacular for a wedding, including everything but a brass band and fireworks, and now you're acting as if everything's agreed upon. I don't get it." She peered at him. "Are we dis-engaged?"

68

"Hell, no." He kissed her decisively. Then he grinned. "I hadn't thought of that ploy, but I'll tuck it back in case it's needed." He silenced her hoot of outrage with another kiss. "No, rest easy." His arms tightened around her. "I merely experienced a moment of enlightenment today."

Her mind skipped back over the day. What had he been up to? All right, she would get to the bottom of this, but he was continuing, unperturbed and still cherubic.

"I realized that everything would come out right."

She waited.

He reached out and traced the line of her cheek.

She shook her head, unwilling to be distracted.

"Why?"

"Because."

Annie gritted her teeth. What a day, dealing with a woman who turned out to be a blood sister to Attila the Hun, surveying the beauties of Chastain in the tow of a formidable eccentric, now faced with this disconcerting behavior from Max. But he was looking at her with an unmistakable gleam in his eyes, and his next actions were predictable. As for his sudden enlightenment, it must mean that he was seeing things her way, but, being Max, he would never, of course, admit to that. Well, that was all right. She could be gracious, too. When they next discussed September, she wouldn't revel in his defeat. As she moved closer to him, she spared one final thought for Mrs.

Webster. The woman obviously was a snake, but that would come out all right, too. Besides, she didn't have to deal with Mrs. Webster until Thursday.

As for now, the night was young.

Her first instinct was to shred the letter.

Her second to hire a howitzer and blast Prichard House and its occupants into oblivion. What the Yankees had not accomplished, one mad Texan would achieve.

"Annie. Annie, honey, whatever is the matter?"

She heard Ingrid's worried chirp through a blood-red haze, but she was too angry to manage even an outraged squall. Wordlessly, she flapped the thick stationery until it sounded like an avalanche on a 1930s radio drama. Ingrid snatched up one of the newly arrived posters of the back wall paintings and began to fan her. "What's happened?"

"I've worked my guts out!" Annie pounded on the cash desk and the skull-and-cross-bones No-Smoking sign skidded sideways. "And now, the day before I'm supposed to make my presentation to the Board, Mrs. President, Mrs. Corinne Prichard Prissy-Ass Webster, sends me *her* outline for a mystery. How about my clues? How about the instruction sheets for the suspects? How about the autopsy report and suspects' statements? I'll have to redo everything! I could murder that woman!"

Annie parked at Lookout Point on Thursday morning and stared grimly across the street at the square fort, home of her present employer, the Chastain Historical Preservation Society. She was still close, blazingly close, to telling the Board members, individually and collectively, to go to hell. Ingrid had soothed; Max had counseled. And, they did have a point. A weak point, Annie felt, but a point. She would still have the fun of creating the clues and running the Mystery Nights, even if she did have to use Corinne's plot. But the thrill was gone. She'd wanted to have her very own mystery, and now she was saddled with that odious woman's creation.

From her vantage point, she could see the front of the old fort and the entry to the parking lot behind it. A cream-colored Mercedes turned into the drive, followed by a faded gray Volvo older than her own, driven by the gaunt redhead she'd met at the Red Cross. Ferrier, that was her name.

Annie took a deep breath. The Board members were gathering. Time for her to arrive, too. And she might still present Madame President with her crumpled letter, now smoothed and stuck into a green folder, and tell her to run her own Mystery Nights. She locked the car, then checked both ways and paused to watch the approach of the magnificent and unforgettable Bentley she'd seen the day Miss Dora took her on a tour. Miss Dora, when not breathing fire and brimstone, had indicated that the Bentley's owner was also a Board member. A sinful one, apparently. Annie glimpsed luxuriant dark hair, enormous tortoise-shell sunglasses, and a slash of bright red lipstick. The car turned onto Lafayette, then slowed to make a left into the lot.

That's the one who gave Corinne a hard time. Annie was all in favor of that. Maybe she could start an insurrection, persuade the board that her original plan was better, get them to okay her mystery and dump Corinne's. Because, actually, it was pretty snappy. Hmm. It would all depend upon how she presented it.

With a decisive nod, she started across the street.

A brown Ford Tempo squealed around the corner and jolted to a stop in front of the Society. A stocky, well-built young man with thick, curly brown hair slammed out of the driver's seat. He had a crooked nose which looked as though it might have been drubbed into football turf more than once. He carried a notebook and a pencil. A couple of extra yellow pencils poked out of the pocket of his short-sleeved white shirt.

She reached the sidewalk at the same time. He saw her and smiled appreciatively, his mouth quirking up in good humor and lessening the predatory look of his misshapen (football?) nose. His admiration was so unstudied that she grinned back. Then he looked past her. His face hardened, hooding his dark brown eyes.

Curious, Annie half-turned and knew her own face toughened, too. America's sweetheart stood on the sidewalk, pointing at the Tempo.

"What is that vehicle doing here? Move it along. You're blocking the entrance to the Society."

From her tone, Corinne Webster might have been addressing the driver of a garbage scow.

The stocky young man ignored her and began walking up the sidewalk.

"Young man, do as I say. Move that car."

He turned as if aware for the first time that she was speaking to him. "Press, lady."

"But you can't come in here." She waved her bejewelled hand toward the Society building.

"Sure, I can. It's a city agency, funded by the city, and there's an open meeting law, lady." He pivoted and continued briskly up the sidewalk.

"You've never come to any of our meetings before." Corinne hurried up the walk after him, her face pale with anger. "If you've come to cause trouble because I spoke to you last week—"

He paused and swung toward her. A muscle twitched in his taut face. "Oh, yeah." His tone was sarcastic. "Gee, I didn't recognize you either. If it isn't Mrs. High-and-Mighty Webster. Sure, you're the dame who offered me money to get out of town. Yeah, I remember you now." There was utter contempt in his dark eyes. "Don't worry, lady, I'm not here on your account. I'm here because the news desk got a tip this was going to be an interesting morning."

He moved on up the sidewalk, yanked open the heavy front door, and disappeared inside.

Corinne Webster stood frozen, her hands gripping the handle of her dhurrie purse so tightly that her fingers turned a waxy white. She wore a black-and-white linen dress this morning and a heavy, beaten-gold necklace with a shiny opal drop. She stood stiffly for a long moment, then stalked forward. Annie glimpsed her face as she opened the door. When it closed behind her, Annie felt her tight shoulders relax. Ah, Chastain, this sundrenched, idyllic coastal hideaway. What next?

A squeal of tortured metal raked the morning quiet. Miss Dora, dressed this morning in a full-skirted bombazine with puff sleeves, turned up the sidewalk, pulling a child's rusted red wagon. A black pillbox hat with a jaunty green plume topped her flyaway silver hair. The raspy voice rose above the scrape of one bent tire against the bottom of the wagon.

"Open the door there, girl."

Obediently, Annie hurried up the walk and pulled open the heavy wooden door and watched in fascination as the gnome-like figure, cane in one hand, maneuvered the wagon. A large hammer rode atop a pile of placards attached to two-foot white stakes, pointed on one end.

Footsteps sounded behind them, and a tall, slender woman reached down to help.

"Good morning, Aunt Dora. It looks like you're all ready for the tour week." Then she straightened, smiled at Annie, and held out her hand. "I'm Lucy Haines, a member of the Board. You must be Annie Laurance, our mystery creator."

Annie took her hand and liked her at once. Her grip was cool and firm, her face serious, her manner formal, but friendly. She wore a gray-and-white striped seersucker skirt and an unadorned white blouse and looked wonderfully normal in contrast to Corinne and Miss Dora.

The heavy, blonde secretary joined them in the entryway. "I'll put the wagon in the storeroom, Miss Dora. I think everyone's here. They're all in—"

The voice full, throaty, and deep, carried as clearly as a Broadway actress's delivery to the farthest stall.

"You've gone too far, Corinne. I won't tolerate this."

Even in the dim entryway with the weak illumination from the wall sconces and the pale squares of sunlight from the deepset windows, the malicious curve to Miss Dora's smile was unmistakable. "Sybil."

Annie felt a quick march of goose bumps across the small of her back. Miss Dora's sandpaper voice oozed simultaneous disgust, pleasure, vindictiveness, and amusement. The secretary peered toward the archway, her eyes wide with distress. The sensible Lucy Haines frowned, and gnawed her lip.

Sybil's deep, vibrant voice quivered with rage. "It is unspeakable."

Miss Dora wheezed with laughter, revealing blackened, uneven teeth. "Come on, girls, let's not miss the show," and led the way through the bricked archway and down a narrow hall to a wider archway that opened into an equally dim, very large room, which held an ornately carved walnut refectory table. One man unknown to Annie sat at the table, but she recognized Gail Prichard, her sometime customer Roscoe Merrill, and the red-headed Edith Ferrier. No one noticed their arrival. All eyes were riveted on two women.

Corinne stood beside the speaker's stand at the far end of the table. Her blue eyes glittered like a southern sea on a blistering day. Annie realized with a twist of shock, however, that Corinne was *enjoying* herself. There was no sense here of a woman beleaguered or defensive. To the contrary, she stood by the table, upright as a goddess on the prow of a Roman ship, and just as arrogant and supercilious.

"Really, Sybil, your attitude is surprising." Her voice was cool, amused, untroubled. "It's a matter of contract, you know. All very clear. You can ask Roscoe."

All eyes, Annie's included, switched to Sybil, posed dramatically in front of the Flemish tapestry that covered a third of the bricked wall behind her. At her first full view, Annie thought simply, "Wow." Voluptuous described Ruebens' nudes and Sybil. And Sybil had the edge. A bitch in heat could not be more frankly sensual. A diamond clip glistened against her midnight black hair. Violet eye shadow emphasized the depth and hunger of equally black eyes. She wore a green jersey dress with a sharply plunging neckline that clung to every generous curve, revealing a cleavage guaranteed to galvanize every male present. She made every other woman in the room look about as attractive as a praying mantis. She turned now and stretched out a hand tipped by talon-sharp, vermilion nails. A diamond large enough to rival the Kohinoor weighted her third finger. A great square emerald glittered in an antique gold setting. Matching emeralds gleamed in a bracelet. "Roscoe, is this true?" The contralto voice vibrated. "Did you have anything to do with this unconscionable exploitation?"

Roscoe Merrill was obviously wishing fervently that he were somewhere else, maybe a far outpost of the Foreign Legion. A fine beading of sweat glistened on his bald head. His expressionless brown eyes avoided both Sybil's probing gaze and Corinne's confident stare, peering down instead at the legal pad on the table. He cleared his throat. "The Museum, of course, felt it imperative to protect its own interests. And, since the paintings have been executed on Museum time and using Museum materials, it is only equitable and reasonable that the Museum should have title to the paintings."

"I can't believe that contract." Sybil stepped closer to the table and bent down to grip his shoulder.

He glanced up, then jerked his eyes away from that enticing cleavage to stare determinedly at the legal pad. A dull red flush spread over his face and bald head.

"It's disgusting. Not only to steal the poor boy's work, but to forbid him to take part in an exhibition! To sabotage his career! Roscoe, you ought to be ashamed." Then she whirled toward Corinne. "And you, you're a jealous, conniving bitch. Just because you're a dried-up, dessicated old woman, you resent anyone who's truly alive. But you needn't think you've won. Just you wait and see!"

For the first time, Corinne's control wavered and an ugly flash of hatred moved in her eyes, but she retained an icy smile. "The Museum's position is irreproachable. And now, it's time for—"

"Mrs. Giacomo, I'm Bobby Frazier, reporter for the *Chastain Courier*." The stocky young man who had smiled at Annie outside pushed away from the wall, and approached Sybil.

Annie put names together. Miss Dora had said she defiled her name, that she was a Chastain. So, Sybil Chastain Giacomo. What price an Italian count?

"Can you tell me a little more about your disagreement here? Is there a problem at the Prichard Museum?" His pencil poised over his notebook.

Corinne reached out and gripped the speaker's stand. "You have no right to come in here and ask questions—this matter is not of public concern."

The reporter ignored her rising voice and,

admiration evident, addressed Sybil. "You're a director of the Prichard Museum, aren't you? Can you tell me what's going on?"

Sybil absorbed his interest automatically, instantly recognized a way to embarrass Corinne, took a deep breath, and let fly. "Why, certainly. Of course I can, Mr. Frazier. I know all about it. Tim Bond—you know his work, of course—is a curator at the Prichard Museum. Actually, he does *everything*. He makes most of the reproductions and cleans old pictures and he paints. Everyone knows he has a *great* future. Corinne snatched him up, because she always wants to own everyone. She told him he could work at the museum and paint all he wanted and he'd have a salary and not have to worry about money at all. But she didn't tell him the contract he signed made all his paintings belong to the museum—"

"That isn't true at all." For the first time, Corinne's voice was strident. "He read the contract. He understood."

"You told him the Museum would be happy to loan his paintings out for exhibits, and there was no question of the Museum keeping the paintings here until Corinne found out that Tim and I—" Sybil's shoulders shifted, and Annie could almost hear the whisper of satin sheets—"are friends. She resents his having friendships. Now, he's had this wonderful offer from a gallery in New York. They want to show all of his paintings in September, and it could absolutely launch his career—and Corinne won't give him permission to take his work to New York!"

Frazier wrote rapidly in his notebook, then turned toward Corinne. "*Has* the Museum refused Bond permission to show his works?"

"The paintings belong to—" Corinne began angrily.

Merrill intervened smoothly, "Mr. Frazier, this matter is still under consideration by the Museum Board and no final determination has been made. I understand there will be further discussion of Museum policy in regard to loan exhibitions at next month's meeting, so it would be premature to announce that a decision has been made."

"Tim Bond's future is at stake," Sybil thundered magnificently, "and I for one do not intend to let the matter drop. Most Chastainians will support me." She paused. Her face was slowly transformed from petulant anger to malignant pleasure. "I'm going to launch a petition drive. I'm going to ask everyone to sign who wants Chastain's most talented young painter to have a chance to achieve success."

"When will you start the petition drive, Mrs. Giacomo?" Frazier was egging her on, well aware that his every question further infuriated Corinne.

"Today. Right now." She reached over Merrill's shoulder, snatched up the yellow legal pad, and brandished it over her head. "Here. I'll start it now." Grabbing a pencil from Frazier's pocket, she scrawled in block letters: PETITION TO FREE TIM BOND'S PAINTINGS. With a triumphant glance at Corinne, she flung the pad down on the table in front of Merrill and handed him the pencil.

Not a muscle moved in Merrill's heavy face. He was as expressionless as a poker player who'd made his last draw. He read Sybil's scrawl, then said temperately, "Obviously, both Lucy and I as members of the Board of the Prichard Museum which would, I presume, be the recipient of the completed petition, are precluded from signing this."

Sybil's sultry eyes traveled slowly from the shiny top of his head to a visible portion of his glistening black leather shoes. Then she drawled, "You never did have any balls, Roscoe." Without waiting for an answer, she shoved the pad down the table toward Edith Ferrier.

Corinne moved like a flash, darting past Sybil to snatch up the pad.

Sybil lunged toward her, grabbing one end.

A sharp crack resounded through the room, and, for an instant, no one moved.

Annie absorbed the tableau: Miss Dora with her ebony cane still upraised, ready to pound the table again; Lucy Haines, lips parted, brows drawn in a frown; Gail Prichard, her hands tightly clasped, watching her aunt in horrified fascination; Corinne Prichard Webster, the bones of her face sharpened by anger, her mouth a thin, taut line; Sybil Chastain Giacomo, triumphant, her tousled black hair an ebony frame for her flushed face; Bobby Frazier grinning, reveling in Corinne's discomfiture; Roscoe Merrill, his shoulders bunched, rigidly controlling his anger; Edith Ferrier wary, her green eyes flicking from face to face; and the sharp-visaged man, whom she hadn't met, beating an impatient tattoo with the fingers of one hand.

Miss Dora broke up the moment, circling the table like a dragonfly, then raising the cane again to bring it down with a decisive whack against the legal pad, still held on either end by Corinne and Sybil. The blow tore the pad from their hands, and it fell to the floor.

"Sybil, sit down. There. By Edith. Corinne, you get yourself up to the table and start this meeting." She swung toward Annie and Lucy. "And you two. Take your places over there." Everyone did just as instructed.

Corinne reached the lectern and began to riffle through a thin sheaf of papers. Her breathing was rapid and shallow. The room pulsed with hostility.

Lucy Haines's low, pleasant voice was in odd counterpoint to the seething atmosphere. "Corinne, we should introduce our guests."

Corinne looked at her blankly.

"Mr. Frazier and Miss Laurance."

Corinne's eyes narrowed, but, after an instant's pause, she brusquely presented them to the Board. "And our members: Gail Prichard, Roscoe Merrill, Sybil Giacomo, Edith Ferrier, Dr. John Sanford, Dora Brevard, and Lucy Haines."

Dr. Sanford. Annie looked at him with interest. The corner of his ascetic mouth turned down in disdain. He had floppy gray-streaked dark hair that curled untidily over his ears, a hawk nose, and impersonal eyes. He sat at the end of the table beside Edith Ferrier, but he ignored her. Edith watched Corinne somberly, and her dour expression contrasted sharply with her cheerful, almost girlish dress, a cyclamen-pink floral print.

Sanford brushed back a drooping lock of hair. "Can't we get this show on the road? I've got to get back to the hospital."

Definitely a Type-A personality. She wondered why he'd become involved in a historical preservation group, which might be expected to pursue a leisurely course guaranteed to drive a man of his temperament mad.

Corinne cleared her throat and briskly described the progress of plans for the tour week. She had herself well under control now. Only the tiny white spots at the corners of her mouth indicated her anger. As her introductory comments wound down, Annie picked up her green folder. She was going to have one swell audience, no doubt about that.

"And now it's time for us to hear from Miss Laurance, who will explain the program she has put together for our house-and-garden-week tours. Miss Laurance."

Still not calling them Mystery Nights. The thought ignited Annie's smouldering anger. How infuriating! Corinne Prichard was such a meddlesome know-it-all that she'd taken over the mystery program, but she still refused to even mention the word mystery. How obnoxious. She had to take a moment, when she reached the lectern, to tamp down her explosive juices.

"Thank you, Mrs. Webster." It wasn't easy

to say, and her voice sounded like thin steel. "It's a pleasure for me to be here."

Fun, fun, fun, the imp in her mind chanted.

"I'm looking forward to the Mystery Nights. I believe we can offer a program that will attract a great many participants."

"How many?" Dr. Sanford barked.

"About a hundred a night," she shot back. The Board members looked startled, but, by God, she'd had enough. "The evenings will begin at six with a tour of the three houses and gardens, followed by a buffet supper on the lawn of the Prichard House. Promptly at seven, the participants will divide into teams and go to The Scene of the Crime. The teams will then study evidence available in the police tent, interview the suspects, and confer to decide who they believe is the murderer."

Dr. Sanford cracked his knuckles. "All right, all right. The mechanics seem sound. Give us a rundown on the murder, then we can okay it."

"It's a Southern Mystery." Not my mystery, she wanted to say. She flicked a brief glance toward Corinne. "We must thank Mrs. Webster for our plot. Our victim is Mrs. Meddlesome Moneypot, owner of the fabulous Familytree Plantation. Mrs. Moneypot is extremely proud of her social position and determined that everyone in her family shall behave as she believes they should. She ruined her brother's romance. She's alienated her husband and niece, and has also made many enemies in town. Her husband wanted to have a career in the foreign service, but she made him resign and come home."

A sharply indrawn breath was magnified by the taut silence.

Annie paused. Was her sardonic reading alienating her audience? Damn it, the room quivered with hostile vibes. She tried to smooth out her tone. "Her husband's been drinking too much for years, but everyone in town is whispering that he's met another woman. Mrs. Moneypot's niece is seeing a man she considers very unsuitable, and—"

A chair moved against the planked flooring, making a sharp high squeak.

"—there are people in town who have reason to hold a grudge against her. She's trying to ruin the life of a young artist—" Annie stumbled over that sentence. How odd. "—she's threatening the marriage of a prominent attorney, the career plans of a doctor, the club election of a society woman—"

Annie paused. Something very peculiar was happening to her audience. As she well knew from her earliest acting days, every audience has its own personality. She would always remember the summer night when she played Honey in "Who's Afraid of Virginia Woolf?" in an outdoor amphitheater in Dallas. It was sultry and thunder rumbled in the distance. The smell of dust, freshly mown grass, and buttered popcorn hung in the still, hot air, but the audience responded on an elemental level to the passion on the stage. It was an audience linked soul to soul with the players, and it was as near exaltation as Annie ever expected to reach.

That was the pinnacle. There had been

other memorable audiences, for good or ill. But there had never been an electric silence quite like this. What the hell was going on?

She stumbled to a stop and stared at her stunned audience. Gail pressed the back of her hand against her lips. Roscoe, looking like a watchful turtle, assessed Annie very carefully indeed, his pale brown eyes narrowed to slits. Sybil was frankly delighted, wide mouth spread in her malicious smile. Edith glared furiously, a bright patch of red staining each hollowed cheek. Dr. Sanford scowled, his restless hand spread flat against the table top. Miss Dora peered at Corinne. Lucy shook her head, as if bewildered.

Corinne's face was as white as ivory, and her dark blue eyes blazed. She pushed back her chair so abruptly that it tumbled to the floor. "I'll sue you," she shrilled at Annie. "You and that disgusting creature." She whirled toward the stocky reporter. "This is your work—and I'll make you pay for it."

Frazier cocked a black eyebrow. "Not me, lady. This isn't my show—but it's a hell of a lot of fun." He turned toward Annie. "Listen, I need a copy of your script. Maybe the *Courier* will run the whole thing." He smiled gleefully. "I'll say you've come up with a Southern Mystery. What did you say the victim's name was? Mrs. Rich Bitch? And who're the suspects?" He looked around the refectory table. "The leading lights of the town?"

The room exploded.

Sybil crowed. "Oh, you got it this time,

Corinne. Jesus, I love it. Hey, I didn't know Leighton was up for grabs. I'll have to take a look. He's always been a good-looking man, and if he's developed a backbone, he'd be worth at least an afternoon."

Miss Dora's wizened face turned plum colored. "Sybil Chastain, don't you know your mama's turning in her grave right this minute, hearing you talk like a harlot."

"I hope she's spinning like a dervish," Sybil said coolly.

Dr. Sanford looked like an enraged eagle. "I don't know what kind of attack is being mounted. But I don't intend to tolerate it. My professional reputation is unassailable."

Gail flushed to the roots of her auburn hair and averted her gaze from Bobby.

"I find it quite unbelievable that I should be held up to public ridicule." Edith's voice trembled with outrage.

"Please, please everyone." Lucy's well-bred voice rose above the babble. "There must have been a mistake of some kind."

Roscoe pounded on the table, calling for quiet.

Not even the urbanity of a John Putnam Thatcher could salvage this board meeting.

"It's a conspiracy. That's what it is. A conspiracy to embarrass me. Well, I won't let them get away with it." Corinne flung out a hand toward her niece. "Don't you see how vile he is?" She glared at the reporter. "He's behind it. He and this girl. He's probably been sleeping with her, and they—"

"Mrs. Webster, you'd better stop." Annie had

never realized that she could bellow. "And you'd better apologize—or I'm the one who will sue. I don't know what the hell is going on here. What's wrong with everybody?"

That brought a moment's stunned silence.

Finally, Lucy spoke apologetically. "It's your murder victim, Miss Laurance. Corinne thinks you're talking about her. It's such an odd coincidence."

"Coincidence!" Corinne's narrow chest heaved.

"Just a few home truths about Chastain's leading bitch—" Sybil began.

To forestall another furious outburst from Corinne, Annie held up her hand. "Let's get a few things straight. I didn't write this murder plot."

"Oh, yes, you did—you and that despicable muckraker!"

"Mrs. Webster, I gather you don't care for Mr. Frazier. That's your problem. I've never met him, never talked to him, and he had nothing whatsoever to do with this murder plot."

"You do too know him. I saw him *smile* at you outside."

The little flicker of fury lapping at her control blazed higher. Annie moved away from the lectern, pushed past the reporter, and stood inches from Corinne.

"Listen very closely. I'm going to say it once. I had never seen this man until I arrived here this morning. He likes pretty girls, so he smiled at me. I smiled back. That's too innocent and genuine an action for you to understand, isn't it, Mrs. Webster? Now, let me make myself perfectly clear. I don't like you, but I also don't like being used. Clearly, I'm the patsy here today. I was set up for this." Moving back to the lectern, she picked up the plan she had received from the Chastain Historical Preservation Society. "Somebody sent this to me. I thought it came from you. The cover letter's signed with your name."

Corinne snatched the six typewritten pages, then scanned the cover letter. "That signature is a forgery." She looked around the room. "This was written on Society stationery."

The implication was plain.

Lucy objected immediately. "That doesn't mean a thing. Everybody in town drops in here from time to time."

"No member of the Society would do such a dreadful thing," Miss Dora insisted.

"I'm going to find out who did this." Corinne's voice was metallic with determination. "And when I do—"

"Best thing is to let bygones be bygones," Roscoe Merrill interjected persuasively. "It doesn't do to take this kind of thing too seriously. You know, women get their noses out of joint, and—"

"What do you mean by that?" Edith demanded shrilly.

"Not a thing, not a thing," he said quickly. "Obviously, this has been a foolish prank." But his voice was worried and tense.

Annie eyed him with interest. Roscoe obviously didn't like this situation at all, and he was determined to get past it.

He held both hands up. "I suggest we get back to the object of this meeting. Our guest has been put in an extremely difficult position. We will have to hope that she will overlook this episode. Ms. Laurance, we agree that you have been victimized, but hopefully we can go forward from here. As I see it, the main problem—"

"The main problem is to determine who perpetrated this outrage." Corinne glared again at the reporter.

Frazier spread his legs and rocked back on his heels. "Nope. Guess again. I wish I'd thought of it. More fun than a whorehouse on Saturday night. But you'd better look among your snooty friends, Mrs. Webster. Who knew enough to dig all this dirt?"

"Young man, your attitude is reprehensible," Miss Dora scolded.

Corinne bit into an idea and clung. "Why did you come this morning," she demanded of Frazier, "if you didn't have anything to do with it?" Then she bent a sharp look at Gail, who began to shake her head in negation.

Frazier's good humor fled. "So now you want to slice Gail up, too?"

"Bobby, don't," Gail pleaded.

He ignored her. A vein throbbed in his neck. "Listen, lady, I'd rather stack crap than have anything to do with you. I'm here today because the city editor got a note in the mail saying all hell was going to break loose.

Frankly, I thought he had a screw loose. You people are usually about as interesting as yesterday's obits."

"A note in the mail," Corinne repeated sharply.

"I'll look into all this." Peacemaker Roscoe held out his hand for the letter. "I promise you, Corinne, I'll get to the bottom of it, if at all possible."

But Annie reached out and plucked the letter from Corinne's hand. "Nope. This letter was sent to me. It's mine. And I'm going to do some investigating myself."

"Young lady, I appreciate your concern, but this is a matter for the Board," Roscoe insisted, flushing.

Who did he think he was? Antony Maitland?

"We can all investigate," she said drily. "I'll send you a copy of it."

"This is all very well and good, and I understand why Corinne and Roscoe and Miss Laurance will pursue this matter, but I do think we must face up to our immediate problem," a reasoned voice urged.

Everyone looked at Lucy.

"After all, the Mystery Nights have already been advertised as part of the house-and-garden tours. I mean, we have only a little over a week before the festival begins."

"Lucy is hewing to the main point," Roscoe agreed. "Ms. Laurance, will you overlook this unfortunate contretemps and create a murder for us?"

8

ANNIE REFILLED MAX'S white coffee mug *(The Red Thumb Mark)*, then her own. Contrary to her usual habit, she shoveled a heaping teaspoon of sugar into her cup and stirred briskly.

It didn't escape him, of course. "Well, old dear, you must be frazzled." He stretched out comfortably, tilting the straight back chair on its rear legs.

Annie looked up from her ragtag collection of papers containing bits and pieces of possible Mystery Nights. "Have you been reading Sayers again?"

He grinned. "Nope. But maybe you should."

"Civilized mayhem as opposed to Southern discomfort?"

"Right." Then his dark blue eyes grew serious. "Actually, why don't you jump ship? Working for those people is like afternoon tea at a nuthouse."

"Quit *now?* Why, I can do any mystery I want to." Visions of plots danced in her head. "Maybe a movable corpse. Like *The Trouble With Harry.* Honestly, Max, did you ever in your life see anything funnier than Harry? Every time somebody buried him, somebody else dug him up."

He rubbed his cheek with his knuckles. "It's comments such as that which make me wonder about you sometimes."

"Oh, my God, it was *wonderful*."

"It wasn't one of Hitchcock's successes."

"Dumb audiences," she said stubbornly. She took another swallow of the sugar-laden coffee. "Or I can do an academic mystery, something on the order of *Seven Suspects*."

"Not unless you want to bore everybody into a coma." He took a big swallow of coffee.

"Or I could go for a grim background, like Moscow in *Angels in the Snow*."

She suddenly felt warm and cozy. Was it the sugar and the caffeine, or the wealth of possibilities that lay before her?

Max tipped the chair upright and leaned his elbows on the table. "What's wrong with good old Thompson Hatfield, the late, unlamented president of the bank? You already had suspects, clues, et al."

"Oh, no. I'm not going to do any mystery where the victim or suspects could by the stretch of anybody's wildest imagination have any relationship to anybody in Chastain, S.C. No, sir." She shook her head decisively. Then she paused and rubbed an ink-stained finger to her nose, resulting in a distinct smudge. "You know, if I didn't have so much to do for the Mystery Nights, I'd hit Chastain like Kinsey Millhone and shake some teeth until I got some answers."

His eyes glistened. "Would you wear tight jeans?"

"Don't be sexist." But it was an absent-minded put-down, and her frown pulled her brows into a determined line. "Dammit, I don't like being used—even if the end result was to take a cut at la piranha."

"Do you think it was a Board member?"

"I don't know. That was my first thought, but I talked to Lucy on the way out, and she said the Board had reported to the Society at the general meeting last month about the plans to have the Mystery Nights, and my name was mentioned then. I do think it must have been done by someone who belongs to the Society. Lucy said people drop in to the office all the time, but I'll bet they parcel out their creamy stationery like gold plate. It's that kind of place."

"Sounds like a good lead. Who had access to the stationery? Let me see the letter for a second."

She rooted around in her piles, found the green folder, and slid it to him.

He read it carefully, then announced, "First, it was typed on a typewriter, not a word processor, because the capital *B* jumps up half a line and the lower case *r* is worn."

"Bravo."

He ignored her sarcastic tone. "Moreover, the typist isn't skilled because the pressure is uneven, resulting in erratic inking."

"Ah, The Thinking Machine at work."

"The allusion escapes me, but I will assume it is apt. Even though machines don't think."

"You, not the typewriter. The Thinking Machine was Jacques Futrelle's detective."

He clapped a hand to his head. "How can I not know of him?"

"Probably because Futrelle went down on the *Titanic* before he had time to write more than two volumes of short stories."

But Max was still analyzing the letter. When he spoke again, the lightness had left his voice. "This is heavy stuff. Somebody *really* doesn't like your Mrs. Webster."

"She's not *my* Mrs. Webster." She sipped at the hot, sweet coffee. "But I don't have time to worry about that mess. I've got to get the Mystery Nights ready to roll—and come up with a plot that can't possibly have anything to do with anybody, living or dead, in Chastain. Listen, how does this grab you? I'll make it a South Sea Island and one of those New England missionaries and he gets involved with this languorous beauty—Max, you're not listening."

He was staring at the letter, his eyes unaccustomedly grim.

Annie whistled.

Startled, he looked up.

"Hey, it isn't all that bad."

"I think it is." His voice was grave. "I don't know. I have a funny feeling."

She quirked an interested eyebrow. "Are you coming all over psychic? Like the tweenie in a Christie country house murder?"

"It doesn't take any psychic powers to pick up bad vibes from this." He tapped the letter. "It's more than an ugly incident. It's dangerous."

She didn't laugh. "I agree," she said reluctantly. "It's just like the *The Moving Finger*. The villagers dismissed the anonymous letters as nasty but meaningless. And they were dreadfully wrong." She picked up the heavy stationery, squinting thoughtfully at the first page. "But surely this was nothing more than an effort to embarrass Corinne Webster. That's all there was to it—and certainly I was a kind of innocent bystander."

Max slammed his fist on the table. "Annie, tell the Chastain Historical Preservation Society to go get screwed."

She laughed aloud. "Oh, my. What a vision that conjures." Then she shook her head. "Nope. They're counting on me."

"I mean it. I think you should drop the whole thing."

"Oh, I couldn't do that. Really. I promised." She reached over the table and ruffled his hair. "Come on, don't gloom. It'll be okay. The letter writer can't fool me—or anybody—twice."

"That's right," he said slowly. "But, I think I'll nose around Chastain, see what I can pick up. That might discourage any further activity."

"Oh, that's a good idea." Once again, she spoke absently, and she gave an abstracted wave as he departed. She could do a Victorian mystery, such as Peter Lovesey's *Wobble to Death*. Or dart back to the days of Richard the Lionhearted as Victor Luhrs did in *The Longbow Murder*. Or attempt the clever twist achieved by Selwyn Jepson when he presented a modern Macbeth in *Keep Murder Quiet*. Or emulate Edward D. Hoch's talent for the preposterous, exhibited so well in *The Spy and The Thief* when his master criminal, Nick Velvet, stole an entire major league baseball team. Or perhaps she should go for that perennial favorite, an English country murder, à la Catherine Aird, Reginald Hill, or Elizabeth Lemarchand...

Max floorboarded the red Porsche off of the ferry. As he drove toward Chastain, gray dust boiled in the car's wake. His urgency surprised him. Damn. Why did Annie have such an indomitably Puritan conscience? He was the New Englander, and he'd never had any difficulty in persuading himself to do whatever he wanted. He thought for an instant of that wonderful *New Yorker* cartoon of the devil explaining to some newcomers that after all, down here it was whatever worked for you. Annie would never receive *that* advice. He sighed. So he might as well stop trying to talk her out of putting on the Chastain Murder Nights. But, dammit, it didn't feel right to him. Maybe if he just sniffed around, the letter writer would lie low—at least until he and Annie were out of town.

The place to start was the Chastain Historical Preservation Society. He followed the plaques into the historic district, took one wrong turn into a dead end, but finally ended up at Lookout Point. He locked the Porsche, dodged through Chastain's version of five o'clock traffic (one milk truck, a station wagon filled with a wild-eyed mother and nine Cub Scouts, a stripped down Ford Mustang, and three Lincoln Continentals) and pulled on the front gate.

It didn't budge. He read the gilt sign. *Hours: 10 to 4.*

Sourly, he wondered why Fletch always found somebody to talk to.

Okay. Four-thirty and nobody home. He kicked the gate. That shut off at least until tomorrow any inquiry into disbursement of the letterhead stationery. But he sure didn't intend to go back to the island without accomplishing something.

Annie had described all the participants in the morning brouhaha. He leaned back against a brick pillar, pulled a small spiral notebook from his pocket, and studied the list of names.

Corinne Webster, the object of attack. An ice maiden busy leeching the vitality from everyone around her. She probably wouldn't talk to him and would be better left for later, in any event.

Sybil Chastain Giacomo. Max's eyes gleamed. Annie described her as a Ruebens nude in an Oscar de la Renta dress. With the mouth of a termagant. Awesome.

Lucy Haines. Sounded nice. Annie said she looked rather serious. A lean, tanned woman with a firm handshake. A librarian.

Roscoe Merrill. A stalwart of the community, obviously. Treasurer of the Society. A lawyer with a face that kept its own counsel. He'd promised La Grande Dame Webster he'd look into the letter, but all the while he kept stressing that it was better to drop the matter.

Dr. John Sanford. Intense, self-absorbed,

arrogant. And something in the letter made him mad.

Edith Ferrier. The letter made her mad, too. Why did she take it personally? And she didn't like Corinne. Why?

Miss Dora Brevard, permanent secretary of the Board, and Chastain's ancient historian in residence. But she seemed to aim her venom at Sybil, not Corinne.

Gail Prichard. The letter writer said Mrs. Moneypot's niece was seeing a very unsuitable man. Obviously, that was a reference to the combative reporter. Max ran down the list again. If he had his druthers, he'd drop in on the luscious Sybil, but he had a feeling— just a faint niggle of warning—that Annie might take that amiss. And the letter seemed far too subtle an approach for Sybil. So, checking the map Annie had loaned him, he began to walk down Lafayette street toward the heart of town.

"She wants the one with the nun who detects."

Annie looked blankly at Ingrid. "Nun?"

"Mrs. Canady. She's called twice, and she insists she wants the new book with a nun."

Dragging her mind back from the depths of its involvement in the rapidly burgeoning plot for the Mystery Nights, she repeated, "Nun?" Then, in a burst of animation, she rattled off, "Sister John and Sister Hyacinthe? Sister Mary Teresa? Sister Mary Helen?"

"A new series," Ingrid offered helpfully.

Annie squinted her eyes in concentration. New series. Oh, yeah. An *ex*-nun. "Ask her if she wants Bridget O'Toole in *Murder Among Friends*?"

As Ingrid loped back to the telephone, Annie gathered up the strands that had been swirling together in her mind: A weekend at an English country home, croquet, tea, and murder. Perfect. Move over Sheila Radley and Dorothy Simpson.

Audubon prints of a red-shouldered hawk and a wood ibis hung against the Williamsburg green wall. Heavy brown leather furniture offered soft-cushion comfort and the aura of a good men's club. A faint haze of autumn-sweet pipe smoke hung in the air.

Roscoe Merrill met Max at the door, offered a brief handshake and an appraising look, then guided him to the oversized wingback chair that faced the desk.

"So you are helping Ms. Laurance with the program for our house-and-garden week." Merrill settled back in his padded swivel chair, his face bland, but his eyes wary.

Max fashioned a genial smile. "Yes, she's hard at work on the nefarious-doings plot now. However, both she and I were disturbed at the trick that was played on her."

Max's good-humored sally evoked no helpful response. The lawyer merely stared intently and said noncommittally, "Unfortunate. Very unfortunate. But just one of those things."

100

Max quirked an eyebrow. "Does this sort of thing happen often within the Society?"

"No. Oh no, of course not. You misunderstand me, Mr. Darling."

Max waited.

Merrill's dry voice was unemotional, a nice match for his measuring eyes. It was easy to imagine him in settlement conferences, cautious, careful, and calculating. He would never give the store away. His pale gray suit fit him perfectly, and he wore his suit coat even in his office. Not a shirt-sleeve man. He had the air of authority to be expected in the senior partner in an old-line law firm. The law books ranged on the shelving behind his desk were leather bound and had been there for a century. The law firm had borne his family name since 1820. Merrill, Merrill, and Merrill.

"Not at all a usual occurrence, of course. I can't think, in fact, of any other example where the Society letterhead has been misused. A shocking episode, upsetting to all of us. No, Mr. Darling, what I referred to was the—" Merrill paused as if in search of precisely the right word—"the proclivity of women, perhaps, to be a trifle more emotional in their responses to certain situations than men. And, of course, the fact that women, because they are not creatures of business, do not realize sometimes the seriousness of what might otherwise pass as a prank."

Max briefly fantasized about Annie's probable feminist response to Merrill's pre-1940 view of women. *Ka-boom.*

101

"As I told Corinne, it will be very much for the better if we all overlook this incident, painful as it was. To seek to discover the perpetrator would avail nothing. Of course, Corinne has a legitimate complaint. Her signature obviously was forged to that missive, but making this a matter of law would bring an importance to it that it certainly doesn't deserve."

Max had a collection of relatives who specialized in obfuscation, so he sorted nimbly through the verbiage. "You think a woman did it. And you don't think it matters."

The lawyer leaned back in his chair and regarded Max over steepled fingers. "I wouldn't go so far as to put it that directly."

Max grinned. "No, I wouldn't say you put it too directly, but that's the substance, right?"

Slowly, Merrill nodded, his pale brown eyes alert.

"Why a woman?"

"It seems to me that it is a distinctly feminine attack." Merrill rubbed his blunt nose thoughtfully. "Obviously, the letter was planned to humiliate Corinne in front of the Board. And the note to the newspaper editor seems an essentially feline touch."

Max was tempted to describe some very feline men he'd encountered in his time, but instead concentrated on prizing loose information. "Did you check on that?"

Merrill pondered for a moment. He obviously didn't relish imparting any information, but finally he conceded. "I spoke to Ed Hershey, the city editor. He received a note typed on plain white paper. No signature. He didn't save it."

So that was that. "Did Hershey print anything?"

"Not much," Merrill said grimly. "Libel *per se*, young man. But the paper carried a general report of plans for the house-and-garden tours and a brief story quoting Sybil about the question of Bond's paintings being exhibited in New York." His mouth compressed.

"What's going to happen there?"

The pale brown eyes regarded Max with about as much enthusiasm as a Republican dowager opening the door to an ACLU pamphleteer.

"That is hardly relevant to the question of the forged mystery plot."

"No?" Max leaned back comfortably in the luxurious embrace of the soft leather. "I'd think it might have some bearing. You suggest the perpetrator is a woman. Maybe Mrs. Giacomo was ticked off enough to put the show together."

For the first time, interest flickered across Merrill's face, followed immediately by dismissal. Max realized with a surge of excitement that Merrill felt certain of the letter writer's identity.

The lawyer said drily, "Mrs. Giacomo is capable of a rather alarming number of rash acts—but this is much too devious—too quiet—for her."

"You know who did it."

Merrill immediately assumed the bland expression of a sunning crocodile. "Absolutely not. I have no more information than you, Mr. Darling." He paused, then reached out and pensively selected a cherrywood pipe from a rack. Opening a wooden canister, he picked out a thick clump of aromatic tobacco and methodically tamped it in the bowl. When the tobacco was lit and drawing, he regarded Max through the smoke. "I assume we can speak confidentially, Mr. Darling."

"Ms. Laurance and I work together."

He blew a cloud of bluish smoke toward the ceiling. "Let me put it this way." How many settlement conferences had the canny lawyer begun with just that tone? "It is inevitable that jealousies arise when women work too hard and too fervently in organizations." He smiled with all the warmth of a robot. "My wife has described situations to me that would shock you, Mr. Darling. I am confident that the unfortunate incident this morning was a direct response to this kind of pressure."

Max wondered if he were being led down the primrose path, but he dutifully responded to the lure. "Did Mrs. Webster clobber somebody in the Society?"

"It could be viewed in that light. There may be some heartbreak here, Mr. Darling. Let us assume, hypothetically, of course, that a woman member has given herself heart and soul to the Society, served it in every capacity, devoted days and nights to its advancement, and then found herself refused the one office she desired. Now," and he spoke precisely, "I wish to make it clear that I am not and will not be construed as referring to any particular individual. But that," and he sucked on his pipe, "could be the answer to it."

"How bitter is this woman?"

"What do you mean?" Merrill asked cautiously.

"How likely is she to sabotage Annie's Mystery Nights?"

"That won't happen. I'm confident that this was an isolated occurrence. It is over and done with. I'm sure of it."

"I don't want Annie embarrassed—or hurt in any way."

"Mr. Darling, you can rest easy. I assure you it's a closed chapter. The only thing that could cause more trouble would be for you to continue to pursue this. I feel that very strongly. And I'm asking you, as an officer of the Board, as a member of our Chastain community, to let it rest. Will you do that?"

Salt water stung Max's eyes, but, blurrily, he could see a familiar—and oh so shapely and touchable—body, or the half of it, beneath the surface. He stroked nearer and reached out and slipped his hand delicately up the back of her leg.

Annie shot out of the water like a Yellowstone geyser, bounced back down in the surf, and flailed wildly toward shore.

Max came up, laughing so hard that he swallowed a mouthful of salt water and began to choke.

She paused in mid-lunge. "You rat! I thought

it was a shark." She squinted at him. "How did you get here?"

"I drove back from Chastain, parked, changed in the cabana—"

She slapped her hand down against the water. "No, I mean *here*. I didn't see you come."

"Actually, my love, a school of hammerheads could have surrounded you. You were staring at the horizon in total absorption. I came up behind you, then swam underwater. The better to pretend I was a shark."

"Max, will you ever grow up?"

"Hell, no." He splashed to her and picked her up in his arms.

"Put me down."

"Hell, no," he said again, enthusiastically.

They toppled backwards, the water roiled, and they came up again, sputtering with laughter.

His report on Chastain could wait until later. Much later.

Annie put a big red X on the paper tablecloth. "And that's where I'll put the corpse."

Max moved his Bud Light for a better view.

The waiter arrived with two Caesar salads. She motioned for hers to be put to one side of the red X.

With true sophistication, the waiter didn't change expression when she said, "I'm going to have her bashed over the head with a croquet mallet."

"Oh, good going," Max murmured, avoiding the waiter's eye.

She leaned back and said in satisfaction, "So, I did pretty well today."

The waiter cut his eyes toward her as he moved away.

"That's great, honey."

"And what happened in Chastain?"

When he finished his report, Annie speared an anchovy. "Are you going to drop it?"

Max scooped up a garlicky chunk of cheese. "I don't know. I guess I'll decide in the morning."

9

MAX WAS SITTING with his tasseled loafers resting on his Italian Renaissance desktop when Barbie buzzed. He flicked on the intercom.

"A lady to see you, Mr. Darling. About a missing painting."

Work.

If he didn't exactly feel a transport of joy, he did feel a moderate stirring of interest. But he hesitated. Did he want to take anything on? He certainly could delve further into the matter of the Forged Murder Plot. But that would just be depressing if it turned out as Roscoe Merrill predicted. Well, it wouldn't hurt to talk to this prospective client. A missing painting.

"Send her in." Max rose and straightened his tie as Barbie opened the door for a little old lady with faded blue eyes, fluffy white hair, and an anxious expression.

"Mrs. Hilliard," Barbie announced.

As Max solicitously directed her toward a chair, he felt her arm tremble under his hand. As he took his place behind the desk, he studied her.

She wore a navy-blue silk dress with a white ruffled lace collar. A brown and white cameo sprouted from the lace.

"What can I do for you, Mrs. Hilliard?"

She looked around nervously. "Do you make records of everything in your office, Mr. Darling?"

For a moment, he was puzzled. "Records?"

"Recordings," she amplified.

So the old darling watched TV.

"No, I don't tape record anything."

"So our conversation is confidential. Absolutely confidential?"

"Yes, of course."

She paused, looked around once more, then said, in a voice scarcely above a whisper, "Mr. Darling, a painting has been stolen from my home. A very valuable painting." Her strained, fuzzy blue eyes avoided looking at him directly, focusing instead on the silver letter opener that Barbie had arranged artistically in the dead center of his desk. "I believe it has been—I think the expression is—hocked. Can you investigate for me, and discover who sold it to this antique shop?"

"Mrs. Hilliard, if your property has been

108

stolen and sold, you should contact the police."

A flush crimsoned her plump cheeks. She clasped her hands together. "The police. Oh no, no, Mr. Darling. Never. Not the police. I just want to know what happened."

It took another ten minutes to soothe her down, obtain the rest of the story, and discover her objective. She wanted him to interview the antique shop owner, get a description of the person who sold the painting, and obtain a sworn statement from the shop owner. That was all.

He stared at her in puzzlement. There was something a good deal more complicated here than a simple theft. The old lady was clearly distraught—and not about a painting. He was intrigued, but if he took this on, it meant he would have to drop his inquiries in Chastain, just as Roscoe Merrill wanted him to. Max had a congenital dislike of doing what others desired. Actually, he hated to miss out on a session with Sybil the Magnificent. And Miss Dora might have an interesting perspective on Corinne and Chastain society. Moreover, Merrill obviously had an axe to grind. He didn't want any more turmoil touching his precious Society. But he was probably on point in his assumption that nothing more untoward would happen in Chastain, and this frail old lady was waiting for his answer as if her life depended upon it. What the hell.

"I'll check into it," he promised.

His new client took a deep breath, as if an

irrevocable step had been taken. "Thank you, Mr. Darling." She gathered up her purse and rose. At the door she hesitated. Again, she didn't look at him, but stared down at the floor. "Now, don't forget. Not a word to anyone— like the police. I just want that written statement."

When the door closed, he scribbled down the gist of their conversation, studied it for a moment with a puzzled frown, then nodded decisively. He picked up the phone and dialed.

"Death on Demand."

"Hi, Ingrid. Annie there?"

"She's gone to Chastain to rent the tents and check the mystery inserts for the tour programs."

"Okay. Tell her I've got a new case, but I'll call her later. Oh, and Ingrid—tell her I decided to drop the letter inquiry. I'm sure the only murder that will take place on the Murder Nights will be the one she's planned."

Dress rehearsal.

Or the next best thing. The meeting room at the Chastain Historical Preservation Society lacked the musty smell of a theater, and the upcoming session wouldn't have the stomach-wrenching sensation of imminent disaster that Annie associated with the night before an opening, but she still quivered with anticipation. Tomorrow was The Day—the opening of Chastain's Fifth Annual House and Garden tours, and the launching of Annie Laurance's first mystery program. She could hear the cheers now. This might signal the beginning of a lucrative sideline to Death on Demand— if the Mystery Nights succeeded.

If. The old rhyme about a horseshoe nail flickered like a ticker tape in the back of her mind, even as she finished putting copies of the character sketches at each place around the refectory table. Damn, if anyone ever had to deal with the incalculability of the human personality, it was she. It had sounded so easy. Put together a plot, drill the cast, plant the body and, bam, start the show. That simple scenario had failed, however, to take Corinne and Sybil into account.

In fact, she had seriously considered canceling tonight's rehearsal. After all, they'd met twice, and the cast members were bright if unschooled in acting. If she'd been able to restrict the rehearsals to cast members, all would have gone swimmingly. The difficulties came from the presence of Corinne and Sybil. She'd made it clear the sessions were intended for the players, and the presence of other Board members wasn't required. Edith and Miss Dora had gracefully, and perhaps gratefully, stayed away. Not so Corinne and Sybil, and Annie could see no way of barring them, especially since Sybil would ignore any polite subterfuge and claw her way with public clamor to the real reason—and that would be appalling. Although Corinne certainly was white meat. It should be obvious to her that Sybil's honey-voiced pursuit of Leighton was calculated solely to infuriate. If Corinne would just ignore her, the game would cease to be fun and a bored Sybil would promptly drop it. But no, Corinne puffed up like an enraged cat, so Sybil smiled and intensified her campaign.

But Annie had a few tricks up her sleeve, too. She would place Sybil as far as possible from Leighton, and she'd persuade Miss Dora to attend tonight, which might slow Sybil down. She wished Max could have come, but he was finishing up his investigation into the missing painting.

"Nothing funny about murder." The hoarse voice scraped Annie's nerves like chalk on a blackboard. She just managed not to leap into the air, but turned to greet Miss Dora, who stood in the archway, peering into the meeting room, her head poking out of a ruffled collar like a turtle surveying the surface of a pond. Tonight she wore a brown bonnet trimmed with dove feathers and sturdily tied beneath her bony chin. "Idle minds are the devil's workshop." She lifted the watch hanging from a thick gold chain around her neck and stared at it accusingly. "Five minutes after eight. Is no one else here?"

Annie was saved from answering as the others arrived in a flurry. She directed Leighton to a seat at the head of the table and put Corinne to his right and Miss Dora to his left—and felt her heart lighten. She grabbed Sybil's arm, managing not to be overwhelmed by the intentionally heady whiff of Diva perfume, and deftly maneuvered her to the chair at the opposite end of the long table. Sybil gave Annie a concentrated look of dislike, then leaned forward, revealing more bust than a lingerie ad, and spoke to Leighton as if the two of them were the sole inhabitants of a desert island. "Leighton, the most exciting discovery!" Her throaty voice promised pleasures known only in the watches of the night. "I've found Great-great-grandfather's diaries—and they start the year the War began, when he was twelve. I can't *wait* to share them with you."

Leighton came up out of his chair, like a silvery six-foot tarpon hooked by a skilled fisherman, and Annie knew a table length wasn't far enough. With Sybil Giacomo, a football field wouldn't suffice.

Corinne looked every day of her fifty-nine years, her cheekbones jutting against her skin, her mouth drawn so tight that hairline wrinkles marched on her upper lip like a stockade fence.

Annie moved to intercept Leighton. She couldn't care less if Sybil bedded him in the foyer, but, right now, her concern was for the Mystery Nights.

She reached out and touched his tweed-clad arm. "Mr. Webster, we're ready to get under way now." She gently nudged Corinne's husband back to his place. Actually, he was attractive enough to warrant Sybil's interest on his own account. Although his face might be a little ruddy from too many bourbons and water, he still possessed an undeniable magnetism, brown eyes, a boyish smile that hovered between diffident and appealing, a big, burly fullback's build, and a courtly manner.

How the hell had Corinne landed him? She realized her smile was almost too warm and knew Corinne would have a stroke if she decided Annie were after him, too. Feeling Corinne's icy gaze on her back, she turned and flashed her a smile. "But first, we'll give Miss Dora some background," and she picked up her own copy of the character information sheets.

She raised her voice just enough to carry over the murmurs of conversation, which immediately fell away into well-bred silence. "Our mystery is set at Gemway Court, the country home of Lord Algernon Eagleton and his wife, Lady Alicia, who will be played by Jessica Merrill." Annie glanced down the table and smiled. Roscoe's wife was a pleasant surprise, vivacious and pretty, with shining black hair and eyes that were a curious cat-like mixture of yellow and brown. Annie wondered what had attracted her to her reserved and balding husband, who sat beside her exhibiting all the personality of a possum in August. Then she directed her attention back to Miss Dora, hoping to restrain Sybil, who was beginning to move restively at her end of the table. "Members of the houseparty, in addition to Lord Algernon and Lady Alicia, are Nigel Davies, Matilda Snooperton, Susannah Greatheart, and Reginald Hoxton. They spend the afternoon playing croquet. Lady Alicia is a croquet champion, but she plays erratically and her team loses. People have commented lately upon her haggard appearance and generally nervous demeanor. The entire house party seems affected by an air of malaise; conversation is strained and disjointed at tea following the croquet. Everyone disperses to dress for dinner. Shortly before seven, Lady Alicia dashes into the upper hall, calling frantically for her husband, Lord Algernon. She announces that her famous ruby necklace, The Red Maiden, has been stolen. All the members of the house party gather in the upper hallway. Miss Greatheart clutches a handkerchief to her face. Mr. Hoxton looks shocked, then angry. Lord Algernon and Nigel Davies discuss calling the local constabulary. But, in the midst of the clamor, they realize that one of the party, Miss Snooperton, hasn't appeared. She is not in her room. Immediately, everyone begins to look for her. Hoxton announces he will check down by the river and dashes out. When she isn't found in the house and Hoxton returns saying there is no trace of her by the river, a wider search is organized and her body is discovered in the gazebo by the pond."

Annie paused for breath and for dramatic effect and scanned her listeners. Leighton smiled up at her with flattering attention. Corinne watched him, slit-eyed. Gail leaned her face against her hand, her thoughts obviously far away. Roscoe sat with his arm on the back of his wife's chair, his fingers resting on her shoulder. Jessica appeared absorbed in Annie's recital. Sybil opened her double-handled Vuitton satchel and drew out an embroidered cigarette case. Miss Dora's snapping black eyes shot Sybil a look of disgust, then moved to Annie with scarcely more enthusiasm.

Annie smiled determinedly at the old lady. "Mr. Webster plays LORD ALGERNON, a stalwart, soldierly figure, known in the village for his champion pigs. He doesn't have much to say, though the village whispers he's been neglected of late, since Lady Alicia spends all of her time playing cards, going to London for several weeks at a time to stay with different friends, playing bridge for money far into the night. He has been very attentive to one of their guests, Susannah Greatheart.

"Lucy Haines plays AGNES, Lady Alicia's maid. Not much misses her notice. She is fiercely loyal to her mistress."

Lucy smiled and bent to whisper to Miss Dora, who pursed her lips and nodded.

"Roscoe Merrill is NIGEL DAVIES, who motored down with his fiancée, Matilda Snooperton, but Nigel, a reserved Oxford don, has been noticeably glum this weekend and was observed by Agnes in a quarrel with Matilda. In his pocket is a love letter from Susannah Greatheart.

"Our love interest, SUSANNAH GREATHEART, is played by Gail." Gail managed a faint smile. "She has known Nigel since their school days and has always adored him. She had expected they would one day marry and was shocked when his engagement was announced to the strongwilled and determined Matilda Snooperton.

"Our last cast member, Dr. Sanford, isn't here yet. He plays REGINALD HOXTON, a man about town in London. No one is quite certain how he earns his living and some men mutter, 'Cad,' when he is about. He's known to follow the races and is quite adept at cards and roulette."

Annie aimed her most charming smile at Miss Dora, whose dark eyes darted from face to face with reptilian swiftness. "Everybody a volunteer, I suppose?"

Taken aback, Annie nodded.

"Amateurs, all of them. And Jessica's much too pretty to play the part of a raddled old gambler. Should have got an older member." She cackled maliciously. "Why didn't you give Corinne a role?"

The juxtaposition wasn't lost on Corinne. Or on anybody else.

Annie wondered wildly why she'd ever thought Miss Dora, with her unpredictable tongue, would be any help at all.

Sybil didn't lose any time. She blew a waft of perfumed smoke heavenward and looked like a wicked but pleased dragon. "Perhaps there should be some changes in the casting. After all, is Roscoe the right man to play a lover? Leighton should have that role."

Lucy trotted to the rescue. "Actually, Miss Laurance has done a superb job—not only in the casting, but the program as a whole. Why, it reminds me of my very favorite mystery writers, Christie and Allingham and Sayers and Marsh. It just couldn't be any better."

Corinne spoke in a carefully controlled voice. "I would under no circumstances consider playing a role in a murder program. I would find it degrading."

"Oh, now, Cory, that's too strong," Leighton admonished gently.

It was like hearing Dr. No called Doc.

He smiled reassuringly at Annie. "Of course the program's good. Very good. I just hope it doesn't take too much acting talent. But I suppose I can stand around and say 'Eh, what,' without too much difficulty. You've put together a good show, Miss Laurance."

Annie knew good-humored "Eh, whats?" wouldn't satisfy the mystery participants. She'd been to several murder weekends and knew the detectives took their tasks with utmost seriousness and fancied themselves as a composite of Holmes, Vidocq, and Maigret, with a dash of Peter Wimsey.

"Most of your time," she said quickly, "will be taken up with answering questions from the mystery night participants. Now, I have a sheet for each of you which contains information known only to you. You can, of course, lie to the detectives on critical points. You are forced to tell the truth only when a detective team formally accuses you of the murder."

"Oh, this is marvelous fun," Lucy exclaimed. "I think I already know the murderer."

"You can't possibly," Jessica objected. "That would outdo even Ellery Queen."

"Ellery Queen?" Leighton's voice was puzzled, and he thumbled through the sheets. "I don't see a character named Queen."

"Actually, this would be a perfect case for Miss Seeton," Roscoe suggested, with a mischievousness Annie would never suspect he possessed.

Miss Dora crisply explained Ellery Queen and Miss Seeton to Leighton, while other voices rose disputing the identity of the murderer.

"Hey, wait a minute. Who the hell are you? Oh no, come on in here." The brusque voice of Dr. Sanford cut through the goodnatured chatter.

Sanford came through the archway, his hand tightly gripping the elbow of a scrawny figure in a navy blue warmup, navy scarf, and grass-stained tennis shoes. "Who's this? She tried to run when I came in."

Despite the dark headcovering, Annie knew instantly. She stalked across the stone floor. "Mrs. Brawley, what in the world are you doing here?" As if she didn't know.

"Oh, Annie, I didn't know you were here."

Sanford released her bony elbow. "You know her?"

"Yes. Mrs. Brawley and I know each other well."

Freed from the doctor's firm grip, Mrs. Brawley gave Annie the look of a rabbit at bay, then bleated, "I was looking for the Inn and made a mistake." She took two quick steps backward. "It could happen to anybody." Then she whirled around and fled.

Corinne arched a thin golden eyebrow. "What was that all about? Was that woman a prowler?"

"Nothing so dramatic. One of my more active customers. She loves to win, and I suppose she

119

couldn't resist the temptation to learn something about the Mystery Nights ahead of time. Actually, no harm done. She didn't hear anything that would give the mystery away." Annie frowned. "I don't like it, though. I'm running an honest Mystery Nights program. Damn, I wish that woman could channel her competitiveness into something useful—like stamping out pornography."

Corinne's face had all the warmth of a Steuben glass polar bear. "I don't see that this is a matter for levity."

"I'm not laughing," Annie replied sourly.

"A flippant remark doesn't hide the seriousness of the situation. Obviously, if the program is compromised, the Board must meet its responsibility."

Annie had a funny feeling, like catching herself on the edge of a twelve-story drop.

"Just exactly what do you mean, Mrs. Webster?"

"The Board of the Chastain Historical Preservation Society represents the community and is responsible to the community for the probity of its programs. We cannot offer a contest in which an unfair advantage has been given to a customer of yours." Corinne pushed back her chair and stood to her full five feet six inches, which gave her the advantage of height over Annie. She stared down arrogantly. "In fact, I believe it must be clear to all the members that this unfortunate and foolish attempt to mix entertainment with our serious exposition of history is a failure and should be dropped."

"All hell broke loose then." Annie pushed back the lock of hair that struggled over her forehead. She still burned with fury. Usually, the serenity of Death on Demand at night with the book jackets gleaming in the dim light could smooth away even the most difficult of days. But tonight's unpleasantness had been scorching.

"I hope you told her to go to hell." Max's normally pleasant face reflected her own anger.

"Oh, I did. In a choice assortment of words." She paused, recalling her tirade with a tickle of pleasure. She hadn't minced words with Mrs. High-and-Mighty Webster. "Of course, I'm not sure how much she heard, because everybody else was yelling—even nice Lucy Haines. But Morgan settled Corinne down in a hurry. He made it clear that we'd signed a contract." Annie grabbed Max's hand. "That was smart of you to insist we do it that way."

He gave her hand a warm squeeze. "Always put it in writing. I knew that before I went to law school." But he was pleased at her gratitude. He lifted his bottle of Bud Light. "Are you still going to go through with it?"

"Go through with it? I intend to put on the Mystery Nights program in Chastain if I have to play every part, answer every question, explain every clue, and play the corpse all by myself." The tightness in her shoulders began to ease. "But I don't have to do it alone. Everybody rallied—and, of course, that hacked her, too. It wasn't the jolliest session I've ever coached, but we worked on the roles for an hour, with Corinne pulsating like a toad and Sybil trying every trick in the book to get closer to Leighton. Honestly, she did everything but unzip his pants."

"Damn, I've *got* to meet this woman."

Annie wasn't amused. "Your father should have warned you about females like her."

"He might have," Max said blandly.

"If he didn't, I am." She sighed wearily and looked around the dimly lit coffee area. "Golly, I'm tired, and I still haven't put all the stuff for tomorrow in my car."

"I'll do it."

"We'll do it together."

Annie drove the Volvo into the alley and parked it by the door to the storeroom. They perched their beer bottles on the car roof and carried the pre-packed boxes from the storeroom. As she lifted in the last one, she said, "Hey, with all the fireworks in Chastain, I forgot to ask about your painting case. Did you solve it?"

Max pushed down the trunk lid. "Yeah." His voice sounded oddly flat.

She peered at him in the golden shaft of light from the lamp at the end of the alley. "What's wrong?"

"It wasn't much fun."

"What happened?"

He reached up and retrieved the beer bottles and handed one to her, then leaned against the trunk. "I feel like a rat. But, I had to put a stop to it. Dammit, love can sure screw people up."

"What's love got to do with a missing picture?" She tilted her bottle and welcomed the sharp taste of the beer.

"Everything. You see, old Mrs. Hilliard is dead crazy about her nephew. She's had a young girl named Edie keeping house for her and running errands. Her nephew, Alec, met the girl and fell for her—and Mrs. Hilliard doesn't think the girl's good enough. The usual objections. No education. No background. Too much make-up. And Alec's the pride of her life. She sent him to college, and he's a rising young junior executive at the bank."

"Did Edie rip off the painting?"

"That's the picture." He grinned a little as Annie winced. "I went to the antique store. Got the description of the person selling it. Right enough, it's Edie. I got the signed statement from the owner."

"So why do you feel like a rat? Looks like Mrs. Hilliard—"

"Sure that's what it looks like. Simple case, right? One more confidential commission executed. But I sat on that statement for a couple of days. I decided to nose a little harder. I hung around outside Mrs. Hilliard's, waited 'til Edie came out and followed her. I struck up a conversation. In a nutshell: her story is that Mrs. Hilliard asked her to sell the painting, and she turned the money over to the old lady."

"I don't get it."

"Neither did I, so I nosed around some more. Found out Alec isn't the sort of fellow to look past the obvious."

Annie understood. A signed statement. Once lovestruck Alec saw it—

"What did you do?"

"She's a sweet old thing. Crazy about that guy." He cleared his throat. "I told her I was on to the scam, and it was no deal."

"So why do you feel so bad?"

"I told you. She's a sweet old thing, and the funny part of it is, I think she's right about Edie."

"When good people do bad things," Annie said quietly.

"All because of love," he concluded.

He upended his bottle, finishing his beer.

She patted his shoulder. "Come on, let's go take a swim. Tomorrow, we'll be caught up in a script, and we won't have to worry about real emotions."

10

IN THE ORDERLY CONFINES of her imagination, Annie had pictured the opening day of the Chastain House and Garden tours: the weather would be April idyllic, soft puffy clouds dotting a turquoise sky; the participants would be genteel, interchangeable with an audience at, say, Sotheby's, and there would be a general aura of Southern elegance, like a debutante's garden party. That was how the month-long pageant unfolded in Charleston's Historic District.

She got it right about the weather. The sky glittered like a blue enamel bowl, and the air was as soft and smooth as Scotch House cashmere. But half a mile from the historic area, she realized the Board of the Chastain Historical Preservation Society had neglected to inform her of some of Chastain's native customs. Cars that had enjoyed their youth in the Truman administration, mud-splashed pickups, and a rickety hayrack pulled by a green John Deere tractor and carrying a bevy of bony teenage girls in long white dresses clogged Montgomery, the main artery (it actually boasted four lanes) to the River. There was a lengthy pause at Montgomery and Federal for the passage of the Chastain High School Marching Band in purple and black uniforms. The musicians were belting out a fairly good rendition of "The Saints Go Marching In" except for the proclivity of one clarinet to squawk on the high notes. Every parking place on both sides of Montgomery was taken. Energetic hucksters held up hand-painted signs, PARKING $5, offering five to ten spots per front yard. Pedestrians thronged the brick sidewalks. They didn't look like garden party goers to Annie: farmers in high-bibbed overalls and women in freshly starched print cotton dresses; teenagers in so many layers of clothing, shirt on sweater on pullover on sleeveless jersey, it was difficult to imagine, much less determine, sex; and tourists of all sorts and shapes, fat, thin, tall, and tiny, but identifiable by the profusion of costly cameras and camera accessories that hung around their necks, including light meters, zoom lenses, filter cases, and even collapsible tripods.

It took twelve minutes to inch across the intersection once the band played past. Annie feared asphyxiation from the bilious fumes roiling out of the Mercedes Diesel in front of her. It didn't improve her humor to recognize the driver as Dr. Sanford, who blasted his horn every foot or two. In a damn big hurry, wasn't he? But he hadn't made any effort to arrive on time for the rehearsal last night. Halfway up the block, he signaled and turned left. By the time she realized he was turning into the alley behind the historic houses, which provided access to the parking lot at the Historical Society, she was past the opening and fated to continue her snail-like inexorable progress forward.

Ephraim Street stunned her. Where yesterday there had been an occasional car and the placid calm of an unhurried backwater, there was today a chaos that at first glance resembled the deployment of several thousand extras in a Steven Spielberg spectacular. Sightseers milled about the street. Booths filled every inch of space along the river bluff, except for a broad space directly across from the Prichard House where workmen tussled with scaffolding to erect a grandstand over-

126

looking the river. In the booths, Annie glimpsed painted wooden ducks; a Statue of Liberty fashioned from fused Coke bottles; hundreds of quilts; shiny wooden signs that announced The Joneses, People Love My Kitchen Best, Use It or Lose It, and Daddy's Girl; stacks of Canton Blue china (manufactured in Taiwan?), and potholders shaped like roosters, cats, baseball mitts, and starfish. Hot dog stands dispensed coneys, chili, and pop, while vendors hawked barbecue, fried shrimp, cotton candy, and egg rolls.

She was halfway into a left turn, although realizing it would be slow going up Ephraim Street because of the crowds, when a whistle shrilled. Jamming on her brakes, she poked her head out of the window.

The uniformed policeman had patches of sweat under his armpits, and he looked like he hadn't smiled in a millenium or so, the frown lines were so deeply engraved on either side of this mouth.

"Closed for the crafts fair. No left turn. NO LEFT TURN, LADY!" The whistle scalded the air.

"I've got to get to the Society parking lot. I'm already late—"

He held a hand behind his ear, then chopped a fist to her right. "Right turn, lady. RIGHT TURN."

She tried again, yelling like a trader in the closing five.

Swiping sweat from his forehead, he lunged to the car. "Lady, no exceptions. The street's closed."

127

"I've got to get to the Prichard House. I'm in charge of the murder."

"No need to get ugly," he yelled back. "I didn't make the street plans. You turn right, or you go to jail."

Twenty-eight minutes later, after a circuitous route that rivaled the complexity of a maze, Annie wedged the Volvo between a yellow Winnebago (Wisconsin plates) plastered with stickers—*Yellowstone's for the Bears, Take Me Back to Texas, My Heart Belongs to San Francisco,* and *Chattanooga Choo-Choo Me Home*—and a black Toyota pickup that smelled strongly of chicken manure.

She unlocked the trunk and looked at the boxes, none of them small, then sighed, and hefted the first one. It was awkward to carry, and she could scarcely see over it. She was rounding the corner when her knees came up hard against a metal obstacle, and she fell heavily forward.

"Here now, Papa, the lady's fallen," a soft country voice called out.

A large calloused hand reached down and lifted her as easily as setting a broom upright, but a hoarse voice howled angrily: "My placards. Don't let those fools stomp on my placards. Clumsy idiots."

And Annie was clambering around on her hands and knees trying to scoop up the mystery sheets which had tumbled from the box. Then she realized she was eye-to-eye with an enraged Miss Dora, equally vigorously pursuing the contents of her upended wagon, which had brought Annie down.

It sorted out in a moment, two friendly Georgians forming a blockade against the crowd. Soon Annie's box was full and Miss Dora's wagon and her placards restored.

Miss Dora gave Annie a venomous glare, then hunkered down and resumed pounding on the placard-adorned stake at the corner of Lafayette and Ephraim streets.

Annie read the message, written in a fine Spencerian script on white posterboard and covered with a protective sheet of Saran wrap:

"Here stood the waggon yards from 1802 to 1825. Cotton was unloaded here and sold for shipment abroad. Due east of this site rose the shops which served the planters, offering clothing for slaves, shoes, harnesses, groceries, satin, laces, and India china."

In the background, pounding continued on the grandstand, holiday banter rose in a Niagara-like roar, and vendors shouted.

Annie rubbed her bruised knees, sighed, picked up her box, and set out for the Prichard mansion.

It was not an auspicious beginning.

Where the hell were the tables? With her luck, they'd been sucked into the crafts fair booths, never to surface again, or perhaps to reappear laden with tinware, log cabins made of matchsticks, or pictures painted-by-the-number of iron-gray Traveller with his black mane and tail. But she had to have tables—

"Miss Laurance."

Annie pivoted. Corinne stood at the top of the marble steps to Prichard House. She wore a sky blue satin-finish wool gabardine that emphasized her youthful figure and the satisfied expression of a chatelaine who's caught the maid snitching a bonbon.

"You certainly took your time getting here this morning. I've been watching for you, and I must say, you're very late."

The box of mimeographed Mystery Nights instructions weighed at least twenty-five pounds. Annie had lugged it from the parking lot, survived her encounter with Miss Dora, and maneuvered through tourists clotted like Devonshire cream on the sidewalks. Her once crisp mid-calf navy skirt and cotton cambric blouse with a deep frilled shawl collar clung limply to her aching body.

She glared up at Corinne. "Why the hell didn't anybody tell me this place would be like Atlantic City when the casinos opened?"

Corinne stiffened haughtily. "Obviously, Miss Laurance, you lack the necessary experience to take part in a House and Garden week. I want to make it clear that I will certainly urge the Board to withhold full payment of your fee if the Mystery Nights are inadequately produced."

Annie's eyes slitted like Agatha's on the approach of a blue jay. "Mrs. Webster, if anything turns out to be inadequate, it won't be the Mystery Nights," and she turned on her heel.

At three o'clock that afternoon, Annie wondered if her brave words could be fulfilled. Clutching a box of clues and a croquet mallet, she stood indecisively on her left foot, and tried to read her smudged list.

Tents.
Chairs. Tables. Platform.
Speaker's stand.
Audio equipment.
Death on Demand display.
Crime Scene materials.

The candy-striped tents were in place, three of them: black-and-white, red-and-white, and green-and-yellow. A large poster was affixed to the main entrance of each: POLICE HEADQUARTERS (black-and-white), SUSPECT INTERROGATIONS (red-and-white), and DETECTION TEAMS CONFERENCE AREA (green-and-yellow).

Where the *hell* were the tables? She'd called three times, and they had yet to arrive. The long conference tables were to be set up in the headquarters tent to hold clues and copies of the suspects' statements, and the round tables capable of seating ten in the other tents.

If there were six of her, it might all come off on schedule. As it was, she felt a frantic urge to race into the Society building to check on the audio equipment and an equally frantic urge to hotfoot it in the opposite direction down the shell path to the pond and strew clues. This inability to decide where to leap next accounted for her storklike wobble on one foot. Fortunately, she did have help. Max had arrived late, of course, held up by the traffic, but he was busy now talking to Harry Wells, the police chief, who had agreed to serve as technical advisor, and Edith Ferrier, obviously in her element, was crisply ordering about the extremely slow-moving minions from the rental company that was providing the tents, chairs, and platform, but that had, as yet, failed to come up with the tables. Meanwhile, Society members fanned out up and down Ephraim Street, making last-minute checks on contents of the rooms to be shown in the three houses. Every so often, Edith introduced Annie to another docent, and she'd now perfected a response to "Isn't it *scary* to plan a murder?"

As she tried to decide which direction to spring, Annie heard Edith's high, rather humorless voice admonishing a catering employee to be careful in firing the butane-fueled steam ovens which would be used to roast the oysters. Out of the corner of her eye, she spotted Corinne making yet another foray. Annie turned to look down the path toward the gazebo. It would be better for her blood pressure if she didn't tangle with Corinne again today.

Then she spotted one of Miss Dora's placards. It was better than Kilroy Was Here, and it gave her an excuse to keep her back to

132

Corinne. She crossed several feet of lawn to read it.

"The earliest home at this site was erected by Morris Prichard in 1746 for his bride, Elizabeth. It was a two-story frame structure built on a stuccoed brick foundation with a hipped roof and a small portico facing the river. It was lost in the Great Fire of 1831. Old Chastainians claim that a grieving spirit, Abigail McNeil Prichard, may sometimes be glimpsed crossing the lawn at dusk in early spring, searching for her husband, Donald, who was killed by the British at the Battle of Fort Balfour, April 13, 1781. The present Greek Revival house was built in 1834 by Abigail's grandson, Nathaniel."

Annie looked across the freshly mown lawn, much of it hidden now by the colorful tents, and she wondered what Abigail's ghost would think of the brightly striped tents, the fluttering groups of women in pastel dresses, and the harried caterers frantically shoving together the last of the serving tables. Tables. That reminded her—she swung around and wished she hadn't.

Corinne stood beside Edith, one hand on the younger woman's arm, the other gesturing at the serving tables arranged on the drive east of the tents.

"I thought we'd included the she crab soup in the menu."

"The Women of Old Chastain are serving the soup and shrimp salad sandwiches this week in their booth."

"Oh." The monosyllable hung like a block

of ice between them. "I suppose it's difficult to decide to whom you owe your loyalty, Edith, when you are active in so *many* organizations. But I do believe you should have remembered that the Chastain Historical Preservation Society is the oldest and most important society in Chastain—and we should, of course, during the Tour Week be offering the best low country food at our buffet." Corinne lifted her shoulders in a delicate shrug. "However, it's too late to make any improvements in the menu now, so I—"

"The menu doesn't *need* any improvement." Edith's deep-set green eyes burned in her sallow face. She looked like a Picasso pastiche animated by hatred: arms akimbo, sunken cheeks touched with fire, black-and-white silk dress, a half-dozen gold bracelets.

Annie held her breath, almost expecting the woman to explode, like a tangle of wire and steel blown apart by dynamite.

Edith's tight, controlled voice rattled off the foods. "We have okra, shrimp, and crab gumbo, oyster pie, shrimp pilau, stuffed flounder, roast oysters, corn on the cob, black-eyed peas with bacon, orange halves stuffed with sweet potato, cheese soufflé with oyster sauce, hush puppies, cheese popovers, lemon chess pie, sweet potato pie, and Carolina trifle."

Even Corinne looked impressed. "Well, that sounds very good." Her cherry red lips formed a patronizing smile. "Edith, you certainly do have a talent for organizing kitchen work. I do hope that you will continue to be willing to exercise your abilities for the good of the Society. I know it was a disappointment when you weren't named to the slate for president, but I'm sure that you will continue to find your natural level." Then she looked past Edith and raised her hand to wave. "Jessica, wait a moment, I want to talk to you."

As she hurried away, Edith remained by the last serving table, staring after Corinne, her face rigid with fury. Annie tucked the croquet mallet under her arm and moved closer, reaching out to touch her arm.

"Hey, don't let her get to you. She's just a bitch."

Edith slowly turned, and Annie was disturbed to see the glitter of tears in her eyes.

"Someday someone is going to kill that woman." She lifted her hands, pressed her palms against her burning cheeks. "Sometimes I wonder why I don't just leave, just say to hell with it all, but Paul and I were so happy here." She tried to smile, but her lips were trembling. "My husband. He died last year, and ever since I've spent every minute with my organizations. But I've always loved it, you know, loved the history and the wonderful old houses and the people, since we first came here when Paul was stationed at Parris Island. Corinne's not typical, thank God. She never lets you forget it if you aren't a native, and she manages to make so many people miserable. Like me. I guess they've told you how she screwed me out of being president of the Society. And it shouldn't matter a damn—but it does. There are so many things that need to be done—"

A soft voice interrupted. "Edith, I know how hard you're working. I brought some lemonade for you and Annie."

Gail Prichard held out a silver salver holding two frosted glass goblets with sprigs of mint poking over the rims, and her gentle eyes offered amends.

Edith smoothed back her curly hair and managed a smile. She had the worn look common to so many redheads in late middle age, and Gail's shiny youthfulness and sleek auburn hair emphasized the contrast. "Thank you, dear. You're very thoughtful."

"It looks marvelous. Let me put my stuff down." The clues could wait for a few minutes. Annie hurried over to the Police Headquarters tent and tucked the mallet and the box of clues behind a folded card table she intended to use for the Death on Demand display. Then, with a grateful smile, she took the goblet. "Thanks for thinking of us."

"I was watching from the verandah. Is everything coming along all right?" Gail's glance at Edith was uneasy.

"Oh, just fine," Annie said quickly. "Except the tables haven't come. I'm going to call again in a minute. The lights aren't working, and I can't get the audio hooked up yet—" She clapped a hand to her forehead. "My God. I forgot to pick up Resuscitation Rhoda! Edith, is the Red Cross closed? Can we get in?"

"She's sitting in the back seat of my car. Let me know when you're ready, and I'll go get her. I'm parked behind the Inn," and she waved her hand generally northward.

Annie nearly collapsed with relief. "Oh, thank goodness. Lord, what else do you suppose I've forgotten?" She dug in her skirt pocket, searching for her list, then panicked, checking her watch again.

"Relax," Edith admonished. "Believe me, I've put on a hundred of these kinds of things. Miraculously, they always come off."

Gail nodded in agreement. "Everything will work out. What you both need is to take a break for a little while. Edith, why don't you show Annie through the Prichard House? She'll be too busy tonight to go through on a tour."

Annie didn't miss the byplay, the obvious flash of reluctance in Edith's eyes, Gail's attempt to reassure Edith that she was indeed welcome. Or the tacit admission when she added quickly, "Corinne's gone over to the Museum. Something more about Tim's paintings."

Annie was worried over losing the time, still concerned about the audio, the tables, and clue strewing, but refusal would thwart Gail's attempt at an apology.

They started in the kitchen of the Prichard House, returning their empty lemonade goblets and meeting Chloe, the cook, who had provided the refreshment. "Of course, this isn't the original kitchen," Edith explained. "As you know, kitchens were separate from the main houses to avoid fires, but this was added to the Prichard House in 1880. The blue Delft earthenware has been in the family since it was bought by a new bride on a trip to Europe in 1817."

As they emerged into the central hallway, Annie realized this was the way Gail had come the day she arrived to scout out the terrain for the Mystery Nights. She recognized the French Empire card table with the dolphin feet and the Chippendale mirror topped by the gilt eagle. Once again the wide double doors on either side of the hall were open. Annie glanced uneasily up at the curving staircase. Today it was empty. Presumably, Corinne was wreaking havoc at the Museum.

Edith led the way into the big drawing room, giving a rapid-fire commentary. "Look at the overmantel with the short pilasters and broken pediment above. Those are original to the house. Note the stucco reliefs of classic figures. And, of course, the decoration in this room is glorious, the dentil cornices and the ornamental plasterwork on the ceiling."

Her deep-set green eyes sparkled as she pointed out the English Regency chairs and an eighteenth-century portrait of Abigail Prichard, who entertained the English general quartered in her house during the Revolution while sending information to Marion's troops by an overseer of one of her plantations.

Looking up at the smooth, young face in the portrait, Annie imagined her listening with grave courtesy to the general, while her heart churned with worry for her absent husband.

In the dining room, Edith pointed out the

silk damask curtains, gold-and-cream patterned Aubusson rug, Hepplewhite sideboard, and reddish-brown mahogany dining table and chairs. "Notice that wonderful Chippendale mirror hanging between the windows."

At the front door, they thanked Gail for the visit, and Edith led the way out. Midway down the marble steps, she paused to gesture at the massive octagonal columns. "Pure Greek revival, of course, and what outlanders always envision when you talk about a Southern plantation house. Actually, not many of the Low Country plantations look like Tara, although that style is common in the South. We're fortunate to have houses of three very distinct types here that have survived to today, and part of the very great charm of Chastain is that the old homes are freestanding on large lots. Many of them are counterparts of true plantation homes. A few, in fact, were boxed up and moved to town by planters trying to escape the bad air. That's what they attributed malaria to, of course. Bad air from rotting vegetation."

It was obvious that Edith adored her adopted home. Annie was impressed by her fund of knowledge and enthusiasm for her topic, even when the house she was describing in such admiring terms belonged to a woman she obviously loathed.

"How long have you lived in Chastain?"

The sparkle dimmed in her companion's eyes. "We came to stay about six years ago, but we had lived here several times over the last twenty-five years when Paul was stationed at Parris Island. He was career military. A lot of military people retire here. We were from Indiana originally. Paul loved to fish and hunt, and I guess there's no better place in the world for that." The emptiness in her eyes echoed her grief. "And now that he's gone... I don't have anywhere else to go. No family." She tried to smile. "Most people here are very gracious and welcoming. But the natives, even the nice ones, always know who belongs and who doesn't. It reminds me of an anecdote by Mrs. St. Julien Ravenel in her book about Charleston. She is talking about a man whom everyone in town liked and admired very much. Then she comments that he was a stranger among them for eighteen years."

"Oh. Wow. And I suppose she said it in all seriousness?"

"Oh, yes, but she meant it quite kindly. Not like Corinne." She glanced back at the Prichard House. "What amazes me is how sweet Gail is. And Corinne tries to run her life, too, of course. If Gail doesn't get free of it, she'll end up warped, just like Leighton. But I don't know of anything short of death that will stop Corinne." She drew her shoulders in, then turned away from the mansion. "Well, let's see. Shall we go left or right? The McIlwain House is quite lovely. It was restored by Lucy Haines."

"Restored?"

"It was a boarding house from the early thirties until she bought it about twenty years ago. Of course, it doesn't have family pieces, but she has purchased some very fine antiques, many of them authenticated to some early families. She inherited a great deal of money from a bachelor brother, and she's really enjoyed working on the old house. It is an example of absolutely lovely symmetry. At one time, it belonged to some distant cousins of hers, so I suppose it's family in that sense."

Annie looked across the lush sweep of the Prichard lawn. Through the low spreading limbs of live oaks, she glimpsed portions of the exquisite Georgian mansion. "A boarding house. That's hard to believe."

"Oh, my dear, if it weren't for the Historical Preservation Society and *very* hard work by its members, we would have only a handful of old houses still standing. You see, this part of town—" her wave encompassed the McIlwain, Prichard, and Benton houses "—has long been encroached upon by the commercial. Over in the next block, past the alley, it's all commercial, although much of it is old, dating at least to the 1840s. Doctors' offices, lawyers. And the library is on the corner directly behind the Historical Preservation Society. That makes it very convenient for Lucy."

An orange WE-RENT-IT truck rattled into the circular drive, jolted to a stop by the buffet tables, then grated screechingly into reverse.

Annie gave one look, leaped down the remaining steps, and hurtled toward the truck, yelling, "Stop. Stop!"

The truck shuddered to a standstill not more than three feet from the yellow-and-green
DETECTION TEAMS CONFERENCE

tent.

Panting, she reached the cab. The driver squinted down sourly at her. "Yeah?"

"You just about knocked down the tent. Do you have the tables?"

"Gotta get 'em close enough to unload, lady."

"You're within three feet—and they won't do us any good without the tents. Put the long conference tables in the black-and-white striped tent and the round tables in the other tents."

Edith joined her. "Now you're all hot again."

"It's all right." She looked around. "You know, I'm almost afraid to say it, but it's taking shape."

And it was. Order was emerging out of chaos. Black and gold balloons tied to the open front gate bobbed in the gentle afternoon breeze. Similar clumps of balloons marked the entrances to the Benton and McIlwain houses. The truck driver and several helpers were efficiently unloading and setting up the tables in the proper places. Servers were unloading food from the caterer's two pink vans.

And Max was industriously arranging the Death on Demand display in the Police Headquarters tent.

Her spirits zoomed. Suddenly, nothing seemed difficult. She beamed at Edith. "I'd love to see the other houses with you, but I'd better check with Max. How about tomorrow?"

As they parted, Annie called over her shoulder. "Would you bring Rhoda to the police tent?"

Yes, it was all falling into place. She might even begin to have fun. Especially if she could avoid Corinne.

Max stood a few feet back from the card table. As she joined him, he shook his head solemnly. "Why just one card table? We need a lot more space."

We. What a nice word it was.

"We've got t-shirts, bookmarks, and the posters." He threw up his hands. "There isn't room for the posters."

"You're right." She looked around and waved energetically at the rental employees. "Hey, bring one of the long tables over here."

"Terrific," Max crowed. "We can hang the t-shirts around the edges, then use the t-shirt boxes to prop up the posters." He opened a box and held up a t-shirt.

A throaty laugh, like the gurgle of an overfed pigeon, sounded behind them. When they turned, Sybil read the legend on the t-shirt. "Let Me Haunt Your House. Oh, God, that's wonderful. Save one for me." She spoke to Annie, but her eyes devoured Max, who was proving a theorem she vaguely remembered from basic biology, something about living plants bending toward the source of light. If Max leaned any farther forward, he was going to topple on his handsome nose.

"Max, this is Mrs. Giacomo, a member of the Board. Max Darling."

Sybil was already past Annie and a scant inch from her quarry. She held out both hands, magenta-tipped nails today and yet another array of gems, two rubies and a winking diamond surrounded by a glint of emeralds. "Max Darling." If her voice went any lower, it would slither on the ground. "I want you to come over here in the shade and tell me all about yourself."

"I know he would just *love* to do that," Annie said sweetly, "but he's promised to go get our victim for us." She eyed him sternly. "The CPR doll."

Max shot a fascinated glance at Sybil, then grinned lopsidedly at Annie. "Sure. I was just on my way. Mrs. Giacomo, I'll look forward to visiting with you later."

As he moved off toward the parking lot, Annie and Sybil exchanged measuring glances. Each understood the other perfectly.

"I'll be sure and save a t-shirt for you, Mrs. Giacomo. And now, if you'll excuse me, I must go strew clues."

Annie crouched in the gazebo, peering at the floor. It was a little on the order of playing Hide the Thimble. Clues must of necessity be in plain view, but not so obvious they bleated. She yearned for the skill of E. C. Bentley, who was a master of slipping unremarked clues into his narratives. She'd stuck the croquet mallet into a clump of reeds by the pond, the handle clearly visible. But it was more difficult in the gazebo. She twisted to look toward the steps. The detection teams would be limited to a view from the steps. Couldn't have them stepping right into the gazebo, or they would mess up some of the clues. And the red herrings, of course.

She opened her clue box, lifted out the crumpled handkerchief with the initials SAG marked in red ink in the right-hand corner, and dropped it near the bench.

"What the hell are you doing here?"

Her head jerked up.

Bobby Frazier, the broken-nosed, abrasive reporter, glared across the placid green waters of the pond at Gail, who stood framed by the dangling fronds of the willows, looking ethereal, vulnerable, and anguished.

Neither saw Annie, still on her hands and knees in the gazebo. Before she could reveal her presence by clearing her throat, Gail replied, "I saw your car. I knew you'd be here."

"Right. I *work* for a living."

The girl jammed her hands into her skirt pockets and looked at him sorrowfully. "Money's awfully important to you, isn't it?"

"Is that what your aunt told you?"

"She told me—" She pressed one hand hard against her trembling mouth.

"Did she tell you I'd called? And called back all week?"

"No."

"The last time I called, she said you never wanted to see me again."

Tears began to slip unchecked down her face. "Just tell me—is it true you took a check?"

"Yeah. Yeah, I did."

She turned and thrashed blindly up the path.

He stared after her. "Goddammit it to

145

hell," he said harshly. Head down, face working with anger, he lunged past the gazebo, following Gail.

In the gazebo, Annie sighed. If anybody wanted her opinion, and no one was clamoring for it, she thought she detected the fine Italian hand of that good old monster Corinne. Shaking her head, she arranged the rest of the clues: the initialed handkerchief, a Turkish cigarette stub, a crumpled note with no salutation that read 'I can't come.' Her last item was an old boot filched from Max. Carrying the clue box, empty now, she paced to the edge of the pond and artistically mashed the boot into the muddy bank. On her way back to the tents, she glimpsed Gail and Bobby on the path behind the Prichard House. They were deep in conversation.

Annie stepped back to admire the five posters, displayed against the backing of the t-shirt boxes. Fabulous. Nobody could pass by those colors without a second look. She only hoped she'd ordered enough—

The thud of running steps cut across the expected background noises, the low chatter of women's voices, the clang of oyster shells being dumped into the ovens, the muted hum from the crowds wandering Ephraim Street. Annie whirled, her pulses racing. Something was wrong.

The running man pounded up the marble steps of Prichard House to the immense front door, and the hammering of his frenzied knock echoed across the lawn. Everyone paused to look his way, the docents, the workmen for the rental company, the catering staff, Annie. And Corinne, who had just appeared, walking up the drive from the gate at Ephraim Street.

"Tim." Corinne's clipped, cool voice overrode the thunderous rapping. He stopped, one fist upraised, then swung around and clattered down the steps. He loomed over her, basketball-player tall, but thin to the point of emaciation. He had a mop of soft chestnut hair that curled on his shoulders.

"You can't take my stuff. You can't do it." His huge hands gripped her shoulders. "You can't do it, I tell you."

"Let go of me." Her tone was imperious, contemptuous.

His hands fell away. His Adam's apple juggled in his throat. "My stuff—all stacked up, ready to be boxed. Who said you could send my paintings away?"

"I am the director of the Prichard Museum. The disposition of our holdings is my responsibility—and I'm responding to a request from some sister museums for a traveling exhibit. You should be pleased, Tim. Your work will be on view across the Southwest for several months."

"We'll see about that." There was nothing sexy or soft about Sybil's voice this time. She faced Corinne with the intractable expression of Daddy Warbucks guarding a mound of gilt-edged bonds.

"I'll kill her. I swear to God I'm going to kill her." A sob hung in the painter's throat.

147

Sybil turned and slipped her arm around him, and it was oddly touching, the young, almost frail, too-tall young man with his soft, curling hair and the voluptuous, lusty woman. "It's all right, Timmy. Don't be upset."

"But she's—"

"No, she won't. I promise you. I'll get your paintings for you." Sybil looked over her shoulder, her face tightening like a leopard's upon attack. Her voice hung in the air, husky and penetrating as the warning rasp of a foghorn. "You haven't heard the last of this, Corinne," and then, gently, she steered Tim toward the street.

Corinne looked after them, a faint flush staining her porcelain-perfect cheeks.

Annie could have turned back to her display. The others dotted across the lawn were picking up the tempo of their interrupted activities. But Annie had had enough. "Do you eat babies, too?" she inquired.

Corinne turned toward her slowly. "What did you say?"

"You heard me. Obviously, you like to take candy away from babies."

"Museum policies are not your concern. You are hired solely to provide entertainment—and clearly that was a mistake."

"Go to hell."

Annie turned back to her display. Behind her, she heard the scrape of Corinne's shoes as she crossed the crushed oyster-shell drive toward the booth.

"What are those hideous things?"

Corinne was looking at the five posters. Her

eyes briefly touched each. The blond man in the gray suit kneeling by a body in a long black overcoat. The naked young woman sitting in the highbacked teakwood chair. The question in the bruised face of the man standing over the body in the beach cabana. The yellow jeep hurtling toward the big man with light eyes. The man with the gun bursting into the cult scene. Disgust was clear in the pinched line of her mouth.

"Copies of watercolors hanging in my bookstore," Annie said furiously. "I run a monthly contest. The first person to figure out the author and title represented by each painting wins a free book—and free coffee all month. If it's any of your business!"

"Get them out of here."

"Over my dead body, lady. Or yours."

11

ANNIE SHIFTED RESUSCITATION Rhoda from one shoulder to the other. Dressed in the rather voluminous folds of a lavender cotton eyelet dress suitable for a 1937 tea party, the rubber dummy was fairly heavy, but as soon as she, or rather the victim, Matilda Snooperton, was in place on the floor of the gazebo, everything would be done.

Everything?

Oyster shells crunched underfoot. A touch of spring coolness wafted out of the long shadows thrown by the live oaks. The air smelled of sun-warmed grasses, pond water, and iris. The serene calm soothed away the last vestiges of her fury with Corinne. By God, she wasn't going to let that poisonous woman ruin the Mystery Nights for her. She'd worked too hard to let that happen. No, she was going to be calm, cool, and collected and enjoy the evening. Which was almost upon her. Had she overlooked anything?

She ran through the list in her mind, checking off item after item. Yes, this was the last task. Perhaps there would be time for her and Max to repair to her room at the Swamp Fox Inn and savor a Bud Light from the cooler she had thoughtfully iced and brought with her. She paused and looked up at the twelve-foot cane stalks, permitting herself a moment to relish her own cleverness. What a quintessentially perfect spot for The Scene of The Crime, isolated yet romantic. She would give pride of place only to the misty, pine-shrouded finger of lake in Theodore Dreiser's *An American Tragedy*.

Shifting Rhoda to her other shoulder, she began to whistle, "Oh, You Beautiful Doll," as she followed the path around the cane thicket and into the grove of willows that encircled the pond. She headed straight for the gazebo, which graced a gentle rise about ten feet east of the pond. A Saran-sheathed placard, slightly tilted, had been hammered into the ground beside the steps since her last visit to the pond. Ah, Miss Dora.

"Superstitions of the Low Country: Danger awaits the unlucky soul whose path is crossed by a rabbit. (Jimmy Carter might believe that one.) Death follows the hoot of a screech owl. Plant corn and boil soap under a waxing moon. A blue-painted door wards off ghosts. Thirteen at dinner signals death. A bird flying into a house or a mirror cracking without cause presages disaster. Never christen a child, marry, or begin a journey on Friday."

Climbing the steps, she scanned the gazebo's hexagonal interior. Good. Nobody had messed with the clues. Kneeling, she stretched Rhoda out on her stomach, arms artistically outflung. She placed the railroad ticket in the pudgy, rubbery right hand, tucked the scrap of stationery with the scrawled, "I can't come," in Rhoda's pocket, the edge just visible. When she stood and surveyed the scene, she frowned. That initialed handkerchief was too visible. Picking it up, she stepped closer to the railing, and dropped it in the shadows formed by the westering sun.

What a delightfully sinister ambience, the lengthening shadows, the brooding quiet, the black, still water. Her eyes narrowed. What was that clump of sodden cloth among the reeds at the marshy edge of the pond? Had it been there earlier? Her gaze traveled out from the bunched cloth, and she saw a hand languidly floating.

Annie didn't give herself time to think. She moved, vaulting over the side of the railing and dropping five feet to the leaf-

151

strewn ground, sprinting to the far side of the pond, then stumbling over knobby cypress roots to splash into the duckweed-scummed water. Her feet stirred rotting vegetation on the mucky bottom. She grabbed at the torso, then her hands recoiled at its lifeless weight. Gritting her teeth, she reached down again, fastened her hands at the waist and tugged. It was hard work. The sticky bottom sucked at her feet. Razor-sharp reeds slashed at her skin, and sweat filmed her face, dripped into her eyes. The cloying stink of dank water sickened her. And sometime during the hideous exercise, she began to scream. She heard her own voice, high and frantic, as if from a long distance.

The body was so damned heavy, and the reeds snagged it, holding it, impeding her. Then, blessedly, there was help, other hands, and, suddenly, they stumbled out onto the bank, and the body lifted from the water, too.

Annie struggled to catch her breath. Lucy Haines, her face gray with shock, stared down at the sprawled figure. "Oh, my God. It's Corinne."

Gasping, Annie dropped to her knees and reached to check the slack mouth for obstruction. Then her hand fell away. CPR wouldn't help here. A concave depression, about the size of the bottom of a glass, disfigured the crown of the blonde head above the right ear. A rusty stain streaked the pond-drenched hair.

Annie looked up at Lucy, whose wide eyes

mirrored horror and the slow dawning of fear.

"This is dreadful. Leighton... Gail. Oh, my Lord." Her lean hands twisted together. Today, probably in honor of the house-and-garden tours, she wore a sprightly figured silk dress with pink and rose flowers and matching low pink heels, dress and shoes now stained with mud and water. The lovely spring dress was in stark contrast to her putty-colored face and the tightly twisting hands with their fresh coat of pink nail polish.

Annie stood and repressed a shudder. "We have to get help."

"I'll go call." Lucy stepped toward the path, then turned back. "I'm sorry. You won't want to stay here. If you go that way," she pointed to a well-defined gray path that curved out of sight behind a screen of willows, "you'll come to the gate into my grounds. I live next door, the McIlwain House. You can call—"

"No, that's all right, Lucy. You'd better go. It will save time. I don't mind staying." That wasn't true, of course. She would have given anything to leave that silent place of death, but it was clearly silly to send a stranger to find a phone and make the proper calls. Time might not be of the essence, but there was no point in squandering it.

Time! Annie glanced at her watch. Surprisingly, very little had passed since she had blithely whistled her way to the gazebo earlier. It was only 5:35. But the tours were scheduled to begin at 6. Everything would be canceled, of course.

Lucy still hesitated, peering anxiously around the quiet, secluded spot. "Do you suppose it's safe? Perhaps you'd better come with me."

Her fear was contagious. Annie glanced, too, at the sun-glossed fronds of the weeping willows, the black, knobby, sinister cypress, the blackish water. Only an occasional rustle as some creature stirred in the reeds broke the silence. The faraway tattoo of a woodpecker sounded. "It's safe enough. I don't suppose there's a mad killer lurking around to bash me."

The brave words echoed hollowly in her mind after Lucy's reluctant departure. She backed away from the corpse, one step at a time, her eyes darting nervously into the thickening shadows. Every crackle of the cane, every vagrant rustle of the willow fronds made her skin prickle.

The sound of running footsteps brought a hot surge of adrenaline. She tensed, ready to run.

Bobby Frazier burst around the cane thicket. Skidding to a stop, chest heaving, he glared down at the sodden corpse. "So the old bitch got it. Where the hell's Gail?" Before she could answer, he gave an impatient jerk of his head, turned, and pounded toward the gazebo.

Annie sorted out the geography in her mind. The path past the gazebo was probably the closest route to the Prichard House.

A siren sounded, than another. Tires squealed; doors slammed. Heavy footsteps came from the direction of the alley, and police spilled into the clearing, led by a heavyset man in a black broadcloth coat, tan trousers, and a white, wide-brimmed cowboy hat. He shot her a cold, measuring look, then approached the body.

No one moved or spoke as he studied the scene, his thick gray eyebrows bunched, his heavy jowls puffed in concentration.

The pond bank reflected Annie and Lucy's struggle to pull the body to land, drifted pine needles scattered, reeds bent and trampled. The corpse lay face up, eyes wide and staring, mouth gaping. That mushy depression in the skull—Annie searched the nearby area. Then she glanced at the pond, and tensed.

The croquet mallet—her very own croquet mallet—floated in the water a few feet from the bank.

"All right." The lawman's voice was a growl, deep in his throat, like a rusty gate opening. His team swung into action: a young, sandy-haired officer shoved short stakes into the sandy soil at four-foot intervals, then began to string yellow tape, a glum plainclothesman with a gimpy leg pulled out a dog-eared spiral notebook and began a painstaking survey of the crime scene, and a red-faced detective with a beer belly lifted a .35 mm camera to record Corinne at her final rendezvous.

The gaily colored lights strung on the gazebo roof for the tour week flickered into life, adding a garish glare to the twilight. Annie swallowed. So the lights were working. Turning them on was a duty she'd assigned to the Society secretary. Even now, bright yellow lights would be glowing in the tents. And all for nothing.

For a moment, there was no sound other than the clicking of the camera, the occasional crackle underfoot as the men moved about. The lawman gave a satisfied grunt, and turned toward Annie.

He walked ponderously, a bear of a man with heavy shoulders and a thick chest. His face was heavy, too, a bulging forehead, slab-like jowls, a triple roll of chins. His watery blue eyes were murky with the memory of too many crime scenes over too many years.

Annie felt the muscles tighten across her back. When he loomed over her, the world shrank to the space between them. She heard his labored, asthmatic breathing, saw the tracery of red veins in his eyes, and smelled a sour odor of tobacco.

"Harry Wells. Chief of police." His tobacco-roughened throat yielded the rasping intro-duction reluctantly. He looked at her without a vestige of warmth.

"Annie Laurance. I'm in charge of the Mystery Nights for the Houses and Gardens tour."

"What's your story?" Those dour eyes gazed at her unblinkingly.

Her story. The unease in her shoulders spread down her back. God, he was hostile, and she hadn't told him anything. She started out, then realized her voice was high and rushed. She took a deep breath and con-trolled her pitch. When she finished, he glanced toward the gazebo, then at the pond.

"You brought the mallet?"

"A prop. It was supposed to be a prop."

"Turned out not to be, didn't it?"

She didn't like his words, or his tone.

"That's hardly my fault," she shot back.

He didn't bother to answer, merely stared at her.

"Look, she was dead when—" She broke off at the sound of approaching voices. Oh, God. She hadn't had time to wonder about Lucy, but she should have expected this.

"There's no mistake, Leighton. Please, you shouldn't—"

"Hurry, John." Leighton Webster came around the gazebo, his hand tight on Dr. Sanford's arm. "You'll see, Lucy, Corinne's just fainted. That's all. John will take care of her. No one would—" His deep voice rumbled to a stop. He stopped in mid-stride. Behind him were Lucy, whose face held no shock, and Gail, clinging tightly to Bobby's arm.

Everyone watched Leighton's approach in profound, stricken silence: Lucy, Sanford, Gail, Bobby, Annie, the police, and newly-arrived Max, Edith, and Roscoe, who had hurried around the cane thicket, drawn by the wail of the sirens and the inevitable groundswell of rumor already sweeping across Chastain.

But Leighton was oblivious to them all. He stared down at the crumpled figure of his wife, his face frozen in puzzled disbelief.

"Corinne?"

"Leighton." Lucy touched his arm, and then gently tugged, but it made no more impression than sea spume against volcanic rock. He stumbled forward and would have torn through the restraining yellow tape, except for the fresh-faced young officer who stepped between him and the barrier. "Sorry, sir. This is a crime scene now, and no one may enter."

Slowly, his stricken brown eyes settled on the detective's face, focused there. "We can't leave her. She's... We can't leave her there."

Chief Wells could move his bulk with surprising swiftness. "Mr. Mayor, I'll take care of Mrs. Webster. You can't do anything for her now. Go on back to the house. I'll come and talk to you as soon as I can."

Mr. Mayor. The note of deference was unmistakable. Wells did everything but pull on his forelock, and Annie's sense of isolation increased. Nobody demanded to know Webster's story. Mr. Mayor? My God, the interlocking power structure in this town was nothing short of incestuous. Did the Websters run everything?

Leighton's dazed face was gray-white with shock. "Harry, who did this? What happened to her?"

"Nobody knows." The massive head jerked in Annie's direction. "She raised the alarm. Claims she found her dead."

Leighton swiveled, looked at her. "Miss Laurance." His gaze swept the gazebo, and understanding moved in his eyes. "The house tours."

"We'll cancel them." Lucy spoke briskly. "We'll take care of it, Leighton. Please don't worry—"

"Cancel?" He shook his large head slowly, then with determination. "Oh, no, we mustn't do that. Corinne wouldn't want us to do that."

"Of course they must be canceled. They should never have been started," Miss Dora hissed. "Strangers tramping through our lives. I told everyone they were a mistake—and look what's happened—murder."

Annie stared at the wild eyes, the straight silver gray hair, the old twisted mouth working with excitement. Where had she come from? No one had seen her arrive, darting swiftly in those high-top shoes, her cane making no sound on the soft ground.

She lifted the ebony stick, pointed the silver tip at Annie. "Ask her about murder. She knows all about how to kill. Maybe she *likes* to kill."

"Oh, now, wait a minute." Max strode toward Annie, reached out and grabbed her hand. "That's damn silly."

"But we never had murder until *she* came." Miss Dora's head jerked and the black feather on her hat vibrated.

Everyone was staring at Annie, everyone but Max, who slipped a firm arm around her shoulders and glared angrily at Miss Dora. The watching faces looked inimical in the rose and yellow glow from the string of lights atop the gazebo.

Miss Dora rocked back and forth. "Cancel them. Yes, cancel them. Or a murderess will move among us tonight."

The hoarse chant had the sound of madness, but Miss Dora's eyes were as shiny and hard as new minted pennies.

Lucy cleared her throat. "Aunt Dora, you'd best go in now. It's getting late. We will cancel the evenings, of course, but Miss Laurance certainly can't be held responsible for this dreadful accident."

"No, no, we won't cancel." Leighton spoke with a dogged stubbornness. "Corinne wouldn't want us to cancel."

Silence hung over the pond and the oddly assorted people standing there. A dragonfly veered away from them to skim over the dark water.

"How can we continue?" Lucy sought out Wells. "A decision does need to be made. People must be arriving even now. The gates open in minutes." She looked at Leighton in distress. "But you won't want Prichard House to be on the tour. That wouldn't do at all."

But Leighton was determined. Perhaps the thought of the gala helped him escape from the reality of his wife's death—if only briefly. "It must go on. That is what Corinne would have wanted. Only the two front rooms are open, and Gail and I can stay upstairs so that will be all right. The tours last only an hour. No, I don't want any of it canceled."

Edith chimed in, "Leighton's right. It will devastate the work of the Society if we cancel."

"Harry, what harm can it do?" Leighton demanded. "And it meant so much to Corinne."

In the instant before Wells replied, even as

Leighton once again insisted that the program continue, Annie surveyed the silent, watching onlookers.

Lucy stood by the distraught widower with brooding protectiveness, giving an oddly militant cast to a middle-aged woman in soiled pink shoes and a muddy dress. Her concerned face was gray beneath her tan, making her coral pink lipstick startlingly bright in contrast.

Gail looked shrunken. Her pale blue eyes were wide and staring, like a child who has wakened in terror from a nightmare. She averted them from her aunt's body and clung to Frazier's arm as she might to a lifeline in a turbulent sea.

The young reporter scrutinized Leighton and the police chief sharply, as if listening for words that weren't spoken. His muscular body seemed ready to spring, and there was about him the look and air of a crouched panther.

Rouge stained Edith's cheeks in bright patches, but her face was composed. Her white cotton pique dress gleamed fresh and crisp. Only her hands, balled into tight fists, betrayed her emotions.

For once, Sanford didn't appear impatient. His hawklike face jutted forward, the smooth skin and hooded eyes expressionless, the thin lips tightly compressed. Annie doubted very much indeed that the dark doctor was experiencing any emotion over Corinne's demise. Why then did he look so wary?

Miss Dora leaned on her stick and glowered malevolently at Annie.

161

Roscoe was as suitably grave as a mortician. Every so often, he glanced up from the body to Leighton and back down again, but he said nothing.

Annie's eyes moved toward the body, too. How odd that so many whose lives had been affected by Corinne now stood assembled at her death. But no grief was apparent in that silent circle, except, perhaps, for Leighton's air of inchoate puzzlement. Instead, Annie sensed a strand of tension, verging on fear, joining them together.

"A vagrant," Leighton said abruptly. "That's what must have happened. Corinne startled someone, a robber perhaps, and she was struck down. We can't let it destroy the work of the Society. It meant too much to her."

Annie wondered if his plea rang as false to other ears as to hers, but the police chief was nodding.

"Be a damn mess with the crowds if they're thrown on their own," Wells said heavily. "Ephraim's jammed right now. All right, open up."

Open up. Just like that. Didn't anybody have any idea of the problems involved? Annie could keep silent no longer.

"Look, I understand Mr. Webster's feelings—and I'm sorry about the crowds, but it just isn't possible! The gazebo—" She didn't want to talk in terms of The Scene of the Crime. Not with Miss Dora's malignant gaze still pinned to her. Backing up, she started over. "All the clues are in the gazebo—and Mr. Webster and Miss Prichard had agreed to play the roles of two of the suspects. I don't think—"

Edith stepped forward. "Of course we can do it. There are others who will willingly take their places. In Corinne's memory, we will do it."

12

WERE THESE PEOPLE CRAZY? Was sudden death merely a piquant addition to their mystery lust?

Apparently so, because the Mystery Night program was a sellout despite the ripple of rumors about Corinne's murder, and tourists without tickets were pressed against the front fence, straining for a glimpse of police and any movement near the cane thicket.

Annie took a deep breath and climbed the steps to the platform facing the tents. She looked out over the cheerful spring scene. Pastel hues predominated in the encroaching dusk, women in pink, yellow, and white, men in light blue, gray, or tan. It might be any church picnic or annual firm outing except for the undercurrent of nervous excitement threading the hum of voices. The lights strung in the live oak trees and suspended inside the tents glowed a soft yellow. Most of the men and women were sitting around the tables under the Suspect Interrogation and Detection

Teams Conference Area tents. A few heartier eaters were in line to refill their plates with Low Country specialties. Her stomach rumbled hungrily. She hadn't even had a bite of the Carolina trifle. She'd been hardpressed to scrub off the pond mud, change into a fresh strawberry-and-lemon striped skirt and soft pink cotton blouse, move the crime scene to the rose arbor just east of the house, drill Max and Edith, who were pinch-hitting for Leighton and Gail as suspects, and make it to the foot of the platform only ten minutes after the mystery program was scheduled to begin.

She looked down the path leading to the pond and wondered if Corinne still lay defenseless on the gray sandy bank, her once lovely face sunken in death, her immaculate wool gabardine dress soiled by water, mud, and blood. A policeman, scarcely visible in the growing dusk, stood guard, turning away venturesome Mystery Night participants. This was the first moment she'd had time to think about her gruesome discovery and its ramifications. That hulking police chief wanted to hear her story—and he had called Leighton Mr. Mayor. But surely he wouldn't cast her as the murderer just because she was from out of town. Her gaze skimmed the crowd surging closer to the platform, and Miss Dora's wizened face popped into view. Annie fought a feeling of panic as she stared into those brooding, hostile eyes. Why had the old lady turned on her? And the answer hung in her mind: because she was a stranger.

Jerking her glance away, she stared down at her notes. She had so many things to remember when she made her presentation, including two gruff demands from Chief Wells. She glanced to her left. The Mystery Night suspects, most of them costumed suitably for an English house party in the late 1930s, stood in a line by the steps. They looked uneasy, their faces strained and subdued in the soft yellow light. And why not? Most of them were a good deal more concerned about the progress of the murder investigation unfolding a hundred yards to the northwest than they were the evening's entertainment.

A sharp voice wafted up from immediately below her. "Are you working on the real murder? Can I help?"

Annie looked down into the fox-sharp eyes of Mrs. Brawley.

Mrs. Brawley stood on tiptoe. "What time did it happen? Maybe I saw something."

"But the grounds weren't open then. What would you have been doing?"

For once, Mrs. Brawley appeared at a loss. Then she mumbled, "Oh, looking here and there. Interested in flowers. Irises." Glancing down at her watch, she yelped, "It's almost fifteen after. You must get started," and she turned and scuttled back toward the Suspect Interrogation Tent.

Swiftly, Annie translated. Mrs. Brawley had made a reconnaissance to get a jump on the other contestants and been prowling around the Prichard grounds. Obviously, she hadn't seen the murder or she would be

regaling Wells and the world with an embell-
ished account. But it meant she'd cheated on
the mystery program, no doubt about it.
However, in the scheme of things, she didn't
at the moment give a bloody damn. Let Mrs.
Brawley win. Just let this horrible, endless week
be over, and then she would be free to return
to Broward's Rock and the uneventful (usually) life of a mystery bookstore owner.

Still, it rankled. She'd gone to a lot of effort
to create a neat mystery, and everybody who
paid their ten bucks deserved a fair chance to
win. But any attempt to disqualify Mrs. Brawley
would delay the beginning of the program yet
again and create an emotional tempest.

So, she loosened the microphone from the
stand. The crowd shifted in anticipation. Her
gaze swept over the throng and rested for an
instant on a very familiar figure, the redoubtable
Emma Clyde, the most famous mystery writer
on Broward's Rock. Emma's stiff bronze curls
had a fiery tint in the fading light. She wore a
lime cotton top and a multi-pleated orange
skirt. Shell earrings with a matching necklace
and three bracelets affirmed a spring outfit.
She looked like a housewife enjoying Wednesday
night bingo, except for the piercing cornflower
blue eyes that even at a distance crackled with
intelligence. For an instant, their eyes met and
held. As always, Annie felt a quiver of unease
in Emma's presence. The woman was so damned
smart. Then Annie grinned and gave a little
wave. If anybody could outwit Mrs. Brawley, it
was Emma Clyde.

As she thumped the microphone, expectancy flickered among the crowd like summer lightning. She gave one last glance at her notes.

"On behalf of the Chastain Historical Preservation Society, I'm delighted to welcome all of you here tonight. It has been my pleasure to create a Mystery Night program for your enjoyment. Before we begin to delve, I want to ask: Did you enjoy your tours of the Benton, Prichard, and McIlwain houses and gardens?"

There was an enthusiastic chorus of affirmatives.

"Did you enjoy your Low Country dinner?"

"Yeees!"

"Are you ready to put together your mystery team and begin the investigation of the English Manor Mystery, a k a 'Alas, A Sticky Wicket'?"

Cheers rose.

"Excellent. We are ready, too. There are a few official procedures to be followed. Participants are requested to form teams of not more than ten members and to elect a Team Captain Detective, who will officially represent the team in the investigation and pose questions to the suspects. The investigation begins after I describe the background to our mystery and introduce your suspects."

Looking out at the sea of eager faces, Annie described the functions of the three tents and the availability of materials in the Police Headquarters tent. "Each team, at the conclusion of the investigation, is to turn in a sealed envelope which contains: 1. The name of the murderer and 2. the reasons why the team accuses this suspect. Now," she leaned forward, slipping in Chief Wells's first order, "it is imperative that you list on the outside of the envelope the name of every member of your team, complete with address and phone number. Failure to include this information will disqualify your entry." Listeners nodded, and some scrawled in open notebooks. "Your entry will be received by 10 P.M. On Friday evening, you are invited to return here for the Denouement Ball, which begins at eight. You may dress as your favorite mystery sleuth or character. Prizes will be awarded for the five best costumes. At midnight, we will announce the winner, that is, the team which correctly identifies the murderer at the earliest time. Finally, one last warning." The low hum of excited voices ceased. These people were serious mystery fans, and they avidly waited to hear Chief Well's second instruction. She spoke distinctly. "The area open to Mystery Night detectives is limited to the tents"—she pointed to each tent in turn—"and to the area around the tennis court, which is just east of the Prichard House. If a member of *any* team is discovered anywhere else, that *entire* team will be disqualified." She smiled. "I know I can count on your cooperation. And now, Mystery Night sleuths, here is your crime."

Heads bent, hands flew, as Annie related the sequence of events at Gemtree Court, the manor house home of Lady Alicia and Lord Algernon: the disappearance of The Red

Maiden, and the discovery of Matilda Snooperton's crumpled body beneath a rose arbor by the tennis court, not far from where only a few hours earlier the happy group had enjoyed croquet. "Detectives are encouraged to study the area near Miss Snooperton's body closely. From police reports, it will be learned that a tool shed near the murder scene has been broken into. There are no fingerprints on the broken lock to the shed.

"You will find in the Police Headquarters tent copies of the statements made by each suspect, the autopsy report, and a table containing replicas of the clues. Each team may make application for one—repeat, *one*—search warrant, which will be granted only if you can convince the magistrate—*me*—" she paused for the laughter which greeted her pronouncement, "that you have sufficient reason. You may sign up at the clue table for your turn as a team to visit The Scene of the Crime."

She tried to ignore a sudden vivid image of the pond and Corinne Webster's crushed skull. In the pause before she forced herself to continue, she heard a contestant mutter happily, "I just love stately home murders. Have you read *Blue Blood Will Out* by Tim Heald?" Her companion nodded enthusiastically. "Loved it. Another good one is *Lord Mullion's Secret* by Michael Innes."

Annie noted that both women, right on the front row, were plump and wore sensible tweeds and sturdy walking shoes. Mrs. Brawley faced sharp competition.

169

"Now, I'd like to present your suspects."

Suspects. Who would be the suspects in Corinne's murder? Other than herself, the stranger in their midst. Discomfort moved in her stomach, and it wasn't hunger. Would Wells remember to cherchez la femme? Or would that be lèse majesté to Mr. Mayor? But the police always looked first at the husband, didn't they? Maybe not this time. Worry gnawed a little deeper.

Jessica started up the steps. Despite her somber face, she was lovely in an ankle-length, leg-of-mutton-sleeved dress of pale yellow organdy.

Suspects. How about the distraught painter and libidinous Sybil? Or the perhaps more than merely eccentric Miss Dora? Or Gail and her unsuitable suitor? And Edith sure as hell—Annie's wandering thoughts quivered, then crystallized. That letter she'd received with the Mrs. Moneypot's mystery plot; it had been full of innuendos about people who hated Corinne!

"Annie."

Jessica's urgent whisper jerked her back to the platform.

"May I present Lady Alicia."

Jessica, her sleek black hair upswept in a chignon, addressed the crowd languidly. "After tea, I rested in my room. I'd quite a headache from our afternoon in the sun, playing croquet." She shaded her dark eyes. "I saw no one. When I was dressing for dinner, I opened my jewel case and found that my famous ruby necklace had disappeared, so I

170

immediately raised the alarm. As for Miss Snooperton, I hadn't seen her since teatime. She was a dear girl."

Brava. An unexpectedly talented amateur actress.

"Lord Algernon," Annie announced.

Max shot her a brief, warning glance as he strode on stage. As always, he carried himself with élan, even in a borrowed tuxedo. He looked every inch a young English lord, tall, blond, and crisply handsome.

"Took a stroll down to the river after tea, but I didn't see anyone." Then he paused, timing it just perfectly to raise doubts among his listeners. "But there might have been somebody over by the arbor. Dashed hard to see in the mist. Damn shame about Matilda. Must've been the work of a tramp."

Leighton asserted that a robber must have murdered Corinne. Nature imitating art? Or had that fragment simply stuck in his mind from his suspect sheet?

Max stepped back beside Jessica, and Roscoe soberly moved forward. As always, he looked reliable, imposing, and excruciatingly boring. He waited stolidly for Annie's introduction.

"Mr. Nigel Davies, the betrothed of our victim, Matilda Snooperton."

Roscoe clipped his speech neatly, reading from his sheet and ignoring the enthralled crowd. "Appalled. Absolutely appalled. Not the sort of thing that happens in our set. Hadn't seen much of dear Matilda since we motored down. Tennis, then croquet. After tea, took a stroll toward the village. Didn't see a soul."

John Sanford stepped forward, quite natty in a light blue cotton suit and a boater hat.

"Mr. Reginald Hoxton, a friend of Lady Alicia's from London."

Unexpectedly, he threw himself into the part, speaking in an ingratiating, oily manner. "Only too glad to help in the investigation. Miss Snooperton a charming gal. First met her this weekend. Left my room after tea. Ran down to my car to get my shoe kit from the boot. Didn't meet up with anybody." He closed with a toothy smile.

Edith was up to any challenge to protect her beloved Society. Though her deep-set green eyes were clouded, she threw herself with utmost seriousness into her role as the love-struck girl, Susannah Greatheart. Her abundant hair covered by a gay pink scarf, she stood with her eyes downcast, nervously twisting a white cambric handkerchief. "Such a shock. I did see Miss Snooperton after tea. I happened to walk down to the arbor, but she was quite all right, oh quite all right, when I left her." She paused, gnawing her lip. "Actually, she was laughing." She held the handkerchief to her face and stepped away.

Edith's rendition of counterfeit distress was outstanding. But the distress emanating from the final player was only too real, though ironically, it was critical to the success of her role. "Agnes, Lady Alicia's devoted maid," Annie announced.

Lucy had changed clothes, but obviously made no attempt this time to dress for a formal dinner at an English manor house. She wore a navy blue skirt and gray silk blouse, and her face scarcely resembled that of the cheerful woman who had been so friendly to Annie. Her eyes looked haunted, and her cheeks sagged. Annie knew her thoughts were far from this platform and felt immediate sympathy. Lucy clutched her suspect sheet in a white-gloved hand that trembled and read in a monotone.

"Happened to overhear Mr. Nigel having words with Miss Snooperton. That I did, early this morning. And later, after tea, I saw Mr. Hoxton with a tire tool, and he looked very disagreeable. And Miss Susannah was crying when she crept up the stairs this afternoon. And there's more that could be said about some of these fine ladies and gentlemen."

And wasn't that the truth, Annie thought grimly. She lifted the microphone and forced a lilt into her voice. "It's all yours, detectives. The suspects will repair to the Interrogation Tent, and I will be in charge in the police tent as Detective-Inspector Searchclue of New Scotland Yard. And—one last point, which I'm certain you will all appreciate—Mrs. Gordon at Swamp Fox Inn has volunteered her restrooms for use by the participants and staff of the Mystery Night. Also, the Inn coffee bar will be open until midnight."

The throng of eager detectives swept toward the tents. It wasn't quite a mad enough rush to imperil life and limb, but it bordered on the frantic. It matched the festival exuberance in Phoebe Atwood Taylor's *Figure Away,* but at least it lacked loon calls and shotgun blasts. The comparison was disturbing, though, when she recalled the fate of the person in charge of that celebration. She started down the steps and saw the dour face of the policeman who'd refused her entry to Ephraim Street that morning. Was he assigned to watch her?

13

IN THE LAST-MINUTE CRUSH around the clue table, Annie tried to answer a half-dozen sharp questions at once, keep an eye on Mrs. Brawley who was edging ever nearer the search-warrant stack, and accept entry envelopes thrust at her with demands for instantaneous time notations. It made the closing minutes on the floor of the New York Stock Exchange seem pastoral in contrast.

Team Captain #3, in his saner moments a courteous druggist on Broward's Rock, waggled his envelope a millimeter from her nose. "We're next!" He thrust an elbow militantly into the ribs of Team Captain #9. "By God, we're *next.*"

Team Captain #9 bared her teeth. "I *beg* your pardon. Some people will do *anything* to win," and slapped her envelope on his.

Grabbing the envelopes, she scribbled 9:48:03 on both, stuffed them in the shoe box cradled beneath her arm, and reached out just in time to pin Mrs. Brawley's hand to the table. "One search warrant, Mrs. Brawley. *One.*"

"We thought you meant *one* for each suspect."

Annie reflected honor on her upbringing by overcoming the impulse to snort, "In a pig's eye." Instead, she gritted, *"One* search warrant to *each* team, Mrs. Brawley. Your team already received a search warrant for the tool shed."

That search yielded Mrs. Brawley's team a card with this information: "The broken lock on the hasp of the tool shed has been wiped clean of fingerprints. The tool shed contains tools and gardening and hobby equipment, including shovels, trowels, hose, putty, paint, the balls and mallets from the croquet game, drills, bits, flower pots, and sacks of fertilizers. Nothing appears out of place. Atop the workbench is a pile of sawdust. On the floor of the shed are found several pieces of gold filigree."

Mrs. Brawley shrieked over the hubbub. "Can we *trade* cards?"

A piercing whistle brought a merciful instant of silence, then Team Captain #4 demanded shrilly, "Is it true Lord Algernon bought that train ticket to Venice?"

Annie ignored him, too, and mustered the strength to shout, "Time, ladies and gentlemen, time!"

Annie stood guard by the trunk of the Volvo, still parked beside the Winnebago in the deep shadows of the Society parking lot. A faint glow from a single light on the back wall of the old building provided the only illumination. She scanned the shadows warily. Nothing would have surprised her at this point. Faked entries. A raiding party on camelback. An offer of a weekend in Rio in exchange for the name of the murderer. She had stationed Edith beside the Death on Demand display on the Prichard lawn while she and Max carried the boxes to the car for overnight safekeeping. There was no point in trying to maneuver the Volvo down Ephraim Street. The booths were closed, but the street still teemed with departing Mystery Night participants, and the odds of finding a parking spot in the Inn lot were nil. Max was making the last trip. She didn't envy him his struggle through the ambling holidayers.

Bright white light exploded beside her. She jumped a foot.

A hearty laugh boomed. "Scared you that time. Just another couple of shots now. Hey, Ms. Laurance, give us the low-down on the murders—Miss Snooperton's and the real one." In the recurring flashes, she saw a walrus mustache quivering with good humor. "I told Mother," her tormentor jerked his head at a dumpling-shaped face nodding in agreement, "this was just the best vacation idea we

176

ever had. We'd planned to go to Europe this summer, wanted to be there for the Wedding, but Mother and I decided there was no time like now to stay home." Mother nodded sagely. "All those bombs. Why, a man would be taking his life in his hands. So Mother read about the house-and-garden tours, and then we saw the bit about the murder, and we just had to come. I'm a sucker for Perry Mason. And can you believe we've got your murder and a real one to boot!" He resheathed his camera, and leaned forward. Annie caught a strong whiff of fresh Juicy Fruit gum. "Tell us now, was that Miss Snooperton a black-mailer?"

Annie caught a flicker of movement at the foot of the Winnebago.

"Come right on out here where I can see you, Mrs. Brawley."

Without a trace of embarrassment, Mrs. Brawley sidled closer to the open trunk. "I had a little thought. If I could just see our entry, Annie, just for a teeny second."

"No." She snapped it with a satisfying sharpness, like the hiss of a plunging guillotine.

"Oh." Mrs. Brawley gave a nervous titter. "I guess Chastain's going all out for the Mystery Nights to assign a policeman to guard the entries," and she looked past Annie.

Annie knew before she turned and saw the sallow face of her favorite traffic cop. "How about that," she managed to say coolly. But her temper never let her quit when she was ahead. "I'm in Room 312."

"Yeah. I know."

She was still staring belligerently at him when Max arrived with the last container. He looked curiously at the newcomers. Annie was in no mood for introductions. She snatched the box from him, dumped it in the trunk, slammed down the lid, and grabbed his arm.

As they rounded the corner onto Ephraim Street and fought their way against the lemming-like stream of exiting gala-goers en route to whatever Bacchanalian delights Chastain afforded after ten o'clock, Max implored, "Hey, where's the fire?"

"Me. I'm mad. Dammit, I'm more than mad. I'm scared. Look behind us. Is that cop coming?"

He twisted his head and gave a low whistle. "Yeah."

"Oh, hell."

Annie stalked up the main walk to Swamp Fox Inn, but Max took her elbow to detour her around to the side. "We'd better go in the back way."

"What's wrong with the lobby?"

"Honey, Refrigerator Perry couldn't heave through that crowd."

"Oh, *double* hell. Max, I'm so *tired*—and I'm starving."

"Not to worry. I spotted a back patio that isn't in use. Leave it to Papa."

She almost retorted sharply that she wasn't Mama (shades of the walrus mustache's Mother), but she had run out of steam.

But she had to admire Max's artistry as he charmed their landlady. Annie leaned against the spotted wallpaper in a back passageway and watched plump, exhilarated Idell Gordon succumb to his charm.

Fluffing her frizzy orange hair, she twittered, "Of course, I know how you feel. Ms. Laurance *needs* a restful dinner. And the coffee bar is packed!" She simpered at Max, thoroughly smitten. "I know what we can do." The "we" was so happily familiar that Annie beguiled herself with a vision of Max and Mrs. Gordon dancing a minuet. "I'll turn on the whirlpool in the patio, and we'll just put on a *tiny* little light, then no one will even know you're there."

As a general rule, Annie considered public whirlpools about as attractive as a lunch date with Typhoid Mary, but tonight her whole body ached with weariness. Manning that clue table had taken the perseverance of a hockey player and the manual dexterity of a card shark, and all the while she had worried about Wells and his stony attitude toward her. "Whirlpool?"

Mrs. Gordon nodded proudly, then heaved a sigh, her protuberant brown eyes mournful. "I had to do it. The Pink Cottage has one, and so does Harbor Lights. And you have to have free wine in the rooms. All the inns do it."

When she checked in that morning, Annie had noticed the bottle of wine sitting on the high nightstand next to the modern-day version of a four poster rice bed. Italian. But there was no handy antifreeze gauge.

"You young people run on up to your rooms and change. I'll bring your sandwiches out to the patio."

As they walked up the hall toward the main stairway, the din from the jammed coffee bar buffeted them.

Annie felt a marrow-deep longing for her lovely, *isolated* tree house on Broward's Rock.

"It's going to be a long week." The worn treads of the staircase slanted to the right. As she started up, the banister wobbled under her hand. "God, a fire trap." And when she opened the door to 312, stale, hot air washed over her.

She turned on the window air conditioner. A faint eddy of slightly cooler air fanned her.

Max stood just inside her doorway, his face determined. "I'm going to see what I can get out of her."

"I doubt if she runs to roast duck."

"Annie, my God, do you ever think about anything but food! I'm worried about your neck."

But Max putting her fear into words triggered a stubborn ostrich-like response. "I don't have anything to worry about," she said loudly.

"Oh, no. Just two extremely public confrontations with Corinne hours before she was mortally bashed."

"Me and everybody else in town," and she told him about Edith, Tim, and Sybil. As she talked, she felt more and more confident. "And there's the infamous letter. Hell, I'm going to laugh when I hand that over to Wells. He can't ignore all those motives." She pushed away the memory of venomous

Miss Dora. "I don't have a thing to worry about—and I'm too tired to gossip with a landlady who twitters."

The phone buzzed.

She yanked it up.

"Your sandwiches are ready, Ms. Laurance."

Food.

A nobler character might have gone to bed hungry to thwart his quest for information. Annie stalked down the slanting stairs.

Max continued to look grave as he pulled out a webbed chair for her at a wrought iron table. Was he trying to make her nervous? Yes, of course he was. She ignored him, though that was hard as they'd both changed to swimsuits, and Max in navy blue boxer swim trunks excited another appetite.

The ham was paper thin, the Swiss cheese brittle, and the white bread store-bought, but it was food. She wolfed three sandwiches as he plied Idell Gordon with questions. Annie shot them a bored glance, which both ignored. My God, who *cared* when Corinne and Leighton got married? Or that Miss Dora was sister to Lucy's mother? Or that Sybil had been married three times, and the last husband was an Italian count who was tragically killed driving a race car at Monte Carlo. She toyed with a fourth sandwich, then picked up her glass of Chablis (of dubious American vintage) and wandered around the shadowy patio. Even in the single light mounted over the doorway, she could see pink paint peeling from the stucco walls. The drooping ferns in the fake blue-and-red Chinese porcelain pots needed a stiff dose of Vertigro. Annie stopped beside the whirlpool, which smelled heavily of chlorine. She squinted at the frothy water, almost sure she saw several bird feathers and the carcass of a black roach. Sitting down, she dangled her legs in the swift, steamy water. And drank some more Chablis, contrary to Department of Health instructions posted prominently on a nearby pillar.

"Of course, she made me so *mad*! So rude and overbearing, but always in this sweet, reasonable tone, as if you were the one in the wrong."

Annie slid over the side and sat on the first step. The water felt good. So Corinne wasn't beloved by Idell either.

"...kept saying the Inn had to maintain standards..."

Too bad Idell hadn't listened.

"...couldn't understand the economics of it. She was *always* rich. What do the rich know about money? I'm trying my best, but everything costs so much. And you can't get good help. One maid was drinking the wine in the rooms and replacing it with water!"

Annie flowed down the steps until the hot water lapped around her neck. The light mounted over the door turned into a nice rainbow when she squinted at it. She could never remember being so tired. And there were three more Mystery Nights ahead—and tomorrow she must persuade Chief Wells how ridiculous it was even to consider her as a suspect in Corinne's death.

"She and Dr. Sanford had the ugliest quarrel. A friend of mine was in one of the patient rooms, and she overheard. She peeked out the door, and she said Dr. Sanford looked *murderous.*" Idell's laughter tinkled insincerely. "Oh, I didn't mean that." But her disclaimer was as phony as imitation alligator. "He really was awfully mad. He wants to expand the Chastain Hospital's program for poor people, and Corinne said that was nonsense, they could go to the county hospital. Dr. Sanford said no, they couldn't for all the things they needed, and then they went at it hammer and tongs."

Annie floated in the bubbly water, and the words danced in her ears like kernels popping in a hot air machine.

"She even made poor Leighton quit the Foreign Service and come back here. He was so handsome then, and he just kind of went to seed." Her voice dropped conspiratorially. "But everyone's noticing how he's taken a new lease on life lately. Lost some weight and been out walking a lot. And sometimes you can't help but think that when a man spruces up, there has to be a *reason.*"

Handsome man. He certainly was. She wiggled in the water. "Good looking," she announced.

There was a moment's strained silence from the table.

"Who?" Max asked stiffly.

"Leighton Webster, of course." Languidly, she pulled herself up, shivered as the cool night air swept over her damp skin, and sank down again. "Mrs. Gordon, do you think he and Lucy might have something going?"

"Lucy?" Her voice rose in astonishment.

"She was certainly protective of him this afternoon, at the pond."

"Oh, no." The landlady spoke with certainty. "No, no, no. Lucy and Leighton are old, old friends, but nothing more than that. Why, Lucy was head over heels in love with Cameron Prichard."

"Who's that?" Annie asked.

"Gail's daddy. You see, it happened this way. Lucy and Cameron fell in love the summer after he graduated from Princeton. They went everywhere together. And then, all of a sudden, Cameron went off to Atlanta. Corinne introduced him to some rich girl there, and he married her. That was Gail's mother. Cameron and his wife were killed in a private plane crash in Louisiana, and Gail came here to live when she was ten. Lucy's just crazy about that girl."

So Lucy didn't care about Leighton Webster. Just an old friend.

Heat coursed through Annie. She should get out of the whirlpool before she dissolved. She rubbed her eyes and stared fuzzily at Max and Mrs. Gordon.

"Of course, people will say anything." Idell's tone indicated her delight in this human failing. "I don't believe a word of it, but some think Corinne cared a little too much about young Tim Bond. Otherwise, why did she get so upset about Tim and Sybil when everybody knows it's right normal for a young man to enjoy an older woman? I think that's why Corinne wouldn't let him send his paintings to New York. She was just jealous."

Fragments of thoughts swirled in Annie's mind. Tim's paintings. The watercolors. Damn good this time, especially the yellow jeep. And the one with the big teakwood chair and the naked girl. Tim wanted to go to New York. Big kid. Why didn't he go? Enormous hands.

"Annie. Annie!"

The call punctured her reverie. Sleepily, she opened her eyes.

Max knelt by the side of the pool, and the rainbow light flickered over his face.

"Come on, honey. You'd better get out before you're parboiled."

"I've got a better idea," she said huskily. "Why don't you get in?"

Max stood on the front steps of the Swamp Fox Inn and relished the feeling of utter righteousness shared by early risers. The Broad River gleamed pale gray in the first pulse of dawn. No one stirred near the empty booths and the grandstand. Closer at hand, crumpled Pepsi cups and mustard-stained hot-dog wrappers littered Ephraim Street. He breathed vigorously, enjoying the fragrance of the purple iris blooming magnificently near the Inn steps. Do Annie good to get up and greet the sun. He was on the point of turning on his heel to go knock on her door, when wisdom prevailed. She would not be pleased. Moreover, she would not be sympathetic to his plan. Dammit, she was in a stubborn mood. What would it take to convince her that Wells was after her? Well, at least he saw the danger. Running lightly down the steps, he turned to his right. Fragile patches of mist rose from the river, swirling like strands of Christmas tinsel in the low branches of the live oak trees. The rhythmic slap of a solitary morning jogger's Reeboks against the sidewalk broke the early morning stillness. Max responded to his cheery good morning and strolled past the crisply white Benton House with its graceful double piazzas. He was intent upon the Prichard House, in all its Greek Revival glory, and what he could see of the extensive gardens. There, far to the back, stood the thicket of cane that screened the pond. He walked as far as the McIlwain fence, then retraced his steps, passing the Prichard House, the Benton House, and the Inn. On the east side of the Inn, on the corner, sat the buff-colored former fort that housed the Chastain Historical Preservation Society. Max turned left down Lafayette, passing the parking lot behind the Society. It was almost full, holding, he assumed, the overflow from the area inns. Halfway up Lafayette, a narrow, dirt alley opened to his left.

The alley was bordered on his left by brick walls or wrought iron fences covered with honeysuckle or shielded by towering pittisporum and banana shrubs. On the right, plainer iron or wooden slatted fences marked the back of business properties. Access was available on both sides for garbage pickup. At the back of the Prichard grounds, magnificent wisteria flowed up to and over the intricate iron fence. Max opened the gate and followed a curving path to the rear of the garages. The path forked there, one branch leading directly to the kitchen steps. He followed the other branch. In two minutes, he had reached the grove of willows and the gazebo. The pond looked dark and deep, sunlight still barred by the surrounding trees. Mist wreathed the trunks of the black-barked cypresses. There was an unearthly oppressiveness about the spot. A fit place for murder.

"Hey, you! Nobody can come through here. Crime scene."

"Sorry. Thought my dog came this way."

"No dog's been through here, buddy. Beat it."

Max lifted a hand and turned back toward the alley. He walked briskly back to Lafayette and turned left.

At the next corner, he started down Federal, his footsteps echoing in the empty street. The locked and shuttered buildings here backed up to the alley and to the houses on Ephraim Street—and to the dark, silent pond.

A granite slab inscribed with ornate cursive writing identified the golden-domed building on the corner as the Prichard

Museum. The paint on the gilded dome glistened as the rising sun spilled down. So this would be the home of the paintings whose ownership was so bitterly contested. Tucking his hands in his pockets, he walked on. Next door was the Chastain Public Library, a cheerful yellow frame with cane-bottomed rocking chairs on the front and side piazzas. The final three adjoining buildings of rose, pink, and yellow stucco housed antique stores, a furniture shop, law offices, and medical offices. He'd already visited one of the buildings, the day he'd talked to Roscoe Merrill in the offices of Merrill, Merrill, and Merrill. Next door, in the pink stucco building, were the offices of Dr. Sanford.

A street-cleaning truck rumbled down Federal's brick paving. A battered pick-up passed with the radio blaring an Eagles tape.

Max found a narrow passage between the rose stucco building and the Chastain Public Library and turned into it. He swiftly crossed the alley and the parking lot of the Swamp Fox Inn and ducked beneath the arch that led into the patio. All nine tables were occupied with Inn guests taking advantage of the free Continental breakfast. Two tables were pushed together to accommodate an octet of chattering garden clubbers engaged in a synthetically sweet struggle over which walking tour to take that morning. "I declare, Beryl, you know I 'specially came to Chastain because my great-uncle Marcus is buried in the St. Michael's graveyard." "Gardens first, I say, gardens first!" "Now, girls, we can all just have a good time today without *any* hard feelings, I know we can."

Annie waved at him with moderate enthusiasm.

"My God," he exclaimed in tones of awe, which were clearly not appreciated, "you're awake."

She sipped coffee, then replied in a carefully modulated voice. "Mrs. Brawley telephoned at six-fifteen. She wanted to know whether Reginald Hoxton's shoes were freshly shined."

"Fascinating the way her mind works." He dropped into the chair opposite her. "What did you tell her?"

She poured a fresh cup of coffee from the server. "This damn stuff's lukewarm. And the croissants are dreadful."

He waited.

"I told her I had no friggin' idea."

"You didn't!"

"*Six-fifteen* in the morning."

"Lovely hour. You should have been up with me."

"I hope you were having more fun than I was."

"I took a walk."

"Your voice is freighted with portent."

He looked over the table, picked up a dog-eared menu, dropped it hastily. "Do you have some paper? A pen?"

She found a crumpled renewal notice for *Time* with a tiny wooden pencil attached.

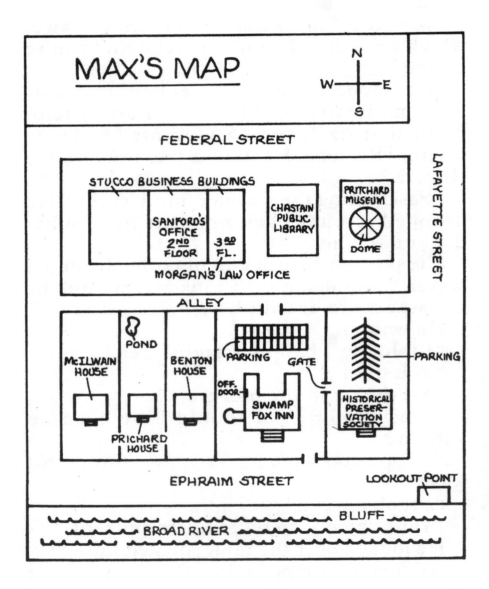

He looked at it in disdain. "I *think* this is a collector's item." Then, hunching over the table he drew a map.

When he was finished, he proudly handed it to her.

She studied it, handed it back, picked up a croissant, and bent it. "Spongy."

"Don't you see?"

"I see that Ephraim Street and Federal Street are parallel."

He poked at the map with a determined finger. "Don't you remember yesterday afternoon, how all those people showed up at the pond? Like a Greek chorus."

"So?"

"They were all within minutes of the pond. *Minutes.* Anyone of them could have clobbered Corinne."

She glanced back down at the map. "I guess so," she said slowly. "Anyone of them could have." Then she grimaced. "But so what? Why do we care? I'll tell you something, Max. I am not going to get involved in another murder hunt. I'm involved in the Mystery Nights, and that's enough to satisfy my blood lust for months." She warmed to her theme. "Correction: for *years*." She started to shove back her chair, then froze, looking over his shoulder toward the arch.

Chief Wells filled the brick entryway, his shoulders almost touching the curved walls. His slab-like face, pocked as old cement, looked ominously grim. Then his questing eyes stopped and focused on her.

14

IN THE SUDDEN SILENCE, his boot heels rasped loudly against the bricks as he crossed to their table. He didn't remove his cowboy hat, and Annie took an unreasoning dislike to the smooth, high, undented crown. Who did he think he was? A Canadian Mountie? He wore gray slacks this morning with his black coat. A black string tie drooped against a faded white shirt. His frosty eyes watched her like a hunter with a 22-inch mallard in his sights.

Whispers, soft as a summer wind in wheat stubble, rippled among the garden clubbers. Annie heard "chief" and "murder" and a sibilant hiss of meaningful "she's." She shared an impartial glare between the brightly curious women and the lawman.

"Ms. Laurance." He moved his pouchy jaws, shifting a wad of chewing tobacco from one side to the other, then gave Max a brief glance. "Mr. Darling." The words sounded like they'd been scraped out of a rusting barrel. "Like to talk to you. At the scene of the crime."

Max smiled pleasantly, but his dark blue eyes were watchful. "Ms. Laurance gave you all the information she had yesterday, Chief."

"Did she? I didn't hear tell about her quarrel with Mrs. Webster." The tobacco bulged against one cheek. "Course, she can talk to me over there," the big head nodded to the west, "or at the station. Her choice."

Annie had always wondered what it would be like to be taken into custody. Her present feelings were as close as she ever hoped to come. She didn't like it, but, mostly, it made her mad. Max was sending an avalanche of silent messages, which she had no difficulty deciphering. They boiled down to: keep cool.

It was still too early for tourists, but an occasional car passed as they headed down Ephraim Street. A street cleaner paused in his sweeping to eye them curiously. No lights shown from the front windows of the Prichard House, and the morning paper lay midway up the gray marble steps. Annie had devoured the headlines in her copy of the *Chastain Courier* over her breakfast coffee. The lead story was topped with a 3 column 48 point bold head:

SOCIETY PRESIDENT MURDERED AT POND

The drop head read:

CORINNE PRICHARD BLUDGEONED; WEAPON IS MYSTERY NIGHT PROP

How dreadful it would be for Leighton to read those blaring headlines. She felt hideously intrusive as the police chief gestured for her and Max to walk up the drive toward the tents, which had a forlorn, after-the-circus appearance this morning.

"Was it right about here?" Wells grated. He spat into the grass, but his eyes never left her face.

"Right about here what?" she demanded.

"That you threatened Mrs. Webster."

"That's unwarranted, Chief." Max's voice was as hard-edged as a meat mallet. "At no time has Ms. Laurance in any way ever threatened Mrs. Webster."

Wells transferred his glower to Max. "Were you here?"

"No. However—"

"Then butt out. I'm asking the girl here."

"That's fine. But I'm a friend of Ms. Laurance's, and I'm telling her that she doesn't have to answer any questions unless she has an attorney of her choice present."

"You a lawyer?"

"Member of the Bar of the State of New York."

Wells lifted a massive hand to scratch at his jaw. "That doesn't give you any right to mouthpiece here."

"Certainly not, and I don't hold myself out as practicing in South Carolina. But there's no law to prevent me from providing Ms. Laurance with counsel free of charge." Max had lost his aura of relaxed complaisance. As he faced Wells, he looked as tough and determined—and handsome—as The Saint at a denouement. Annie loved it.

Wells masticated his tobacco for a long moment, then without a word, turned back to Annie. She savored it as a victory, but realized with a sinking heart, that the skirmish was far from over.

"I got a witness, heard you tell Mrs. Webster she'd be a dead body if she didn't get off your case."

Annie seined through yesterday's encounters. Oh God, the watercolors... The entire infuriating scene sprang into her mind, and once again she throbbed with anger.

"She was really a bitch," Annie exploded.

Max sighed wearily and rolled his eyes heavenward.

Wells looked like a hammerhead positioning himself for the kill.

"I mean really! She insulted Edith Ferrier, who's worked her tail off for the Society, then she twisted the knife in that poor kid painter, and, finally, she went after my posters. I wasn't having any."

"So when you met up with her at the pond and she started in again, you picked up that croquet mallet and let her have it." His words bounced like boulders down a hillside, gathering force as they came.

Too late, Annie remembered Max's signals. So what the hell. She couldn't go head-to-head with Wells. He was too damned big, but she glared up at him and spit back, "Absolutely not. I didn't see her again until she was dead— and that wasn't my pleasure." Actually, her stomach gave a decided lurch, remembering that dented skull. "Look, you're off on the wrong foot. Frankly, I don't care *who* crunched that awful woman, but there's a big field out there."

"Nobody else threatened her. And you and she had a knock-down-and-drag-out fight at the rehearsal Sunday night, and she ticked you off first thing Monday morning 'cause you were late. It all got to be too much, didn't it?"

"Chief, that woman was ripe for murder. She'd infuriated everybody who knew her. She poisoned everything she touched. Have you bothered to look around? You haven't even asked me about the letter that listed all the reasons everybody wanted to kill her. What kind of investigator are you? If you've got so many big-mouthed witnesses, surely somebody's told you about the letter."

Wells looked exquisitely bored. "Yeah, I heard about it. That letter you *say* you didn't write."

"Obviously, she didn't write it," Max interjected. "How would she get stationery from the Chastain Historical Preservation Society? How would she know the dirt on everybody in Chastain?"

Wells shrugged. "That letter don't mean a thing. Just some woman with her nose in the air." So he'd talked to Roscoe Morgan. "I don't need any fancy-dan fiction to find a murderer when I got two people hot and heavy with Mrs. Webster."

"Two people?" At least she wasn't the only candidate for the county jail.

Wells paused to expectorate a long stream of tobacco juice, then rubbed a heavy hand over his mouth. "Yeah. You and that smart-ass reporter."

Two outsiders. Annie could almost hear the click of the cell door.

196

"How about Edith Ferrier? And Tim Bond? And Sybil Giacomo? And everybody else mentioned in the letter?" Hands on her hips, she glared at him.

"Little lady, I don't give a damn about that letter. Now you tell me this—who picked the pond for a murder spot? Who carried the weapon there? And who knows all about killin'?"

An ear-splitting roar echoed up from the river. Annie pressed her fingers briefly to her temples.

"The speedboat races," Max observed. "They get underway about eleven."

Sightseers eddied up and down Ephraim Street, drawn to the booths which were beginning to open.

"All this place lacks is a Coliseum with lions."

Max grinned and stuck his hands in his pockets. "Maybe next year."

"This year the sport's going to be feeding me and Frazier to the local gendarmes."

The high keen of a revving speedboat almost drowned out her words.

"Oh, good grief. Let's see if we can find a spot quiet enough to despair in."

But the lobby of the Inn teemed with culture-hungry tourists.

A fat lady stuffed into an orange polyester slack suit pouted in a corner. "I don't see why Mildred *always* has to have her way."

Mildred, prim and purposeful in a restrained

gray shirtwaist, brandished her guidebook. "The McNeil gardens are second only to Middleton Place. And *that's* where we're going."

Idell Gordon spotted them, and gestured energetically at the message slot for Room 312.

Max made it to the ferry wharf with ten minutes to spare. He wriggled impatiently in his seat. He wished he were with Annie, but they needed that letter containing the Mrs. Moneypot's mystery plot. If the chief wouldn't investigate its origins, by God, they would.

The cellular telephone rang.

He snatched it up, then relaxed at the sound of his secretary's voice. God, he wouldn't put it past Wells to clap Annie in chains at any minute.

"London called."

"The Queen, or the Prime Minister?"

"Neither," Barbie replied seriously. Max admired her efficiency but regretted that her sense of humor was on a level with Agatha's. "Mr. Ronald Harrowgate called from Sotheby's. He said the matter could be concluded for 200 pounds."

"Great. Call right back. And tell them to send it Federal Express."

"Across the Atlantic?"

"Sure."

As he hung up, Max grinned. At least *something* good was happening this morning. It wasn't an expensive gift, but it was a momento she would cherish. And, when she was ecstatic with delight, well, that would be the time to spring his *new* plan for the wedding.

Three cheery toots of the whistle signaled the ferry's approach. Max looked across the sparkling water. As soon as he had the Moneypot's plot in hand...

Gail was waiting on the kitchen steps for Annie. She wore an ankle-length gray cotton skirt, a high-necked white blouse with a lacey front panel, and a pale yellow cummerbund. Her thick, shining auburn hair was twisted into a severe bun, emphasizing the circles beneath her eyes and her pallor.

"I'm sorry to ask you to come to the back. Leighton's in the drawing room with some cousins from Savannah." Her hands twisted nervously. "You're awfully nice to come at all."

Although she had her own objectives for this meeting, Annie couldn't have refused the piteous message Idell had handed her. *Please come. I need help.—Gail P.*

And Gail did look damned vulnerable, frail, and grief-stricken. For just an instant, Annie felt a flicker of irritation. Where was the girl's gumption? Then she thought of Corinne's steel strong will and the years she'd had to dominate this gentle creature.

"Certainly I've come. What can I do?"

"I saw you out in front. With Chief Wells. Did he say anything?" She waited tensely for Annie's answer.

Annie saw no point in advertising her own predicament. She replied judiciously, "He

199

was interested in what Corinne did yesterday." Which was a very delicate way of putting it.

"Did he—did he mention Bobby Frazier?"

Annie couldn't decide how to field that one, and she waited long enough that Gail assumed the worst.

"Oh, I knew it." The girl clung to the wooden railing. "He's prejudiced against anyone different. I'm so afraid he'll try to blame Bobby."

"Being from out of town isn't sufficient grounds for a murder charge," Annie said firmly, mentally crossing her fingers.

Gail shook her head hopelessly. "You don't understand. Bobby and Corinne—"

"Why did she want him out of town?"

Gail stared at Annie as if she'd suddenly sprouted horns. "How did you know that? How did you ever know?"

The morning's on-shore breeze rattled the glossy magnolia leaves and whipped the frothy lace at her throat.

"Last week at the Society meeting, the famous one where I read the letter—" Gail nodded, her eyes never leaving Annie's face— "before we came in, Bobby and Corinne had a spat on the sidewalk and I heard him say something about her offering him money to leave town."

Gail gripped Annie's arm. "Did you tell Chief Wells?"

"No. But look, Gail, something like that can't be kept quiet. I'm sure I wasn't the only one who heard it. Lucy was coming up the sidewalk just then, too."

"Oh, Lucy would *never* tell. She knows how I feel about—" Gail flushed. "I mean, he's awfully nice. No, Lucy won't tell." Then her cheeks burned a deeper red, and she released Annie's arm. "I'm sorry, I can't ask you not to speak out. But it isn't nearly as awful as it sounds. If you just let me explain, you'll see it doesn't amount to anything!

"I met Bobby last fall when he came to do an article on the Museum. I work at the Prichard Museum. I'm the curator." Quiet pride shone in her eyes. "That's what I studied at school, art history. And I don't have the job just because of my family. Even Bobby sees that. He told me so." A smile touched her drawn face. "Bobby's not like anyone I ever met before. He's so strong and quick, and he says what he thinks, always." She looked at Annie with a flash of rare defiance that made her look radiantly beautiful for a fleeting moment. "I like that."

Annie knew directness could have its advantages. She thought of Max, whose mind was positively serpentine. And she enjoyed that, for all the frustration it could engender. Weddings with 500 guests indeed!

Gail's moment of courage faded. "My aunt didn't like him. She said he wasn't—" she jerked her head angrily "—wasn't a gentleman. She told me not to see him anymore." She darted a defensive look at Annie. "He kept on coming to the Museum. And we went out for lunch, and sometimes we met for dinner."

"Corinne didn't know?"

Gail lifted her chin. "I finally decided we

weren't going to sneak around anymore. I told her I was going to see him when I wanted to."

"Is that what prompted her performance the day I came to look at the grounds?"

Gail avoided Annie's eyes, staring down at the lake-blue amethyst ring on her right hand. "That was just Corinne being Corinne."

"Why were you so angry?"

"Because—because I couldn't believe what she'd done." An echo of that anger throbbed in her voice now. Her blue eyes enormous, the girl struggled to breathe, and Annie remembered the dreadful moments in the exquisite front hall of Prichard House. "She offered him money to leave town—and he took it." Gail looked at her imploringly. "You won't understand. I almost didn't understand, when I found out. I felt like a fool, that he hadn't cared for me at all, that he was just interested in money. Then, yesterday, he was mad, too, and he yelled at me to look at the canceled check before I made up my mind. I called a friend who works at the bank, and she checked for me. Bobby's endorsed the check over to the National Children's Fund."

"So he took the money, just like he was being bought off, then turned it over to charity? She must have been furious." Oh, what she would have given for a glimpse of Corinne's face when she discovered Bobby's doings!

"He doesn't care about money. When I told her yesterday afternoon, she said he was a thief and a cheat, and I told her she was an ugly, jealous old woman." The fire died in her eyes. "I didn't know anything was going to

202

happen to her. I told her there wasn't anything she could do to keep us apart. She said if I saw him again, I wouldn't get a penny of my parents' estate. But when I told Bobby, he didn't care about that at all."

The back of Annie's neck prickled.

"This happened yesterday afternoon? You found out about the check and quarreled with Corinne, and then you told Bobby all about it?"

Gail nodded.

Annie approached from another angle. "How could she keep you from inheriting?"

"Oh, she could do it," Gail explained reluctantly. "She had the power under Daddy's will to decide if I should receive the bulk of the estate on my twenty-fifth birthday, or on my thirtieth birthday. Yesterday she said I'd never get any of it. But Bobby said she could take her precious money and—" She paused, blushing. "He didn't care at all! He said we'd do fine without a dime from anybody."

And Chief Wells would be as likely to believe that, Annie thought, as he would to believe in little green men serving pink champagne in the mansion gardens at midnight.

"What time did you talk to your aunt yesterday?"

Gail's face again looked shadowed and pale. The vivacity drained away. "It must not have been long before...it happened."

"But you were mad at Bobby when you talked to him at the pond."

Gail drew her breath in sharply. "Were you there?"

"I was putting some clues in the gazebo. Neither of you saw me. When you started talking, well, it seemed like a bad time to speak up."

"That was *before* I talked to Corinne. Bobby chased after me, and made me listen. That's when I called the bank, then I marched in to Corinne and told her she was trying to embarrass me and make Bobby look bad, but it wasn't going to work. Then I found Bobby out in the grounds, and we worked it all out. Afterward, I went to the Museum. It always makes me feel better to go to the Museum. I'm putting together a new exhibit of Victorian wallpapers. I love the names of some of the patterns. They're so grand. Bachelor's Pear Vine. Oglesby Damask. Fuschia Trellis. Hewes Parlor Paper."

But Annie scarcely listened. She was sorting out the timing.

1. Bobby and Gail at the pond.
2. Bobby follows Gail.
3. Gail and her aunt quarrel.
4. Gail and Bobby talk on the Prichard grounds. Gail tells Bobby, whee, all is fine, I'm being disinherited, but whither thou goest, etc.
5. Gail to the Museum.
6. Bobby where?

Wherever he was, he carried with him a gilt-edged motive. As did Gail.

Annie looked curiously at the girl, who had the relaxed air of someone who has told it all and found it less awful than expected. Didn't she have the slightest idea that she had now provided both herself and Bobby with enormously satisfying reasons to murder her aunt?

"So you see," she concluded, "once Bobby knew I was going to keep on seeing him, he didn't have any reason to be mad at Corinne anymore."

Annie nodded solemnly.

Then worry clouded the pale blue eyes looking at her so earnestly. "But I'm afraid Chief Wells won't understand."

Annie felt confident Gail's concern was thoroughly justified.

"So that's why I asked you to come over. Roscoe told me that you and Mr. Darling have some experience with murders. The thing is, do you think you could help figure out what happened to Corinne?"

"I'd sure like to—" Annie began.

"Oh, that's wonderful! You're wonderful!"

Annie felt on a level with a charlatan advertising radio waves to rid a house of termites, but when she saw the effect of her response on Gail, she couldn't backtrack. The girl looked as if she had been suddenly reprieved from the gallows.

"There's no way I can ever thank you enough!"

"Please don't try," Annie said feebly, wondering how she was going to explain this to Max.

Gail had the grace to look embarrassed. "I was just sure you would help, so I've already called Lucy and persuaded her to talk to you. You'll go see her first, won't you?"

The lady in front of Max couldn't decide. Did she want *"Chastain. Two Hundred and Fifty Years of History,"* or *"Interiors of Low Country Plantations?"* Then she held up *"Southern Gardens, Their Majesty and Magnificence."*

"That's the one," Max encouraged. "No one should come to Chastain and leave without that book. The gardens, you know."

She glanced up at him and the frost in her eyes melted. "Oh, do you really think so?"

"Absolutely. Cross my heart."

He smiled genially at her as she paid, received her change, and slowly yielded her place.

The Society secretary, eyes bleary with fatigue, looked up gamely.

"Yes, sir. What can I do for you?"

"Can I buy you a beer?"

Louisa Binning brushed back a tangle of peroxided curls. "That's the nicest thing anybody's said to me all day." Then she looked past him and sighed. "But I can't leave. You have to make hay, etc."

"You think they'll all buy books?" He tilted his head at the two-deep line that stretched behind him out the propped open door and all the way to the sidewalk.

"My dear, they buy *everything*!"

"I'll buy a stack of ten, any ten, you pick 'em, if you'll give me a few minutes time."

She laughed goodhumoredly. "Talking to

you—and to everybody—is my job. You don't have to buy any books."

Max took out his wallet, picked out a bill, and dropped it into a wooden box shaped like the fort, varnished a golden brown, and carrying the painted legend, *Gifts for Chastain.* Then he reached into his inner jacket pocket, pulled out a thick envelope, and handed it to her.

"How did the writer of this letter get the paper and the envelope?"

She emptied the envelope, glanced at the cover letter, then stiffened. "Why, this is the letter..."

He nodded.

She was still studying the sheets, and her mouth formed a silent O.

Max had the silky feeling of delight akin to rolling up three oranges on a slot machine.

When she looked up, worry lines bunched around her eyes. She stared past him at the restless line of tourists, then pushed back her chair.

"Ladies and gentlemen, there will be a slight delay in filling your orders. Please feel free to look over our brochures, and you will enjoy walking through the fort. You will find musket slits in the east wall. I will reopen the desk as soon as I have restocked the books. Thank you for your patience."

Then, in a low voice, she turned to Max. "Come back to the stockroom with me, where we can talk."

15

A S SHE CLIMBED THE shallow front steps of the gracious Palladian portico of McIlwain House, Annie couldn't resist a glance to her right, but banana shrubs masked the wrought iron fence, affording not even a glimpse of the Prichard grounds. The sweet scent of the shrubs mingled with the smell of freshly turned dirt in the flower beds by the steps. It couldn't be far to the pond, though, for Lucy to have heard her screams for help.

The front door was open. Annie rang the bell and looked through the screen door into the hall. Lucy came slowly, her footsteps heavy with fatigue. She seemed to have shrunk since that day they first met. Annie remembered a vigorous woman with a country road stride. The woman holding open the door seemed frail. Her voice was flat. "Gail said you might come. I don't know what you can do, but I'll help if I can."

The heart pine flooring of the entry hall glistened in the early morning sunlight that splashed through the open door of the dining room to the east. Lucy slowly led the way to the drawing room. Annie looked around appreciatively. No expense had been spared in restoring this room to grandeur. Bois-de-rose silk hangings framed the tall windows and emphasized the rose background of the Aubusson rug. The wallpaper was a rich floral print of peonies against a cream background. Rose and cream, too, dominated the upholstery of the Chippendale-style furniture. The most remarkable piece was a mahogany china breakfront, holding a Blue Canton dinner service.

Lucy gestured for her to be seated. "Won't you have some coffee?"

Annie accepted immediately. The morning offering at the Swamp Fox Inn had a taste like lukewarm dishwater with a dash of instant coffee. Lucy's coffee had the dark, winey taste of chicory, and the warm, homemade doughnuts she brought were superb.

Lucy smiled as she ate with relish, but didn't touch her own pastry. "This was a recipe of Corinne's. We made them often when we were girls." Her voice was controlled, but a sense of anguish hung in the room, not so much grief, perhaps, as sorrow at the passing of long ago days.

"You had known her for a long time," Annie said softly.

"A very long time." Lucy turned the small garnet ring on her little finger and shivered, then looked up apologetically. "I'm sorry. You want me to help. What can I do?"

Annie put down her coffee cup. "Tell me about her. What she was like?"

Lucy had large, expressive eyes. It was as if an opaque curtain fell. "You met her. Corinne was what she seemed to be, a beautiful, willful, determined woman." Her voice was studiedly neutral. "She wasn't all good or all bad—like most of us. She had very decided views on everything, on life and love and what was suitable and what wasn't. Usually, she meant well—or thought she did. The only difference between Corinne and most of us was that she would have her way, at all costs."

"You were good friends."

"We grew up together."

"Is it true—that she kept you from marrying her brother?"

For a moment, Lucy's pallid face was absolutely blank, then a lopsided smile faintly touched her lips. "That old story. Lord, don't people ever forget anything? And Cameron's been dead now for a decade or more." She gave an impatient head shake. "People always think that if you never marry, it's because no one asked you. And that's not true. No, Corinne had nothing to do with my turning Cameron down." Her lips closed into a thin line. "And that's all I intend to say about that."

Again her eyes dropped to the garnet ring, and she moved it around and around.

Annie knew she was skating on thin ice. "That morning at the Society when I made my presentation, everybody—but me—knew the fictional victim was Corinne. The story listed a bunch of people who had motives for murdering her."

Lucy stiffened. It was so quiet Annie could hear the tick of the Dresden clock on the mantel.

"It said her husband was playing—"

"You can't pay any attention to that letter!" She leaned forward, gripping the chair arms. "Please, it was—oh, it's just a scurrilous piece of nonsense. I told Chief Wells this morning that it didn't amount to anything—and he agreed with me. Can't you just let it drop?"

"Let it drop? Why, it's the best lead we have! And obviously, the writer was right on target about Tim Bond and Sybil and Edith Ferrier. And certainly about Gail and Bobby. So why not—"

Lucy's eyes flashed. "Have you come here expecting me to tell you every nasty bit of gossip I know? I'm sorry, Ms. Laurance, but I'm not playing that game. That letter was just a meanspirited attempt to embarrass Corinne. To take it seriously would be absurd."

Annie tried to suppress her anger, but she knew her response was crisp. "Is it absurd? I don't think so. And I intend to find out the truth behind it."

"You must do what you feel is right." But Lucy's face was drawn into a tight frown.

"All right, I will. And I wonder if the Chief might be more interested in that letter when he finds out that on Monday afternoon Corinne threatened to keep Gail from receiving her inheritance, and Gail told Bobby? What kind of motive do you think that is?"

"Gail would never injure anyone, and certainly not Corinne." But the sick anxiety in her eyes showed how deep the barb had gone.

"Perhaps not. But she's crazy about Bobby

211

Frazier—and Chief Wells is sniffing after him. And, as a matter of fact, after me. I'll lay you odds of ten-to-one he puts either Bobby or me in jail by week's end."

"That's dreadful." Lucy's eyes were wide and shocked.

"I think so, too. That's why I'm here. I've *got* to find out who hated Corinne and why." She leaned forward. "Won't you help me?"

Lucy picked up the silver server and poured a stream of fresh, hot coffee into Annie's cup. Her gaze roamed restlessly from the iris-filled Delft vase on a Chippendale table to the gleaming bronze andirons at the fireplace. "There isn't evidence enough to arrest Bobby—or you." Her eyes flicked to Annie's face. "It's all just circumstantial evidence— isn't that what they call it?"

"Juries have been known to convict on circumstantial evidence."

"Oh, it won't happen. It won't."

Annie was torn between compassion and frustration. Lucy was so evidently upset—and so determined to protect her friends and neighbors. But it was disconcerting to see her willingness to jettison Annie or Bobby.

"So you won't help me?"

"My dear," her voice was bone-tired and defeated, "I would help you if I could. But I can't."

Max refused to reveal his discoveries until they had eaten, even though it took a forty-five minute wait in a line that snaked from the marina parking lot to the restaurant, The Pink Carrousel, atop the bluff.

Annie brought him up to date on her talks with Gail and Lucy, then suggested, "We could go to a fast food stand."

"I do not eat fast food." There was a monumental dignity in his pronouncement.

"That's un-American."

"Did you know that the rate of heart disease in China is less than—"

She reached up and put a finger to his lips. "Love, I don't give a damn."

When they were finally seated in the outdoor garden, the table listed unsteadily to her right and gnats hovered in a friendly gray cloud.

The menu featured a jaunty merry-go-round, pink, naturally, on a beige cover and 12 pages of offerings.

Max sighed. "A menu this extensive presupposes a microwave."

"*Everybody* uses a microwave."

"Not in a first-class restaurant."

It only took twenty minutes for the harassed waitress to reappear for their order.

"Taco salad and a pink limeade."

Max avoided gagging and ordered, "Baked scrod, steamed broccoli, and a Bud Light, please."

She grinned at him.

"Taco salad is a gringo invention," he admonished.

"Don't try to sound authoritative about Mexican food. That's my province. And taco salads have an honorable history—"

"If you include junk food in culinary history, perhaps."

"Ah, refried beans, fajitas, sopapillas dripping with honey and powdered sugar. Heaven in Texas on a Saturday night."

"If we're going to talk about the components of a heavenly Saturday night, in Texas or—"

"Down, boy. We're talking food."

Their drinks arrived, and he averted his eyes from her gloriously red cherry limeade. She sucked noisily on her straw.

"I do have news," he said portentously.

"Better than mine, I hope. I didn't get any change at all out of Lucy."

Max pulled two envelopes out of his pocket, tossed them to her.

Annie felt the thicker one, poked inside, and recognized the famous mystery plot letter.

"I've seen—"

"Put it on the table. Then put the sheet from the other envelope beside it."

He crossed his arms and smirked in satisfaction.

She glanced at the new sheet, read: "The quick brown fox—" then exclaimed, "It matches. It matches! Where did you find it? How did you find it?"

"The old Remington at the Chastain Historical Preservation Society."

"Oh." Her voice sagged. "Hell, I thought maybe we'd learned something."

Max held his tongue until the waitress unloaded his scrod, which looked like it might rival the Sahara for dryness, and Annie's salad, which appeared disgustingly delec-

214

table, the guacamole a luscious green and the taco shell crisp and light.

"I found out a terrific amount." His fork stuck in the scrod. He yanked it free and used it as a baton, tapping the beer bottle for emphasis. "One: The letter must have been written between March 12, when your name was first mentioned as the prospective mystery expert—"

Annie poked at the bobbing lime in her glass and frowned at him skeptically. "And who told you that? A flea in the woodwork?"

"Louisa Binning, the Board secretary. She types up Miss Dora's meeting notes. It's all there, in black and white."

For the first time, Annie looked interested. "Okay, the letter must have been written between March 12 and—" she paused, figuring "—and say around March 24, because I got the letter on the 26th, and we have to allow time for delivery."

"It's postmarked the 24th."

A grin tugged at her lips. "Very good, Sherlock." She balanced a piece of shell heaped with taco meat. "But that gives us a ten-day period—so how does it help?"

"The Remington was at Crosswhite's Typewriter Repair Shop March 10 through the 19th. But here's the meat: Louisa insists the letter couldn't have been typed during hours when the Society is open and that includes the weekend of the 22-23rd when the Society hosted a local China painting display."

Annie chewed reflectively on a morsel of taco shell. "So somebody got in and used the typewriter at night on either the 19th, 20th, or 21st of March." She scowled. "How could anybody get into that place at night? The walls must be two feet thick."

"That's the point." His voice oozed satisfaction. "It would take a broadaxe to make a dent on those doors, and the windows are too small for anybody but a midget. Besides, there were no traces of a break-in."

"So how did anybody get in?" Her face brightened, and she answered her own question. "A key. Max, the typist had to have a *key*!"

Max interred the remains of the scrod beneath some watercress and prodded doubtfully on the mushy broccoli. "And who has keys?" he prompted.

"Okay, you're wonderful, Maigret. Share with me the results of your investigation."

"It's a nice, small list. The members of the Board and Louisa Binning."

"Oh, sure. Sure. It certainly figures. That means somebody was enjoying the hell out of my presentation of the Moneypot's plot." She wriggled her shoulders in distaste.

"Maybe. Maybe not. A Board member or anybody with access to a Board member's keys."

"Like Leighton."

"Or even Merrill's wife."

Annie pushed her plate away. "That brings up a critical point. Did the letter give somebody there a murderous idea? Or is the letter writer the killer?" She banged a small fist on the table and beer foamed over the top of Max's glass. "Why won't Wells listen to us?

The letter is absolutely critical. Whether Lucy admits it or not, the woods are full of suspects, including Leighton, Dr. Sanford, and Roscoe Merrill. And if Wells won't investigate them, we will!"

The spicy smell of cedar potpourri didn't quite mask the underlying odors of burnt coffee, chlorine, and unswept corners. The bar of sunlight which flooded in as they opened the front door revealed, too, that the black-and-white tiled entry of Swamp Fox Inn was long overdue a good scrubbing. Annie thought longingly of the exquisite cleanliness of Death on Demand, but soldiers of fortune had to make camp at the battle site. At least it was quiet this afternoon; the indefatigable tourists were out thirstily absorbing Chastain culture.

"Miss Laurance. Oh, Miss Laurance!"

The foyer, with its scuffed tile floor, led directly to the old-fashioned oak counter. A desk littered with letters, brochures, empty soda cans, a greasy box with two soggy glazed doughnuts, and a flyswatter shared space with a Depression-era switchboard and a wall letter box with numbers affixed for guests' rooms. Idell Gordon stood on tiptoe behind the counter. She wore a dark brown cotton dress with speckles of lint from the dryer.

Reaching up to the slot for 312, she pulled out a scrap of paper. "For you, Miss Laurance. Chief Wells left word for you to call. I have the number for you." She pushed forward the telephone that sat on the counter. Her protuberant eyes glistened with curiosity.

"Oh, thanks so much. I'll call from upstairs."

Annie was pink with suppressed giggles as she unlocked the door to her tiny room. "Did you see her face? She was *quivering* for me to use that phone so she could hear."

Max draped himself comfortably on her bed. "Either way, your call has to go through her switchboard, sport. I'll bet a scrod (you eating) that she listens in."

"I don't gamble," Annie countered righteously.

She pulled up a wicker chair next to the telephone stand and dialed. She was put through immediately.

"You called?"

"Oh, Miss Laurance." The greeting sounded like a dungeon door dragging against twelfth-century flagstones. "Thought you might be interested in the autopsy report."

"Yes, of course." Alarm tingled down her spine. Why tell her?

"The skull injury was caused by the end of the croquet mallet. But it wasn't the cause of death."

"It wasn't?"

"She drowned."

Annie remembered the heavy, wet figure face-down in the duckweed-scummed water.

"Medical Examiner figures someone struck her from behind, and she pitched forward into the water."

She tried to picture it. Corinne arguing, then swinging around arrogantly to walk off. No,

Corinne must have turned away and faced the pond, and someone snatched up the mallet and flailed out.

She had a funny feeling of ESP when Wells's heavy voice grated, "Hard to picture why she would turn her back on somebody, look out at the water."

There was something about him that brought out Annie's combative streak. "Oh, I can think of a lot of reasons. She and this person were standing there gazing across the pond, and the other person stepped back and let her have it."

"That's not the way I see it."

She didn't like his tone. At her frown, Max swung off the bed.

"No," Wells rasped. "I see it this way. She's quarreling with somebody and turns away and starts to leave, and then she's struck from behind and plops forward."

She didn't relish being his straight man, but she couldn't resist asking, "How could she have drowned, if she fell forward on the path?"

"Drowned?" Max mouthed.

Wells bulled ahead. "Her killer realized she was still breathing, but it's too late then to back down, so the murderer pulls her around and shoves her into the water and holds her head down." His heavy breathing echoed on the wire. "You were goddamned wet and muddy, weren't you?"

She got it then, like buckshot between the eyes. "Now, wait a minute, for God's sake. I was trying to get her *out* of the water."

He didn't say a word, just stood there and

breathed, and Annie felt like a hapless soprano being stalked by the phantom of the opera. The *jerk*. Trying to use psychological warfare on her.

She opened her mouth for a withering reply, but he beat her to it.

"And the only fingerprints on that mallet are yours. Clear as a bell most places; smudged and partial on the grip."

She felt the icy calm that precedes panic. "Of course my prints are on it. I carried it down to the pond. I brought it to Chastain. I must have touched it hundreds of times."

A worried frown creased Max's face.

Once again, that infuriating, accusatory silence from Wells.

Her fingerprints. That simple statement indicated a great deal of police effort directed at her. "How did you get my fingerprints?"

"Frank Saulter. Broward's Rock police."

"You're a busy little man."

Max immediately began a frantic waggle of sign language.

"Too bad you're wasting your time and the taxpayers' money. Listen, Chief, I've got some information for you. The letter—you know which one I mean—the letter that lays it out about who hated Corinne and why— okay, that famous letter was typed late at night on the old Remington right next door from here at the Society. It was typed after hours on either March 19, 20, or 21. Now, nobody broke into that massive old fort—so what does that mean? The typist had a key. That's right. And you know who has keys to that building? Only the members of the Board of the Chastain Historical Preservation Society. I'm telling you that whoever wrote that letter was either the murderer—or has a hell of a good idea who the murderer is. And I think I know who wrote that letter."

Even in her fury and despite the chief's stertorous breathing, Annie heard a telltale gasp. So Idell wasn't missing out on much.

But she didn't care who heard what she said.

"I'll tell you who wrote that letter—Who knows *everything* that goes on in town? Who's a thwarted old spinster who hates *everybody*? Who's the only member on the Board who *wasn't* listed as a suspect? I'll tell you—Miss Dora!"

Max made an "Oh-God-I-can't-believe-it" face, then drew his finger across his throat.

But there was no stopping Annie now. "So you just keep on hounding innocent people and see how much good it does you. If you won't find out the truth, I will!"

M AX BELLOWED IN HER EAR. "We don't have time to do this!"

"We'll take time!" she insisted. Then, standing on tiptoe, she struggled to see over the bobbing heads. "For Pete's sake, what is that awful noise? And why are people jumping around?"

He reached up and grabbed a gnarled live oak limb and nimbly hoisted himself up. Dropping down in an instant, he yelled, "It looks kind of like a cross between square dancing and tap dancing."

"Oh, of course. The cloggers," she shouted.

"Don't be silly. They don't have loggers in South Carolina."

She gestured helplessly toward the side street, and, heads down, they fought their way into the less densely packed mob on Lafayette. The thunderous clacking was reduced from the roar of an approaching subway train to merely the thunder of nearby surf.

"Clogging," she explained. "I read all about it in the Chastain House and Garden Tour brochures. It originated in Ireland and Lancashire, England, and it's here by way of Appalachia. That bit of news was tucked next to the information about the magic shows on the hour at Prichard Museum. And the flea market in the Armory. And the praline eating contest in the basement of the Methodist Church." She grabbed his arm, and they broke into a half trot. At least they were moving against the traffic flow now.

"Is there any other excitement you're keeping from me?" He darted a worried glance at his watch. "Annie, your cast is going to show up in twenty minutes for a warm-up."

"They'll keep. And everybody did swell last night. This is more important."

She did slow for a moment, however, at the

corner of Ephraim and Prince streets to point up a curving drive at the greenish-gray plaster of a Greek Revival mansion. "Lady Lust lives there."

"Sybil Giacomo?" It would not be inaccurate to say his tone quickened.

Annie shot him a disgusted look. "The one and only."

"Hey, why don't we talk to her now? We need to find out where she and Tim were when Corinne was killed."

Annie grabbed his arm firmly. "Tomorrow."

But when they reached the long, dark line of wrought iron two doors down, she felt a funny little thump in her chest. The late afternoon shadows threw deep pools of shade across this immense stretch of lawn. Spanish moss hung in ghostly filaments from the live oaks. The day was still and somber, and the sweet scent of the pittisporum hung in the air like a powerful perfume, dizzyingly.

She pulled open the gate with its ornate pineapple motif. The reluctant shriek of the metal was worthy of Inner Sanctum's finest hours.

Midway up the stately avenue of live oaks, she stumbled to a stop. "Look, there's another one." She might have been pointing out a tarantula.

This placard was bound with scratchy brown twine to an especially low and thick branch:

"This live oak was the site of eight recorded duels, only one of which resulted in death. The facts are these: Harold Anderson Chastain derided the conduct of Judge Arthur Winyard, declaring him to be the servant of the factor and disloyal to his duties as a magistrate. The judge's son, Thomas, sought out Mr. Chastain and, after a heated exchange, struck him with a riding crop. The men met in combat at the hour of noon on August 18, 1805, each walking twenty-five paces, then turning to fire. Mr. Winyard was mortally wounded and died at the scene. He was 22 years, 8 mos. and 6 days of age. Mr. Chastain suffered a grievous injury and passed from this earth on September 6, 1805, at the age of 32 years, 9 mos., and 17 days."

She shivered, and the chill came from more than the sunless dark beneath the trees.

"She's *crazy*," Annie whispered.

She took Max's arm again, purely for companionship, of course, and they continued up the shell drive. In the silence, oppressive after the roar near the riverfront, the sound of their footsteps carried clearly.

A low tabby wall enclosed the house, which was built of brown-toned plantation bricks. Four huge tabby-covered Doric pillars supported a two-story verandah and a flat roof with a balustrade around the top. They mounted the steps. A rattan rocker faced the front yard. Annie knocked vigorously.

They might as well have pummeled a tomb door in the Valley of the Kings. No sound. No movement. No response.

"Dammit, she can't accuse me of murder, then go to earth like a rat in a burrow."

But Miss Dora's house brooded in the light

of the setting sun, impervious to Annie as it had proved impervious to intruders throughout its history.

Frustrated, Annie lifted both fists and pounded again, but with no more effect than before. They were turning to descend the steps, when she reached out, gripped Max's arm.

"Look. There. Did you see?"

"Where?"

"The window. That curtain *moved*. I swear it did."

Annie stared at the dusky folds of velvet, pressed against the pane. Was there a slit there, a fine line open to vision? Were malicious black eyes staring out at her?

They gave it up, finally, and started down the steps, but Annie knew she was engaged in a duel. A duel of wits that might prove deadly.

Annie was forewarned for Tuesday night. She had, after all, survived Monday night, the kick-off of the English Manor Mystery, a k a "Alas, A Sticky Wicket." Ingrid was on duty in the Police Headquarters Tent, emphatically instructed to be certain that each team received only one search warrant and warned to be suspicious of everyone, especially sturdy little old ladies with angelic expressions. Further, she was keeping a vigilant eye on the clue table. Tonight Annie intended to personally roam the Suspect Interrogation Tent to ensure that the Mystery Night detectives stayed within some bounds of reason.

After she made her brief speech intro-
ducing the suspects, she followed them and
the charging crowd to the tents. She waved
at Max, who was busy signing up teams to visit
The Scene of the Crime, now moved to the
rose arbor near the tennis court. Ingrid
flapped her hands frantically. Annie started
toward her. She was dodging her way around
clumps of conferring detectives, when a
piercing voice demanded:

"How about the real murder, Ms. Laurance? Are you snooping around?"

Walrus Mustache, beaming genially, hefted
his camcorder and focused. Mother bounded
forward, microphone outstretched.

Annie had often wondered what it would
be like to be the cynosure of all eyes; abruptly,
she knew. A hush fell, like the dead air at a hurricane's center.

"Understand you and the police chief had
some words."

The intelligence-gathering capabilities of
the Sticky Wicket detectives should be studied
by the CIA for possible emulation.

"We have discussed the crime," she answered
carefully.

"Come on, now, girl. Let us in on the real
scoop."

"I don't really know very much—"

A disappointed collective sigh rose.

"—but I can tell you this much."

The quiet was absolute.

"It looks like the murderer is someone
who had known Mrs. Webster very, very well."
She waved her hand, smiled, and turned

away. Let Chief Wells stuff that in his jaw and chew it.

She was in high good humor when she reached a besieged Ingrid and the clue table.

"Aren't there supposed to be *five* exhibits?"

She glanced down at the table, which held a train ticket, a crumpled initialed handkerchief, a Turkish cigarette stub, and a note that read *I can't come.*

She felt disgust but no real surprise. These addicts were capable of anything. "Somebody's ripped off a clue," she muttered to Ingrid. "I'll be right back." Thank heavens, she had duplicates of all the clues at the Inn. Replacement seemed simple enough, but she hadn't taken into account the limpet-like qualities of the detectives. She was accosted three times en route to the front gate, then had to struggle through the county-fair-strength crowd on Ephraim Street. This evening, the free entertainment featured a ventriloquist with a talking banana. Fortunately, the Inn was just the other side of the Benton House. She wormed through the coffee bar patrons, raced up to her room, grabbed the cast of a footprint, and hurtled back downstairs.

Idell poked her head out of the untidy office behind the counter.

"Miss Laurance, oh Miss Laurance!"

"Sorry, I'm in a hurry—"

"Miss Laurance, do the police think the person who wrote that letter to you is the same as the murderer?"

Halfway out the door and barely paying attention, she yelled back. "Maybe. Maybe not."

She replaced the pilfered clue, then began to circle unobtrusively. At least, this investigation was proceeding smoothly, although not everyone appeared enchanted with her Stately Home murder. A skinny man in black-checked trousers perilously held up by yellow suspenders snarled to a fat woman in pink tights, "This is a sissy kind of murder. As far as I'm concerned, you need a hero." He paused, then said gruffly, "Down these mean streets—" "Oh, my God," his companion groaned, "if you're going to quote Chandler..." Annie turned away to hide a grin. In the Interrogation Tent, Team No. 4 concentrated on the search, and its captain, a white-haired Chastain lawyer, bore down on Reginald Hoxton.

"Can you tell us how you earn your living, Mr. Hoxton?"

Sanford lolled back in his chair, a wolfish smile on his dark face. He wore a pale yellow shirt with a round white collar and pale blue slacks. It wasn't nineteen-thirtyish, but he was the epitome of a man from whom you wouldn't want to buy a used car. For the first time, Annie suspected the abrasive doctor of having a sense of humor.

"Investments," he replied airily.

"Investments in what, Mr. Hoxton?" the lawyer persisted.

"One business today, another one tomorrow."

"Perhaps your real business is taking advantage of women, Mr. Hoxton."

"Those, sir, are scurrilous words."

"Oh? Can you explain the testimony of

Lady Alicia's maid? She tells us Lady Alicia owed you 3,400 pounds."

"Lies, all lies."

"Agnes tells us you have badgered her poor mistress for huge sums of money, claiming she owes them to you for losses at cards. Is this true, Mr. Hoxton?"

Smiling, Annie moved on and came up behind the circle of questioners around Agnes.

Her smile faded. Poor Lucy was obviously miserable. She sat unsmiling and rigid in her chair. Tonight she wore an attractive black-and-white silk dress and white gloves. Her face carried an unaccustomed splash of color on each cheek, and Annie knew she'd tried to use make-up to hide her pallor. Lucy listened attentively to her questioners, answering each question dutifully, but her gloved hands were clenched in her lap.

"Agnes, what exactly did you hear Mr. Nigel say to Miss Snooperton?"

Lucy glanced down at her prep cards. "It was shocking to me, sir, *that* I can tell you. Mr. Nigel was all upset. He kept saying he wanted to know how long she'd been seeing Lord Algernon on the sly. Miss Snooperton denied it had ever happened. Mr. Nigel said he wasn't going to marry anyone who would lie to him, but Miss Snooperton told him he'd given his word and she wore his ring and it would be a scandal if he broke it off. Mr. Nigel stormed away, but she called after him that she'd talk to him later, as they'd planned."

Team Captain No. 6 probed deeper. "Funny

how you can see and hear so much about everyone but your mistress. Tell us now, when was the last time you saw the necklace in her possession?"

Lucy's distrait silence was perfect. Finally, she responded sharply, "I know that necklace like my own hand. I saw it that very morning. But you can't fault me for having eyes and ears, and Mr. Nigel's not telling all he knows."

A high, sharp voice urged her teammates, "Oh, let's hurry. Let's get a search warrant against Nigel Davies."

Annie would know that voice anywhere. As the team members broke into a trot, heading for the Police Investigation Tent, she called out, "Mrs. Brawley."

Slowly, reluctantly, a slight figure with a fox-sharp face paused for an instant.

Annie reached out, gripped a bony elbow. "You were here last night."

Mrs. Brawley lifted her chin defiantly. "I have a ticket tonight, too."

"That isn't fair."

"There's not a thing in the rules that says you can't come every night, if you buy a ticket." Mrs. Brawley shook free of Annie's hand. "And I bought a ticket for every single night." She darted away.

Annie stared after her.

Obviously, it was cheating. By the time she'd been on four different teams, it would be a bloody miracle if she weren't the first to figure the mystery out.

But Mrs. Brawley was right. There wasn't a single thing in the rules to prevent it.

It was not, Annie decided, a surprise that so many murders occurred, but so few.

She stalked after Mrs. Brawley and her team, and arrived in time to see the members receive their information from the search warrant on Nigel Davies.

They learned: Nigel Davies had been expected to marry his girlhood sweetheart, Susannah Greatheart, and friends had been surprised when his engagement to the worldly Miss Snooperton was announced. Nigel and Miss Snooperton had been observed quarreling, with Nigel threatening to break the engagement. The search of his room at the Manor revealed a note from Miss Greatheart, which threatened suicide if he did not return to her.

With happy clucks of anticipation, the team rumbled off en masse to return to the Suspect Interrogation tent and a session with Miss Greatheart.

Annie glanced at her watch. Nine-forty. Thank heavens, the madness would soon be over.

"Miss Laurance."

She knew that voice, too.

"Could I talk to you for a minute?"

It was politely phrased, but Bobby Frazier's tone brooked no disagreement. His face was shadowed by a tall, perfumed pittisporum shrub.

"Certainly."

He jerked his head toward the Benton House. "Let's walk over by the fence."

They found an oasis of quiet near the gate between the two houses.

In the yellowish glare of the overhead security light, he looked drawn and tired, tension lines bracketing his mouth.

"What did Gail tell you?"

Annie didn't like his peremptory tone.

"Why don't you ask her?"

Frazier swallowed jerkily. "Look, I've got to know. I've got to know what the hell is going on."

"Pick up a phone," she retorted. "Call her."

"I can't." He grabbed a bar of the fence. He should have looked inoffensive, a young man in khaki slacks and a yellow sports shirt with pencils poking out of the pocket, but he reminded Annie uncomfortably of a predator crouched to spring, every muscle taut, every nerve stretched to the highest pitch. Then, with evident effort, he smoothed out his tone. "Look, Miss Laurance, I just want to know what she told you. It's no state secret, right?"

"She told me about her talks with you the day Corinne was murdered."

His hand tightened convulsively on the bar. "You may have gotten the wrong impression."

She waited.

"Gail's a nice girl, but she's not interested in me—and I'm not interested in her."

"Oh?"

"Yeah. We're just friends. That's all."

"I guess you forgot to tell her."

He reached out, gripped her arm so tightly that Annie gasped softly. "What the hell do you mean?"

Because his tone frightened her, Annie responded fiercely. "Gail is a nice kid, Mr. Frazier. She doesn't know any better than to tell the truth, and she's telling everybody—and I'll bet that includes Chief Wells—that you didn't give a damn about her not having any money and you intended to go on seeing one another."

"Oh, shit." His fingers unloosed her, and he banged through the gate and was gone.

Annie stared after the yellow shirt until it was swallowed by the darkness. What did that mean? Nothing good for Gail. Was this a less than graceful effort by Bobby Frazier to remove himself from suspicion?

Annie sighed, turned to return to the fray, and froze. Was there a rustle in the bushes behind her? Swinging around, heart thudding, she peered into the shadows. Yes, there was movement and a dark splotch of cloth. Suddenly, she shivered. The bushes lay quiescent now. But she had glimpsed a wizened face and malevolent eyes.

Hadn't she?

With a feeling of horror, she plunged up the path toward the tents.

17

ANNIE WATCHED IN DISMAY as Max poured their coffee. "Can't you see? It's *yellow*. It's not even brown."

"We could walk down the street to the Harbor Lights. I understand they have wonderful Belgian waffles and excellent coffee."

Annie glowered down into her coffee cup. "She'd find out, then we'd never get another word out of her."

"I'm not sure she knows anything." Max's tone was reasonable.

"She *has* to. She's too nosy not to know something useful. Shh-h. Here she comes."

Idell Gordon swept into the patio, smiling in satisfaction at the crowded tables. She stopped beside Annie and Max.

"Good morning. And how are our detectives this morning?" she asked archly.

After a restless night on a lumpy mattress, a two A.M. search for a three-inch cockroach, and a rapid approach of a crise de nerfs because of severe caffeine withdrawal, an honest reply quivered on the tip of Annie's tongue. However, she forced a grim smile and remained tactfully silent.

Max, annoyingly, rose gallantly to his feet.

"Will you join us for some breakfast, Mrs. Gordon?"

"Oh, my dear boy, I've been up since dawn. A proprietor's work is never done, you know." She waved him back to his seat. Her protuberant, questing eyes dropped to the newspaper, the Wednesday edition of the *Chastain Courier,* with its screaming headlines about the investigation into Corinne's murder. "Did you notice who wrote the story?"

She didn't have to say which article.

They nodded. It was bylined to Bobby Frazier.

"What would Corinne think, if she knew?"

Considering the question rhetorical, they waited.

This morning, Idell had ill-advisedly chosen to wear a faded pink shirt and tight white polyester slacks. Neither were flattering. She stood by their table and stared down at the newspaper, her eyes shiny. "Did you see where Leighton is offering a $5,000 reward for information leading to the arrest of the killer?" She looked at them sharply. "Are you going to try for the reward?"

Max shook his head. "No. We hadn't even thought about it."

"Are you?" Annie asked.

Idell stepped back a pace, a hand at her wrinkled throat. "Oh, no, no. Of course not. How would I do that? Well, enjoy your breakfast. I must check the kitchen now," and she scuttled away.

"She has something on her mind," Annie

observed, tartly, "but it will be a cold day in hell before she tells us."

"Do you really think so?" He yawned and picked up the paper.

Annie sighed and took another sip of what purported to be coffee. "Anything new in the story?"

"A few things. Let's see, Mrs. Webster was last seen by the cook, starting down the path from the kitchen steps. That was about five o'clock. Nobody admits seeing her after that time."

Annie fished the spiral notebook out of her skirt pocket and flipped to a fresh page.

5:00—C. W. leaves Prichard House.

5:30—Annie discovers body.

She checked back at some earlier notations.

4:25—Annie at gazebo, Gail and Bobby arrive and quarrel.

4:30—Bobby follows Gail, tells her to find out what happened to C. W.'s check.

4:35—Gail to Prichard House, calls back, quarrels with C. W.

4:50—Gail leaves in search of Bobby, finds him, tells him C. W. intends to block her inheritance. Gail returns to house, Bobby where?

5:00—C. W. leaves house. Why?

She studied her times. "Where was Corinne going?"

"Since I don't specialize in seances, I can't tell you."

"Max, be serious. This is important. Why did Corinne leave the house? Where was she going?"

"Maybe she was ready for the start of the evening's festivities."

"It wasn't time. The gates were to open at six. So where was she hotfooting it at five?"

He put his hands behind his head and stared up at the three stories of balconies, which slanted suspiciously toward the patio. "One good earthquake and I'll bet this place collapses." At her impatient wiggle, he held up a broad hand. "I *am* pondering. Why did Corinne leave the house? Oh, offhand I can imagine at least six reasons. She wanted to come and harass you a little more. She was going to check on the arrival of the caterer. She decided it was an opportune moment to commune with nature. She had a secret lover, and they planned a rendezvous behind a yew hedge. She was on her way to Roscoe Merrill's office to deal him a little grief, or ditto Dr. Sanford. That's six, isn't it?"

"Five o'clock," she muttered. "She must have had something specific in mind. It wasn't time for the gala to start, and she'd already been on my case several times. No, this is important. We've got to find out *why* she left the house."

Chloe was small, dark, and weary. "No'm, Miss Corinne she didn't say nothin'."

Sunlight sparkled in the immaculate kitchen of Prichard House. The copper cookware above the chopping block glistened. The smell of apple pie and roasting meat hung in the air, but there was no corresponding holiday mood. Chloe was preparing food for the family after the funeral that afternoon.

She looked at them with teary eyes. "She was upset, and walking mighty swift."

"Do you think she was on her way to meet someone?"

Chloe kneaded her hands against her crisp white apron. "I don't know. She'd had too much upset. Miss Gail's a foolish girl, running after that upstart young man. She ought to have listened to Miss Corinne. And they'd fought something awful, and Miss Gail burst out of the house. Then the phone done ring."

Annie leaned forward. "Was it for Mrs. Webster?"

The little woman nodded lugubriously. "Yes'm. She said, sharp like, that her mind was made up, that's all there was to it. Then I went to the pantry. In a minute or so, that was when she left."

Max frowned. "Where was Mr. Webster while all this was going on?"

"In my study."

Leighton Webster stood in the doorway to the kitchen, his heavy face cold and unfriendly. There was no genial charm in his manner today. His powerful hands were bunched into fists at his side.

Max was always willing to try. He smiled goodhumoredly at Webster. "We're trying to discover your wife's destination when she left the house. Did you happen to hear any of her conversation on the phone?"

"I was not in the habit of eavesdropping on my wife. Furthermore, I believe the police are in a better position to ask questions such as these." His eyes flickered over them dismissively. "I understand Gail's asked you to investigate, which I consider absurd—and offensive."

"Why do you object to our trying to discover the murderer?" Annie demanded.

Leighton rubbed a hand across his cheek, then sighed heavily. "I don't know what happened." Truculence gave way to uncertainty. "I can't believe anyone would hurt Corinne intentionally, and certainly not anyone she knew. It had to be a stranger, one of those dreadful things that can happen." He looked at them in mute appeal. "Don't you agree?"

"It could be," Max said gently.

"You're going around, talking to people. Ask them if they saw any strangers."

"It wasn't a stranger."

Leighton and Max both stared at Annie.

"How could it have been?" She lifted her hands in a query. "Think about it. Corinne turned her back on the person who struck her. It *had* to be someone she knew—and didn't fear."

"I don't believe it. I'll never believe it." Leighton's voice was rough with anger.

"Why not? She'd made everybody in town mad—and how about you? After I read that letter at the Society, didn't she ask you whether you were involved with another woman?"

Annie was aware in the shocked silence that followed of Max's incredulous glance and of Leighton's sudden immobility.

She'd prodded a raw wound. There was no righteous anger of the innocent.

He made no answer at all, but looked past them, as if they weren't there, misery and heartbreak in his eyes. Then, without a word, he turned and stumbled blindly from the room.

Annie and Max were silent as they headed down the back steps of Prichard House. They started down the path toward the pond.

"Poor bastard."

"I know. I'm sorry," she said defensively.

"That's all right. God knows he should be at the top of Wells's list."

"Except Wells can't see past the fact that he's mayor." Annie scuffed through a covering of pine needles.

"Do you suppose he did it?"

Reaching up, she grabbed a crinkly handful of Spanish moss. "His insistence on the mysterious stranger makes me wonder."

They came up on the gazebo. Beyond it the pond lay placid and blackish-green without a breath of breeze to stir the reeds. Their footsteps echoed in the morning air as they climbed the steps. They sat down on the wooden benches, and Annie stared glumly at the place where Corinne's body had lain.

"It makes a hell of a lot of difference whether somebody got mad at her and serendipitously picked up the club and swung, or whether somebody lured her down here with murder in mind."

"Why?" Max asked.

"A difference in the kind of person. Take Leighton Webster for example. I can't imagine him plotting a murder in advance. He's too much of a gentleman. But if he got mad, and there was a weapon handy—"

"Why would he be quarreling with her at the pond? They had that enormous house to quarrel in."

Annie shot him an appraising glance. "I think you're sorry for him. Maybe Leighton had just asked her for a divorce, and she'd said no deal, he couldn't have one. Chloe may have been mistaken about the phone; maybe Corinne was talking to Leighton. She was mad, so she stalked out to take a walk. He went after her, found her at the pond, they continued fighting, and whammo."

"Maybe," Max said doubtfully, scuffing the dust with his shoe tip. "That would be unpremeditated, but I think the murder was planned to the last detail. Somebody knew that mallet would be here, called Corinne, and talked her into a meeting. That's how I see it."

She tapped her fingers impatiently on the arm of the bench. "What we need is some clever analysis of our suspects. Kate Fansler *always* figures out how everybody's mind works."

"I'm agreeable, whoever Ms. Fansler may be. What do you suggest?"

"Some tête à têtes."

Edith Ferrier reluctantly invited them inside and led the way to a side piazza. Cheerful red and black cushions made the white wicker furniture comfortable. A partially completed yellow afghan lay atop a wicker coffee table.

She gestured for them to sit on a divan and took her place opposite in a straight chair. She looked at them unsmiling, her heavily mascaraed jade green eyes wary. "I don't know why you want to talk to me." Her chin gave an infinitesimal backward jerk.

Here, you couldn't hear the tourists. Bees droned in the honeysuckle that nuzzled the verandah balustrade. Swallowtail butterflies flitted near a blossoming dogwood with white flowers as brilliant as a snowy peak. The manicured garden, though much smaller than those of the show houses, was April perfection, but the tension on the porch was thick enough to cut.

"We're talking to everyone who had a motive to kill Corinne." Annie knew it was the equivalent of a flung gauntlet, but why not?

Again, that nervous tic, but Edith kept her awkwardly rouged face impassive. "That doesn't include me."

Annie continued on the attack. "You were the clubwoman mentioned in the letter."

"No one can prove that." Her fingers nervously worked the pleats in her navy silk skirt.

"It's obvious. And you admitted on Monday, when Corinne was deviling you, that she'd kept you from being president of the Society."

Edith picked up the afghan and began to crochet, her eyes intent on the flashing hook.

"I am busy with a number of organizations. Certainly, I can find plenty of opportunities to fill my time, and there are many in Chastain who appreciate my efforts."

Before Annie could speak again, Max knocked his knee against hers and smiled winningly at Edith. "Actually, I've been looking forward to our chance to visit with you."

The crochet hook eased to a stop.

"Since Annie and I are strangers, we have to depend upon others for information about Chastain and the people who knew Corinne. As a mainstay in the city's power structure, it seems to me that you are an invaluable resource with your contacts, and, even more importantly, that you are singularly well qualified because of your extensive volunteer work to be able to look past the obvious and give us real insight into personalities."

Annie would have gagged except for the magical effect of this honeyed flow upon Edith. She was settling back into her chair, the afghan draped loosely over her lap, and a faint flush of pleasure stained her powdered cheeks. "I've dealt with all kinds of people over the years, Mr. Darling, and, let me tell you, I can see through a false face pretty quick."

Max beamed at her. "I knew you were the right person to talk to."

Annie might as well have been invisible. She stifled a malicious urge to give a piercing whistle.

Max's voice was as smooth as chocolate mousse. "Tell us about the Board members. What are they really like? And who do you think wrote the letter?"

Edith's face sharpened, like a hawk preparing to dive. "You're right, of course." Her voice was more animated than Annie had ever heard it. "It must have been done by a Board member. And I think I know which one."

She paused and received the attention she sought. "I think Gail wrote it."

"Gail!" Annie's voice rose. Max nudged her again, harder.

"You can only push any living creature so far. Corinne was killing that girl, crushing the life out of her." Edith's voice vibrated with emotion.

"Would Gail know all of the things in the letter?" Max asked.

Edith moved her hands impatiently, jangling her silver charm bracelet. "Of course, she would. She lived in that house. And everyone in town knows how Corinne and John Sanford were wrangling over the hospital funds, and about Tim's paintings and Sybil." She paused, and a frown drew her carefully lined brows down. "I don't know about Roscoe, though. I had heard a few whispers, something about some young woman lawyer in Atlanta. I suppose if I'd heard, Gail could have heard." She tossed her head and her red-gold hair rippled. "It's like Gail, though. A weak person pushed to attack and doing it secretly."

"So you don't think John or Roscoe were likely to have written the letter?" Max persisted.

Edith didn't dismiss them outright. "Oh, I don't think so. It's too calm and studied for John. As for Roscoe—actually, Roscoe is a very complex man. You rarely know what Roscoe is thinking; he keeps his own counsel. He seems so dry, such a stick, but I don't think

244

he really is. He's absolutely crazy about Jessica. That's why I thought that story about a girl in Atlanta might be false—but he did seem upset when you read the letter. I was watching him, and his face went absolutely livid for a minute. So I can't imagine that he would have written it."

"Unless that was a particularly clever double bluff," Max suggested.

"What would that achieve?" Edith asked reasonably. "No, I can see where John and Roscoe would have the necessary knowledge, but they both seem unlikely."

"How about Lucy? She's an old Chastainian," Max observed.

Edith nodded. "Oh, yes, she is. And I've heard, too, that Corinne ruined her romance with Cameron. But that was a long time ago. Isn't it a little late to try for revenge? So far as I know, they were on the best of terms. In fact, I guess Lucy was about Corinne's only friend."

"How about Sybil?" Annie ignored Max's involuntary wriggle and concentrated on Edith.

"Sybil." Edith dropped the name like a pound of butter in boiling chocolate. "Ah yes. Sybil."

For the first time in their acquaintance, Annie saw a glint of humor in those huge green eyes.

"I'd like to think it was Sybil. Everyone believes Sybil capable of anything outrageous, but frankly it would take too much time and be much too subtle for her." Her mouth

245

curved in a sardonic smile, admiration mixed with disgust. "If you dumped Sybil in the middle of the Sahara, there would be a half dozen sheikhs there within the day. There's something about her—"

Max opened his mouth, intercepted Annie's glare, and wisely remained silent.

"She sends out signals," Annie said dryly.

Max opted for a diversion. He ticked them off on his fingers. "So, John's too abrupt, Roscoe's too careful, Lucy's too unlikely, Sybil's too—impetuous. You think it's Gail."

"I'm afraid so."

But Annie was shaking her head. "You're both wrong. It's obvious as it can be. Miss Dora wrote that letter."

To her surprise, Edith was adamant. "Oh no, she wouldn't do that. No, you have to understand Miss Dora. She's devoted heart and soul to Chastain, to its history, its traditions. Nothing matters as much to her as Family. She wouldn't do anything to harm the Society."

"Just strangers she sees as a threat," Annie muttered. "Like me."

Annie wasn't enchanted about their next interview, but she realized it was necessary.

It didn't improve her humor to see one of Miss Dora's placards posted on the main entry gate.

"The present structure, built in 1833, is the third home at this site. It is Chastain's oldest surviving Greek Revival home. (The Prichard

House on Ephraim Street was built in 1834.) The first home at this location was built by Chastain's founder, Reginald Cantey Chastain, and the property remains in the Chastain family to the present day. The younger son of an English settler in the Barbadoes, Chastain established the settlement which bears his name in June of 1730. Of an energetic and adventurous nature, he came to the province of Carolina at the age of 23 years and, within five years, amassed a fortune to compare with those of the factors in Charleston. He was a well-built man, standing almost six foot tall with curly chestnut hair and eyes of the palest green. He was married to Anna Margaret Hasty on January 9, 1736, and they had five sons, Thomas, Nathaniel, William, Percival, and Harold."

Reginald was probably a rapacious swashbuckler. Sybil no doubt came by her appetites honestly. Heredity, Annie decided, was an awesome force. She glanced up at Max, who was striding eagerly toward the marble steps, his dark blue eyes gleaming with anticipation. Perhaps she should give some thought to Mendelian truths before September.

Max poked the doorbell, then bent down to whisper. "Look, honey, why don't you let me handle this one?"

"Are you suggesting that I lack tact?"

"Mmmm," he said, displaying his own exceptional perceptiveness, "let's just say, I think this one needs a man's touch."

"Ooh-la-la," she hissed as the door opened. Annie immediately felt like a pile of sun-

bleached bones. Today Sybil wore red. Flaming
red. A red that rivaled that of the San Francisco fire. She was riveting in a linen dress that
most women would categorize as skimpy
even while recognizing a Bill Blass original
and lusting in their hearts. Whether for the
dress or a little of Sybil's panache, it would
be hard to say. Who else but Sybil, at her
age and voluptuous state, could look magnificent in a dress that ended three inches above
the knee? When she turned to lead the way
down the hall, navigating on four-inch red
leather heels, the curving hem rose high in the
back, revealing more leg than a rack of lamb.
She managed to overshadow even the
spectacular length of hallway with three intri-
cately patterned oriental rugs and a spectacular
four-tiered crystal chandelier.

Sybil led the way to the library. The
Pompeian red walls certainly provided a
dramatic backdrop for her raven black hair,
Annie thought cynically. She dropped into
a Queen Anne wing chair with embossed
creamy satin upholstery and waved them
negligently toward a Chinese rosewood couch
with scrolled back and arms. As they sat,
Sybil deftly fitted an extra-long menthol-
tipped cigarette into an ivory holder, lit it,
and blew a cloud of minty smoke. She gestured
at a heap of brightly colored brochures and
magazines spread across the mahogany
Sheraton drum table.

"I've had the most marvelous day." Her
throaty voice was as mellifluous as the warble
of feasting doves. "Trying to decide just how

the exhibition folder should look." At their blank silence, she crossed one silk-clad leg over a knee, and jounced her foot impatiently, exposing a well-endowed thigh. "Timmy's NewYork exhibition, of course." Her crimson lips curved in open amusement. "What's wrong, sweeties? Do I seem to lack a funeral air?" She shrugged, and Annie sourly noticed that the dress also provided ample view of fulsome breasts. "Don't worry, I'll be at the funeral. But I don't believe in crocodile tears. And, certainly, it does solve a problem for us."

"Have you expressed this sentiment to Chief Wells?" Annie inquired.

She tapped the cigarette in a silver ashtray. "Oh, he won't bother me," she said carelessly. Her eyes, as black as licorice, swept Annie, but with as little interest as an electronic eye in an elevator. "I was talking to Leighton. He told me Wells is after you. Or that reporter."

"Hasn't Wells even talked to you?" Annie demanded, feeling her cheeks heat. "Doesn't he know how you and Corinne were feuding about Tim's paintings?"

"I don't know." Her indifference was monumental. "Now, let me ask you, don't you think two paintings per page at the most?" She reached out and picked up a brochure. "Here's a good one from a recent sale at Sotheby's. What do you think of this format?"

Annie would have exploded, except for the viselike grip Max wisely planted on her wrist. She swallowed angrily, and glared at him. He'd pay for this—later.

"Sybil, I know you don't think it's too important," Max said smoothly. "But we're trying to account for everyone's whereabouts at the time of the murder. Can you tell us what you were doing?"

Those pit-black eyes moved to Max, lingered on his face, moved slowly down his body.

"What you were doing," he repeated stoically.

"Oh sure." She smiled, and this one was X-rated. "Sure. I was making Timmy feel better." She put the cigarette holder in her mouth. "We were upstairs in my room. For a long time."

Annie was still seething as they fought their way up the marble steps to the double, fourteen-foot-tall bronze doors that marked the entrance to the Prichard Museum. It was slow going because everyone else was herding down the steps. When an elbow cuffed her in the ribs, Annie snarled, "Hey, watch where you're going!" "Honey," a soft voice soothed, "you're goin' the wrong *way*. There won't be another magic show for twenty minutes." But, finally, a bit battered, they reached the doors, and Max pulled one open. They stepped into a magnificent rotunda, and Annie was delighted to see only a sprinkling of tourists. She was, all things considered, getting tired of tourists, no matter how many t-shirts they bought from the Death on Demand display.

Sunlight sparkled through the stained-glass dome, illuminating the glass cases that sat around the perimeter of the circular room.

Annie paused by the first one, which contained a silver-plated reproduction of a silver trivet created in 1763 by a London artisan. Other cases held reproductions of authentic colonial pieces, including candlesticks, doorknobs, wall sconces, and bookends. A neatly printed card in the corner of each case announced: *Replicas created by Tim Bond, artist-in-residence, Prichard Museum, Chastain, S.C.*

A brisk young woman greeted them eagerly. "I see you are interested in our reproductions." Perhaps they were a welcome change from the magic devotees. "Prichard Museum is famous for the quality and quantity of its reproductions, and, in the bookstore, we have a catalog which lists all of our offerings. If you would like to tour the Museum, tickets are two dollars each. The Prichard Museum was built in 1843 as a meeting place for the Chastain Thursday Night Club. As you can see, it is built on three levels, and the supporting columns are Doric on this floor, Ionic on the next, and Corinthian on the third. The ballroom is on the second floor and is still used today for the winter balls."

"We would love to see the Museum," Annie said, "but today we've come to see Tim Bond. If you can direct us to his office..."

"Oh, certainly. This way." She led them through the bookstore in an ornate sideroom to a back hallway. "Tim's office is in the basement. Now, these stairs are dreadful. Watch your step as you go down. The offices are to your right." She opened the door, and the faraway bang of a hammer echoed up the stairwell.

Annie led the way and was glad of the advice. The steps pitched so steeply that she had to cling to the metal banister for balance. A light dangled from a cord at the landing. Unshaded bulbs hung in various parts of the basement, providing brilliant circles of light that emphasized the dark reaches between them. The rhythmic thud of the hammer masked the sound of their footsteps on the cement floor. They passed a door labeled Darkroom and a second one with Curator stenciled on it. A third door, a dingy yellow, bore a placard with the warning POISON. Tables and workbenches paralleled the corridor. At the far end of the basement, Tim Bond stood beside a cluttered workbench, driving nails into the ends of a crate. The light here was very bright, a circle of yellow against the blackness of the cellar's recesses.

"Hello, there," Max called out.

For an instant, those narrow shoulders stiffened, then he turned and faced them, hammer in hand. The harsh light bleached the color from his gaunt face. In silence, he watched them approach. He wore a paint-spattered shirt and frayed cut-offs. His sea-green eyes had a wild look, like a horse ready to bolt. He shifted from one big foot to the other.

"What do you want?"

"We just wanted to visit with you a little," Max said soothingly. "What are you working on?"

Tim sniffed around the question as if

expecting a trap, then answered sullenly. "I'm crating my paintings, getting them ready to go to New York."

Annie twisted to look at the canvases lined up in a neat row. "That's pretty important to you, isn't it?"

"Any reason why it shouldn't be?"

"Was it important enough for you to kill Corinne?" Annie asked abruptly.

His Adam's apple jerked in his throat. "Hell, no." But his voice was shrill.

"You were mad at her. She wasn't going to let you go to New York. She was sending your paintings on a tour."

Tim licked his lips. "It would've been all right. Sybil was going to make her give me my stuff."

"How could she do that?" Max asked.

His eyes slid away, focused on the white pine board. "I dunno." He lifted the hammer, slammed the nail in solidly.

Annie raised her voice. "Where were you when Corinne was killed?"

He stood very still, hunched over the crate, then, with a look of great cunning, said, "How should I know? I don't even know when she was killed."

"Don't you read the paper?" Max asked.

The big head swung toward him. "Why should I? I don't care."

So much, Annie thought, for rapport between patroness and artist.

"Where were you between 5 and 5:30?" she asked briskly.

"Oh. Here and there," he said vaguely. "I

don't pay much attention to time. I don't even own a watch."

A telephone jangled behind him. He reached out a big hand to pick up the receiver. "Yeah." His pale eyes flickered from Max to Annie, then his face reddened, until his skin was scarlet to the roots of his soft, curly hair. "Oh, yeah. They're here. Okay."

He hung up, then glared at them defiantly. "I was with Sybil. I was with Sybil the whole time."

Annie pulled the booth door shut, which immediately made it airless and hot, but there was too much noise from the parade proceeding up Federal to the accompaniment of a rousing "Stars and Stripes Forever" to leave it cracked. While she waited for Gail to come to the phone, she entertained herself by admiring Max's sun-touched profile through the smudged window.

"Hello?"

"Hi, Gail. This is Annie. I'm sorry to bother you, but there's something we really need to know."

The tiny sigh on the other end said more clearly than words that Gail was disappointed in the caller. Hadn't she talked to Bobby yet?

"What can I do for you?"

"Who is Leighton involved with?"

Now the silence tingled with dismay.

"I know," Annie continued quickly. "You don't want to say. I understand that. But we

have to talk to everyone concerned—and
believe me, it's up to me and Max. Chief
Wells isn't talking to *anybody* but me and
Bobby."

"Oh, God." Silence again, then a hoarse,
unhappy whisper, "Peggy Taylor. She teaches
at Chastain High."

18

THE SWIMMER KICKED a steady four beats per
stroke, and her elbows came high as her
hands knifed cleanly into the water. At each
end of the pool, she made swift, nicely executed flip turns.

Annie waited patiently beside the diving
board. The water glinted satiny green beneath
the overhead lights, and the heavy smell of chlorine hung in the still, moist air. The high
school secretary had directed her to the pool.
"Miss Taylor works out at noon every day, but
she won't be finished yet."

The swimmer neared the deep end, but
instead of flipping, she surfaced and clung to
the rim. Shaking her hair back, she glanced
around the deserted pool, then up at Annie.
"Are you waiting for me?"

"Yes. I'd like to talk to you for a minute, Ms.
Taylor."

She pulled herself up and out of the pool,

without apparent effort. She had a swimmer's body, lean, firm, and shapely.

A woman more different from Corinne Webster would be hard to imagine.

Peggy Taylor moved with the unselfconscious grace of a superbly conditioned athlete. Her Lycra racing suit revealed high breasts, a narrow waist, slim hips. She pulled off her goggles, looked curiously at Annie, then held out a firm hand. "Peggy Taylor."

Annie shook her hand. "Annie Laurance."

"What can I do for you?"

"You know Leighton Webster."

Peggy's face closed, became carefully blank. "Yes."

"You know, of course, that his wife was murdered."

"Why have you come to see me? I didn't know Mrs. Webster." Her voice was even and colorless.

"But people say you knew him very well indeed."

"People be damned." She stared at Annie, her tanned face set and stiff.

"Do you think he could kill his wife?"

"No." Her voice was harsh; the denial was explosive. But her gray-blue eyes were full of fear. She slapped a hand against the webbing on the board. "That's absurd. Leighton isn't that kind of man. He's gentle and kind and honorable."

"Have you spoken to him since Monday?"

"No." She looked away from Annie, stared down at the water lapping against the lane ropes.

"When did you last talk to him?"

She didn't want to answer that question. Her reluctance quivered between them. Finally, grudgingly, she said, "A week or so ago. I don't know exactly."

"Had you quarreled?"

"Oh, go to hell," Peggy cried. She grabbed up her towel and stalked away.

"Where were you Monday afternoon?" Annie called after her.

The slim figure paused. For a moment, Annie was certain she would not answer, but then Peggy Taylor looked back. "In a bloody faculty meeting that ran late." Then she headed swiftly toward the girls' locker room.

Annie stopped at a pay phone in the main hall of Chastain High and dialed the Prichard House again.

It took a minute, but Leighton Webster came on the line.

"Mr. Webster, I just talked to Peggy."

There was a sharply indrawn breath. "Miss Laurance, I find that an unwarranted intrusion in my life."

"I have just one question. What happened the last time you saw her?"

"She didn't tell you? No, I don't suppose she would. Actually, Miss Laurance, it might interest you to know that she told me of her future plans. She has joined the Peace Corps. Peggy's leaving Chastain when school ends next month."

Even the cheery smell of pipe smoke and the club comfort of the richly padded brown leather armchair couldn't offset Roscoe Merrill's icy reception.

"Mr. Darling, I don't appreciate your telling my secretary you wished to see me about a murder. That kind of loose description can give rise to heated imaginings."

"I assumed your secretary was discreet."

A dull flush rose to Merrill's cheeks. "She is, of course. Nonetheless... Well, you're here. What do you want?"

"Where were you at five o'clock Monday?"

"Here."

"With a client?"

"I'm not too sure of the time. Perhaps. But I may have been working on a will."

"Don't you keep time slips?"

Wariness flickered in Merrill's hooded eyes. "Of course. I could check them."

"Why don't you?"

"I will—for the properly constituted authority."

Obviously, Max didn't qualify, and, equally obvious, Merrill had no intention of being helpful.

"Anything else, Mr. Darling?"

Max decided Annie's rhinocerous approach sometimes had its good points. He stretched out comfortably in the enfolding softness of the leather chair. "Just one thing. Does your wife know you're involved with another woman?"

"That isn't true!"

There was a ring of sincerity in the pronouncement that brought Max up short.

Merrill sat like a bronze Buddha behind his desk.

"Then why was Corinne threatening to tell her that you were?"

Merrill began to roll a pen in his fingers, his eyes seemingly intent on the leisurely revolution.

Max pressed ahead. "You can't deny you were the lawyer mentioned in that letter."

The pen moved faster.

"The letter made it clear Corinne intended to tell the lawyer's wife."

Merrill's chair creaked as he leaned back and stared up at the beamed ceiling. "For the sake of argument—and I wish to make it clear that this constitutes no admission of any kind—but just for the sake of argument, let's talk for a moment about the lawyer mentioned in that letter. You will remember the letter indicated Corinne felt the lawyer's wife had a right to know of an incident?"

Max nodded.

"Corinne believed one act of unfaithfulness should be reported to his wife, no matter how happy the marriage in question. Now, this lawyer—" he paused and the muscles worked in his jaws—"has a marriage everyone envies—and rightly so." He gave Max a considering glance. "I would imagine it is the kind of marriage you hope someday to have with Miss Laurance."

Max felt a tightness in his chest. That dry,

unemotional voice and, beneath it, a passionate caring.

Merrill threw down the pen and looked past Max at the painting of the wood ibis. "That kind of marriage is made up of many things. It's made up of love and passion and friendship and laughter—and trust. That lawyer's wife has always trusted him implicitly, and rightly so." Merrill rubbed the side of his face. "Now, let's talk for a moment about that lawyer. He's middle-aged, and he's always been faithful to his wife. He's involved in a lawsuit in Atlanta. There's a young woman lawyer, a rather lusty, hungry young woman lawyer, representing a co-defendant in the case. They work together very closely for several months, and he's quite aware that she is available. He isn't interested." Now he paused and took a deep breath. "Unfortunately, he's human. The night the case is won, they return to the hotel, he has too much to drink—and the young woman lawyer—"

Max waited.

Merrill's mouth turned down in a humorless smile. "Of course, it is an uncanny fact of life that you always see someone you know when it is least convenient. In this case, Corinne was staying at the same hotel." He picked up the pen again, balanced it in his palm. "The lawyer was unfaithful to his wife. On any serious level, it is meaningless, which his wife would both understand and appreciate. On another level, the knowledge of this incident would destroy that absolute trust." His hand closed convulsively around the pen.

"It would not destroy a marriage, Mr. Darling, but it would blemish what has been perfection." Merrill cleared his throat. "As you must appreciate, keeping this incident secret is important to this lawyer. Yet, I think you would agree that preventing his wife from learning of this stupidity would scarcely warrant murder."

Annie caught up with Max as he was turning into the yellow stucco building where Dr. John Sanford had offices on the third floor.

On the way upstairs, she told him about Peggy and Leighton. "Don't you see? She must have given him an ultimatum. Get a divorce, or she would leave town."

As they reached the third floor landing, Max observed reasonably, "This is the 1980s. Why not just get the divorce?"

"Maybe he's too honorable."

"Is it more honorable to bash in your wife's head?" He opened the office door.

Even empty, the rectangular waiting room had a cramped appearance. Cheap plastic straight chairs were wedged around three walls, and tattered copies of *Sports Illustrated, Guideposts, Reader's Digest,* and *McCall's* were stacked on a chrome-edged coffee table. A rustle of papers beyond the untenanted counter indicated someone was present.

Max punched the bell on the formica-topped counter.

A sweet-faced nurse with thick glasses poked her carefully-coiffed head out of an adjoining room. "Sorry. Doctor doesn't hold office hours on Wednesday afternoons."

Max leaned on the counter. "He's here, isn't he? They told me at the hospital I could catch him here."

"Yes, but he doesn't hold—"

"Tell him Max Darling and Annie Laurance want to talk to him about Corinne Webster's murder."

She raised an eyebrow, then withdrew into the adjoining room. In a moment, she returned and gestured for them to come through the swinging door.

Sanford was in his office, which overlooked the cobblestoned alley.

"No Wednesday afternoon golf, Doctor?" Max asked.

Sanford ignored the pleasantry, and looked at them with cold, brooding eyes. He looked capable, confident, and controlled. If he had a bedside manner, he kept it under wraps.

"I'm busy," he said brusquely. "What do you want?"

Annie pointed at the window behind him, which framed a portion of the McIlwain House and the Prichard grounds. "Did you happen to look out that way Monday afternoon?"

He shrugged his thin shoulders impatiently. "I've got better things to do than stand at my window."

Max took it up. "What were you doing at five on Monday?"

Sanford beat a silent tattoo on his desktop with his right hand. "Finishing up patient folders for the afternoon."

"In here? By yourself?"

"Right."

"Can anybody vouch for that?"

His chilly eyes moved toward Annie. "I was here when Leighton called."

"That was at five-thirty." Max didn't amplify, but the implication was clear enough.

For the first time, a smile touched that swarthy, intense face. "Plenty of time to meet Corinne, bang her over the head, and get back here. Is that what you mean?" His laughter was a cynical bark. "Actually, I'd liked to have strangled her a hundred times, but they don't include justified homicide in the Hippocratic oath."

"Why did you want to strangle her?" Max asked, with the politeness a dozen governesses had instilled in him.

"Did you ever deal with Corinne?" Disgust weighted Sanford's voice. "God, that woman. The brains of a flea, and the tenacity of a leech. And selfish! All she thought about was the Prichard name, the Prichard House, the Prichard Museum, and, God forbid, the Prichard Hospital. She figured it was some kind of personal fiefdom just because her precious great-grandfather founded it. Do you know what she wanted to spend money for?" He slammed his hand on his desk, and papers slewed. "A restoration of the lobby to its original state in 1872. Jesus. And when I wanted to increase the hours for outpatient consultations..." His eyes glittered. "Stupid, bloody bitch."

"If you felt that way about restorations, why

are you on the Board of the Historical Preservation Society?"

He looked at Annie as though he ranked her intellect on a level with Corinne's. "This is a small town. A damn small town in the South." His voice capitalized it. "It's a pain in the ass, but you have to play the game to get along with people. And the game in Chastain is historical preservation."

"Why come here? You could have set up a practice somewhere else, couldn't you?"

For a moment, the anger and irritation left his face, replaced by eagerness. "Oh no, I couldn't go anywhere else. This is one of the best places in the world to study parasitic diseases. I came here to work with Byron Fisher." He looked at them expectantly, but when the famous name didn't impress them, his face wrinkled in disgust. "Why, we've got research underway here that isn't duplicated anywhere." His eyes alight with excitement, he drew sketches, cited tables, described his laboratory.

"Was this part of your work at the hospital?"

Once again, his face reformed into an angry glower. "Certainly. It was understood when I came."

"Was Corinne in favor of this use of the facilities?"

"What do you think?" His snort was contemptuous. "But I would've gotten my way."

"Was she trying to block your plans?"

Sanford leaned back, placed his supple hands flat on the chair arms. "Oh, yeah. But

I have a way of winning." Then his mouth twisted in a sardonic smile. "Without resorting to murder."

Max fastidiously averted his eyes from Annie's chili dog and root beer. They'd made two stops for lunch. One at the hot dog stand for her order, the second at a seafood restaurant for his shrimp and crab salad and Bud Light. There wasn't a spare foot of space along the bluff, so they finally ate standing up at the corner of Lookout Point, then dashed across Ephraim to the Inn. There was just time to change for the funeral.

Every seat was taken at St. Michael's. Annie realized anew how important a figure Corinne had been in Chastain. The family sat in the first pew on the lesson side of the aisle, looking rigidly ahead. Gail sat between Lucy and Miss Dora. The priest made no mention of murder as he intoned the stately funeral service from the Book of Common Prayer, but Annie sensed a peculiar undercurrent in the sanctuary. Instead of the usual quiet reverence that underscores an Episcopal service, she felt an unmistakable air of tension, a mixture of grief, fear, and pernicious curiosity. As they rose for the recessional, and the pallbearers walked up the aisle beside the casket covered by the silk funeral pall, sidelong glances followed its progress, then turned toward the family. Was it her imagination or was there almost a tiny pool of space around each person who had been associated with Corinne?

After the final prayer, Leighton took Gail's elbow as they left the pew. Lucy and Miss Dora came after them. Lucy pressed a gloved hand to her mouth. Miss Dora stumped up the aisle, her wrinkled face as dark and unreadable as mahogany.

Annie spotted Roscoe, his eyes downcast, his balding head bent. Jessica held his arm tightly. Edith Ferrier stared straight ahead, her face solemn. Tim Bond yanked at his collar, making his tie hang in disarray. Sybil strode forward as if she couldn't leave the church soon enough.

Out in the bright afternoon sunlight, the mourners—or those who had attended the funeral—began to drift toward the bright striped tent that marked the open grave. Corinne, of course, would be laid to rest in the graveyard, which held dead kinsmen back to Morris and Elizabeth Prichard, who died of yellow fever in 1766. A gap opened in the crowd for the family to pass through. Once again, Annie pondered the kind and quality of the sidelong glances directed at Leighton Webster.

Edith stopped beside Annie and Max. "My God, doesn't Lucy look awful."

Lucy's thin face was gray with faint splotches of make-up high on her jutting cheekbones and a thin red line of lipstick on her mouth. Her cheeks were sunken; her navy blue silk dress hung on her. She carried a prayer book in gloved hands that trembled. Her eyes followed the casket, but every step seemed an effort.

"I can't believe she's taking it so hard."

"They were friends for a long time, weren't they" Max asked.

Edith fell into step with them. "Oh, sure. They grew up together. But if that old story's true, she ought to clap her hands at Corinne's demise. I'll tell you, if somebody'd ruined the love of my life, I wouldn't count her as a friend."

That old story. Annie glanced across the crowded churchyard and caught another glimpse of Lucy, who did indeed look dreadful. Then she glanced at Edith, whose dark brows were drawn in a tight frown. No, Lucy and Edith weren't cut from the same cloth. Unlike Lucy, Edith would be a good hater.

"Oh, Lord." Now Edith's tone was sympathetic.

Peggy Taylor would be a standout in any crowd because of the aura of health and vigor that she carried with her. She was especially noticeable today, waiting in the shade of a weeping willow near a mossy gravestone, just beyond the path. When Leighton Webster, walking heavily, came even with her, he paused for an instant. He lifted his hand. There was an open hunger in his eyes.

She stared at him, her eyes aching with questions.

Then it was over, the moment gone, as he moved on, walking toward the gravesite, ignoring the crowd's murmurs.

Peggy Taylor looked after him. Her face crumpled. She held a handkerchief to her mouth and turned and walked swiftly away.

"She's afraid he's guilty. Poor devil."

Annie wondered who Edith was calling a poor devil. Leighton—or Peggy?

"And look there."

Annie looked past Max. Bobby Frazier stood at the edge of the crowd, his eyes on Gail's slender figure. And what did his gaze hold? It was hard to know, but she felt certain she saw a jumble of emotions and an agony of indecision. He took a step forward, as if to walk to Gail. Gail looked up, saw him, and her face brightened.

He took one step toward her, then swung around, head down, and walked away.

19

"**W**ASN'T IT A LOVELY funeral?" Idell's froglike eyes glistened with pleasure. She still wore her funeral dress, a shiny black polyester. She leaned on the Inn counter, obviously eager to talk.

Lovely? How lovely is it to watch lives disintegrating from the pressures of public and private suspicion?

"Everyone came," Idell prattled on. "Corinne would have been pleased."

Certainly Idell was. She radiated good humor, and something more. Excitement? Anticipation?

How much did Idell know about her recently deceased neighbor and those who hated her? Swallowing her distaste, Annie leaned on the counter, too. "Mrs. Gordon, I'd *love* to have your opinion on this case. You know these people *so* well. You must have a great deal of insight into who Corinne's enemies really were."

The landlady bridled with pleasure. "I know a lot about people, that I can tell you. Why, you'd be surprised what you learn running an inn. Why, people can be just dreadful!"

Annie lowered her voice. "Now, just between us, what do you think about Mayor Webster?"

"Oh, poor Leighton. She led that man around like he had a ring through his nose. I thought it served her right when he took up with that Miss Taylor. Met her out on his walks."

"Do you think he would have asked for a divorce?"

For an instant, genuine sympathy gleamed in those shiny brown eyes. "I would have hoped so, but Leighton always was such a gentleman. Even the way things are today, everybody getting divorced, I don't believe he could have brought himself to do it. Poor Leighton."

Was he too much of a gentleman to murder his wife?

"But Leighton didn't do it. I'm sure of it."

There was such a ring of confidence in her voice, Annie looked at her in surprise.

Idell's gaze fell away in confusion, and she began to rearrange the drooping daffodils in the tarnished holder next to the telephone. "These flowers. Must see to them. It's better to have fresh every day."

Feeling that her prey was slipping away, Annie plunged ahead. "And you knew Corinne as well as anyone."

Idell was suddenly less absorbed in the flowers.

"Oh, yes, of course. Known her forever!"

"How did she seem the last time you spoke to her?"

"She was *impossible*. No wonder she got murdered." Idell yanked viciously at a dead bloom. "Always trying to cause trouble. She said the Board was going to have to bring me into court if I didn't shore up the fence between the Inn and the Society Building. Claimed it was unsightly for visitors. Well, why couldn't the Society help? I need every penny I can get to keep the Inn going, with utilities going up every year and people using air conditioners even in April. I told her I couldn't do it, and I didn't have the money to go to court. Oh, she was a mean person."

"I guess it did make it hard, having the common boundary with the Society."

Idell looked at her gratefully. "Well, you run a business. You can understand. And the Inn is all I have." There was a note of fear in her voice, the spectre of old age and no money and all her assets gone. But there wasn't the least bit of concern about her quarrel with Corinne. Obviously, Idell didn't see herself as a potential suspect. So scratch that dark horse.

A sudden thought struck Annie. "You're right next door to the Society. Did you happen to look out that way—" She paused and thought. "It was one of three nights in the middle of March that we think the letter was typed next door. The nights of March 19th, 20th, and 21st. I don't suppose you saw anyone going in or coming out of the building after hours?"

Idell's eyes slid away from Annie. Then she shook her head vigorously. "No. But I remember the middle of March." She touched her jaw. "Oh, I had an awful toothache."

Annie stood in the middle of the room, holding the large cylinder of cardboard that contained the five Death on Demand mystery prints, and checked to see if she'd forgotten anything. Max had already taken down the stacks of mimeographed sheets with the Mystery Night information, the autopsy report, the suspects' original statements to police, and the clue box. She was walking toward the door when the phone rang.

"Hello."

"Miss Laurance."

Chief Wells's voice reminded her of gravel being dumped from a truck. Annie gripped the receiver tightly and knew her voice was strained when she answered. "Yes, Chief?"

"Got a tip on the murder."

She waited.

"Got a waiter here from a restaurant over on Broward's Rock. Says he thinks he's got a description of the killer. Cute blonde about twenty-three or so, gray eyes, good figure."

"Oh, now wait a minute—"

The heavy voice rumbled over her protest like a steamroller squashing rocks. "Know what he overheard? Girl said she'd decided to bash the lady with a croquet mallet."

"I was talking about the Mystery Nights plot," she said furiously.

"So you admit that's what you said?"

Annie phrased it very carefully indeed. "On the occasion in question, I was describing to Mr. Darling the means by which the mythical murderer in the mythical Sticky Wicket murder intended to attack a *mythical* victim."

He wheezed loudly. "So you say."

"So I say."

"You'll be at the Prichard House tonight?"

"I'm not fleeing to Timbuktu, if that's what you're asking."

There was a long pause, and she thought she detected the juicy mastication of a tobacco wad. She wondered if there were a Mrs. Wells.

"Smart ass talk won't get you far, young lady."

"I understand you haven't even bothered to talk to Sybil Giacomo and Tim Bond."

His voice scraped like flint on a fire rock. "I can manage my own investigation, young lady. And I'll tell you this much, if I can prove either you or that reporter had a handkerchief on Monday, I'll arrest you."

"A handkerchief?"

"Yeah. Think about it, Miss Laurance."

Annie thought about it as she introduced the suspects for Wednesday's Mystery Night. She thought about it all evening, between frantic moments of the Mystery Night. Why a handkerchief? As a matter of fact, she never carried one. Which would distress her maternal grandmother, who expected a lady always to possess a dainty, lace-edged hankie. But hankies went out with garters and girdles. Who, today, carried a handkerchief? Apparently not Bobby Fraizer, either. If the killer carried a handkerchief, that narrowed the circle indeed. At one point, she whispered her query to Ingrid, who with a true librarian's skill could be expected to find the answer to any question. She came back in less than half an hour with this news: Leighton, John Sanford, and Roscoe, as might be expected, always carried handkerchiefs in their left hip pockets. Tim Bond, also as might be expected, owned not a single handkerchief, although he occasionally wore a ragged red bandana. Gail didn't carry handkerchiefs, but sometimes Edith, Lucy, and Sybil did. Miss Dora, of course, was always equipped with one.

Her head spun.

A hand tugged at her arm. "Miss Laurance, there's a discrepancy."

It was hard to say whether Mrs. Brawley was delighted or offended. Her nose wriggled with eagerness.

"What's wrong?"

"Last night Lord Algernon said that he gave Miss Snooperton the ticket to Venice on the Orient Express *before* they played croquet. Tonight, he said he gave her the ticket *after* they played croquet." She waited eagerly.

"Very good," Annie praised. "We'd better take care of this at once."

Mrs. Brawley padded happily alongside Annie to the Suspect Interrogation Tent. Annie patted her on the shoulder, then stepped up to Max and whispered in his ear.

He grinned and said firmly, "I gave the ticket to Miss Snooperton before we played croquet."

Annie and Mrs. Brawley exchanged satisfied smiles. Annie moved slowly around the tent. She paused behind Lucy, who still wore her navy dress and white gloves. She looked bone weary, but perhaps all of this at least took her mind off of the murder for awhile.

Sanford continued to play his role with panache.

Mrs. Brawley's team (No. 7 tonight) clustered around him. This time, Annie noted with amusement, Mrs. Brawley was Team Captain, and savoring every moment of it. She leaned forward, finger waggling, a picture of ruthless inquisitorial determination.

"Mr. Hoxton, have you ever before been a guest at a country home where a jewel theft has occurred?"

Sanford stroked his chin. "Ah, my dear lady, perhaps. It's so hard to remember when one is so often a guest."

"You can remember," she snapped.

"I do believe there was one instance. At Lord Healy's home, Castle-On-The-Thames. I think I recall the disappearance of a diamond brooch."

Mrs. Brawley stalked nearer. "Was that theft ever solved?"

"I don't believe so, dear lady."

"Did you then enjoy a spurt in your income, Mr. Hoxton?"

He registered shock. "That is an unwarranted assumption."

Mrs. Brawley raised a hand. "It is time to demand a search warrant of Reginald Hoxton's room and its contents."

Her group stormed triumphantly after her and received this information: In the pocket of Hoxton's trousers worn that afternoon, the police laboratory (with emphasis on the second syllable) discovered a fragment of gold, apparently from a jewelry setting, and a trace of putty.

Smiling, Annie moved on to Edith, playing Miss Susannah Greatheart.

An eager questioner demanded, "Isn't it true that Miss Snooperton had stolen Nigel Davies from you, and you quarreled with her shortly before her murder?"

Edith dabbed at her eyes with a crumpled linen handkerchief. "Oh no, I never quarrel with anyone, and I felt certain Nigel would come to his senses when he discovered that Miss Snooperton was involved with Lord Algernon."

"And how did you know this?"

"Why, dear Lord Algernon felt I would be sympathetic to his problems. He was trying his best to be rid of Miss Snooperton. He thought her a dreadfully fast young woman, who had tried to ensnare him with her wiles. I do find Lord Algernon to be such a gentleman."

After a hasty consultation with his team, Team Captain No. 3 brayed, "We demand a search warrant against Miss Greatheart."

The warrant revealed: A ruby necklace stuffed in among Miss Greatheart's lingerie, and a bloodied croquet mallet thrust deep in her wardrobe. Upon investigation the necklace was declared a replica of the missing Red Maiden, and the mallet was identified as the murder weapon.

Taxed with these facts, Miss Greatheart broke down, declaring she had been framed. "Someone must hate me very much."

Team No. 3 stampeded to surround Lord Algernon. The intensity of their questions delighted Max, who responded with élan.

"I had broken off my involvement with Miss Snooperton. Fact of the matter, gave her a ticket to Venice this morning, then wrote her a note I couldn't meet her at the arbor after tea."

"Was it your note that was found in her pocket?"

"Must have been."

"You say you were finished with Miss Snooperton. Was she finished with you?"

"Felt like Nigel had taken me off the hook there, getting himself engaged to her. Damn disgusting the way he was treating Miss Greatheart. Tried to cheer her up."

"Isn't it more, Lord Algernon, that you were exhibiting your longtime weakness for members of the opposite sex other than your wife?"

"Oh, that's a rum suggestion. Besides, Alicia's a sport."

He finally admitted, though he downplayed its significance, that he'd had a few angry words with Miss Snooperton at the rose arbor, but he insisted that he left her alive with the clear understanding their affair was ended, whether or not she accepted the ticket to Venice.

Team Captain No. 8 demanded a search warrant against Lord Algernon, and these facts were unearthed: A packet of angry letters from Miss Snooperton threatening to reveal their affair to Lady Alicia unless he made a substantial settlement upon her. One letter stated: *Cough up or sweet Lady Alicia will learn about our weekend in Nice.*

From there Team Captain No. 8, a mild-mannered professor of medieval poetry at Chastain Community College, bounded across the grass to attack Lady Alicia.

Jessica Merrill, stately this evening in an ankle-length pink-and-white dimity dress, faced the barrage of questions with haughty disdain.

"Was I aware of an involvement between Algernon and Miss Snooperton? Why, of course not. That is truly absurd. And, of course, even it it were true, I would merely

277

pity the poor boy to have become entangled with such an unattractive and predatory woman."

"Didn't you earlier say Miss Snooperton was a dear girl?"

"Oh, did I? Perhaps. I've no real opinion in the matter."

"How much money did you owe Reginald Hoxton, my lady?"

"Merely a small debt between friends."

"But how could you hope to pay it off? You have no money of your own, have you?"

"There was no pressing need to resolve a trifle between friends over a card game."

"But Miss Greatheart says she heard him threaten to tell Lord Algernon if you didn't pay up?"

"She must have misunderstood. Such an insipid young woman."

Jessica Merrill refused to buckle beneath the spate of questions. Lord Algernon had harummphed and said Lady Alicia was a sport about his extra-marital activities. How would Jessica Merrill feel about her husband's involvement with a predatory lady lawyer?

Every so often, to the enormous disappointment of the besieging detectives, one or another of the English Manor suspects would hang a Back Soon sign in their chair and slip away for a few minutes of rest or refreshment.

When Jessica took her break, Annie followed her out to the main sidewalk. As she hurried to catch up, she overheard a middle-aged woman returning to the detection area tell her friend, "This has just been the most fun I've had since I was seven and my mother gave me *The Clue In the Album.* Doesn't the investigation remind you of the house party at Lady Billington-Smith's in Georgette Heyer's *The Unfinished Clue?*" Her companion nodded energetically. "Oh Hetty, I know just what you mean. I keep remembering Chayning Court in Gladys Mitchell's *Speedy Death.*" Buoyed by her eavesdropping, Annie spurted ahead and called out, "Jessica," as her quarry turned into the inn.

"Oh, hello, Annie. Decided I needed a drink. God, it must be exhausting to actually be a suspect in a murder investigation."

Annie settled for an enigmatic, "I suppose so," rather than a query about Roscoe's emotional temperature.

They settled in a corner of the coffee bar, which offered a very limited drink list, coffee, house wine, white and red but provenance unspecified, and a bottled wine cooler. They both opted for the last.

"One more night," Jessica sighed.

"It's good of you to keep up, considering the circumstances."

Jessica poured the cooler slowly over the ice, then picked up her glass. She looked very self-possessed, her dark hair curling softly away from her face, her large, attractive eyes meticulously outlined in eye shadow. She smiled at Annie. "It's been difficult, of course. Corinne has been our friend for many years. I know she would have wanted the garden nights to continue, and, of course, as a member of the Board, Roscoe certainly feels a responsibility to see that the Society's efforts aren't damaged."

"Did you like Corinne?"

Those large eyes returned Annie's gaze steadily. "That is a remarkably tactless question at the present time."

"Being one of two primary suspects in a murder investigation has put tactfulness pretty low on my priority list."

Jessica sipped at her cooler. "Roscoe doesn't think anyone will be arrested. Apparently, there is no direct physical evidence linking any one person to the crime scene, and he says it's very difficult to sustain an arrest or obtain a conviction without clear-cut evidence or a confession." She smoothed her softly waving black hair back from an unlined forehead. "It will probably be one of those famous unsolved mysteries."

"That's pretty lousy for everybody. Me included." And especially, Annie thought, for Gail and Bobby, and Leighton and Peggy. "And I'm not at all sure Wells won't jump on Frazier or me, just to quiet the newspapers." Annie thumped her glass onto the cocktail table. "Dammit, Wells won't even *talk* to people who could have done it. Like Sybil and Tim." Then she glared defiantly at Jessica. "Or Miss Dora."

To her surprise, Jessica was neither shocked nor outraged. Instead, her eyes narrowed thoughtfully. "Miss Dora."

Annie tried to interpret Jessica's Madonna-like face, so smooth, calm—and masklike.

"It's funny you should think of Miss Dora. She's such a fixture around Chastain that no one even sees her, despite those out-landish clothes and her hats." Jessica smiled, but her brown eyes were serious and intent. "Miss Dora has spent her life trying to pre-serve Chastain's history. That is all that mat-ters to her, that and family. She opposed almost every innovation Corinne proposed for the Society. Miss Dora hates these garden weeks. She thinks Chastain should belong to its own and never to outlanders." Jessica toyed with her lapis lazuli necklace. "But, of course, it's absurd to imagine her creeping up behind Corinne and striking her down."

Annie almost corrected Jessica. No one had crept up behind Corinne. Corinne had turned to walk away. But it didn't really matter.

Jessica took a last swallow, smiled. "Well, I suppose we'd better get back—or the detec-tive teams will track me down here."

As they rustled in their purses for money, Annie asked quickly, "Had you talked to Corinne recently?"

Jessica's hand momentarily froze, then she lifted out her billfold. "Yes. Last week." Her voice was placid.

Annie added her portion to the tray. "What about?"

"Nothing special. She called me to ask if we should add a new line of reproductions at the Museum. I'm rather an authority on colonial glassware. She wanted my opinion."

It was so smooth, so easily delivered, and, Annie felt certain, absolutely false. Especially when she looked into those eyes, now curiously defiant.

"You and Roscoe have a wonderful marriage."

Jessica didn't challenge the non sequitur. She merely nodded as she pushed back her chair.

Annie rose. "I don't suppose the same could be said of Corinne and Leighton."

"I wouldn't know."

"Rumor has it that Leighton was involved with a young woman."

Jessica forced a smile. "That happens, doesn't it, when men reach a certain age. It usually isn't of any importance."

And with that, Annie realized that Jessica Merrill knew full well about Roscoe's lapse, and, if the matter were ever raised, would dismiss it as unimportant. The corollary being, of course, that if it didn't matter to her, it certainly couldn't provide a motive of any kind for Roscoe to silence Corinne.

But had Roscoe known—in time—how his wife felt?

The detective teams swarmed into the Suspect Investigation Tent full of last-minute questions.

"Miss Laurance, did the lab report say that footprint by the body belonged to Nigel Davies?"

"Yes."

"How about that broken lock on the tool shed? Did it have any fingerprints?"

"No. It was wiped off."

Fingerprints. Wiped off. Why did Chief Wells want her or Bobby to have a handkerchief?

A high squeal of sheer excitement erupted from Mrs. Brawley when her team received a search warrant to Reginald Hoxton's car. In the boot was found one of the croquet balls. It had been tampered with, and secreted within it was a handful of red rubies.

She was marking times on the last envelopes, when Bobby poked his head in at the main opening. He looked around, glared, and left.

Max plumped the final box down next to the wall. "Next time you plan a Mystery Night, I'll hire a pack horse."

"Next time I plan a Mystery Night, you can buy me a one-way ticket to El Paso. It would be more fun."

He sighed and draped himself against the poster of the rice bed. "How about a drink?"

She shook her head wearily.

"Rain check? I'm bushed."

He didn't even protest.

She didn't blame him. The room was stuffy and airless and about as comfortable as a wadi in the Sahara. Damn Idell. You couldn't leave the room for five minutes without her slipping in to turn off the air conditioner. Crossing to the window, Annie punched the button. After a shuddering cough, it slowly ground to life. She glanced out, admiring the patterns of shadow the moonlight splashed across the grounds and the Society Building next door.

The Society Building. If only stones could talk. Who had typed that letter after hours? If they only knew that....

20

A S ANNIE LIFTED the brush to stroke her hair, a shriek from downstairs knifed through the thin wooden door. She stared at her early morning reflection in the mirror, her eyes startled, her mouth parted in surprise. A second scream resounded, louder still and with a growing undercurrent of hysteria.

Something was very amiss within the stuffy confines of Swamp Fox Inn. Max burst through their connecting door, and Annie grabbed her shorts.

He looked tremendously relieved, then his eyes widened with pleasure.

She stepped into the shorts and pulled on a t-shirt. They moved toward the door. Max opened it, and they scrambled through at the same time.

On the balcony, the sounds of distress were louder still, and the words bubbling between sobs brought them both pounding down the stairs.

"Dead...horrid...sticky and wet...oh my God, dead..."

The assistant manager shook the shoulders of the gray-haired maid. "Shut up! You're going to wake everybody up. Dammit, Frieda, you're not making any sense. Shut up! Who's dead?"

"Idell. She's laying in there..."

The assistant manager and Annie and Max turned at once, abandoning the sobbing Frieda. They halted abruptly in the open office doorway. Idell Gordon sprawled stiffly on the love seat behind a small glass-topped coffee table. A decanter sat on a Chinese lacquer tray. She still wore her black polyester funeral dress, and it pulled at the seams against her ungainly pose. Staring eyes were fixed on the ceiling. Her face was pinkish, and her mouth agape, the lips strained back in a twisted smile.

The young man made a noise deep in his throat and backed up, crushing Annie's foot. She yelped; he jumped, glared at them, and yanked the door shut. "I've got to call the doctor."

"And the police," Max added quietly.

A woman in the knot of guests clustered behind them began to whimper.

"Everybody go to your rooms, please. We'll be talking with you as soon as possible. If you have important business, Sergeant Harkey will take your name. Back to your rooms please,

ladies and gentlemen, we have an unex-
plained death here, and it will take time for
everyone to be seen. Back to your rooms,
please."

Annie leaned disconsolately against the
window, an elbow on the hiccuping air conditioner.

"God, it's my fault. It's my *fault*."

"How old was she?"

"I don't know. Fifty-five. Sixty? She'd be
older if—"

"A grown woman. If she knew who the
murderer was, she knew who to tell. Chief Wells.
That she didn't tell him is no fault of yours.
Besides, it doesn't sound all that clear-cut to
me that she knew."

"She's dead."

"Okay. Good proof. But nothing she said
to you yesterday was that obvious."

"I guess you're right. But she was excited—
and positive Leighton wasn't the killer. She
must have seen someone slipping out of the
Society late at night." Annie whirled around,
paced to the door. "Wells *has* to listen to me
now."

A vein pulsed in Wells's bulging forehead. The
wad of tobacco in his cheek was motionless.

"She was excited! And she asked if we were
interested in the reward. Chief, I'm sure she
saw the letter writer."

His big hands balled into fists. "I got a
murder here. Another one. And it's the kind
of murder smart people try. So I don't give

286

a damn about that stupid letter. I want to know how many times you came back to the Inn last night?"

Wells had ordered Annie to stay in her room, but Max made forays in and out, and he picked up quite a bit of information from other guests. Idell had been quite cheerful the last night of her life, visiting animatedly with various guests. She hadn't changed from the dress she wore to the funeral. She ate dinner in her apartment on the east side of the second floor, and was on duty at the desk during the early evening, giving way to the night clerk at nine P.M. When found Thursday morning, she was dressed as she had been the night before. She was in her office, which was to the left behind the counter area. A door from the office opened out into the Inn grounds. That door was open. The office light was on. On the floor, where it had fallen from her hand as she fell back in a seizure, was a single sherry glass. The sherry remaining in the glass had spattered on the wooden floor. The glass with its dried residue had been sent to the laboratory for examination, as had the crystal top of the sherry decanter. The sherry too, had been sent to the laboratory. Beneath her body, crushed against the faded damask rose upholstery, was the Wednesday afternoon issue of the *Chastain Courier*. Red pencil circled Bobby Frazier's byline to the lead story, and red pencil underlined the sentence reading: *The bereaved widower is offering* *a $5,000 reward for information leading to the arrest and conviction of Mrs. Webster's murderer.*

After the last policeman finally left, Max and Annie slipped out the back door.

Annie glanced back over her shoulder. "Do you suppose Wells will arrest me if he finds out I've left my room?"

Max wasn't worried. "No. You just hacked him, bringing up the letter again."

They took the alley to the McIlwain grounds. Annie stiffened at the back gate, pointing to the placard jammed into the grayish dirt.

"Although this is now known as Whitsett's Alley, after the proprietor of a print shop which stood here in the early 1800s, this is the site of the earliest Chastain racecourse, which was laid out in January of 1735. Races began in February and nearby planters entered the pride of their stables. Prizes included silver cups, bowls, or salvers. Race week culminated annually in the Jockey Ball, which opened with a stately minuet but included vigorous country dancing. Supper might have included baked turkeys, terrapin stews, iced cakes, partridge, quail, and goose, Madeira and Port wines, and punch."

Annie glanced wildly around. "That old woman is everywhere, but you never see her. It's giving me the creeps!"

The gate screeched like a cat with a stepped-on tail, and Annie jumped a foot.

"Gothic heroine," he murmured.

"Don't be obnoxious," she retorted.

They found Lucy at the side of the house, pruning a wisteria vine. She wore a floppy pink gardening hat, a denim skirt, and tailored cotton blouse. At the sound of their footsteps, she looked up, took a deep breath and visibly gathered strength.

"I suppose it's true." But she didn't need their confirmation. "I don't understand it, though. Corinne and Idell had nothing in common. Oh, they knew each other, of course. We all know each other. We've lived here so long, and we are neighbors. But why would anyone kill both Corinne and Idell? I don't suppose Idell had a heart attack?" She looked at them hopefully. "Could it be that?"

"They aren't sure yet what killed her," Max said, "but I heard the cops talking about poison. That's what they're looking for."

"It doesn't make any kind of sense. Not Idell."

"Actually, it does make sense." Annie described Idell's interest in the reward, and the idea that she may have seen the writer of the plot letter.

Lucy's face looked as though it had been chiseled out of pond ice.

"Louisa Binning insists the letter must have been written after hours," Max explained.

"And that means the typist had a key to the Society building."

Lucy drew her breath in sharply. "That's dreadful." If her face had looked worn before, now it appeared absolutely stricken. "Oh, my God. Someone with a key." Then she shook her head. Her voice was high. "Chief Wells doesn't believe the letter matters."

Annie looked at her gravely. "Don't you see how wrong that is? Lucy, please. You know these people. You know everyone who could have gotten into that building. Won't you help us? Won't you tell us what you really think?"

For an instant, Annie felt that it trembled in the balance, because Lucy understood.

Who could better judge the motives and passions of her longtime friends and neighbors? Lucy knew them all:

Leighton, the charming, handsome, not-so-grieved widower.

Gail, the emotional, love-struck, frightened niece.

Bobby, the abrasive, tough, self-serving reporter.

Roscoe, the self-contained but passionate lawyer.

John, the ambitious, determined, aloof doctor.

Sybil, the lusty, willful, spoiled sybarite.

Tim, the gifted, immature, self-centered artist.

Edith, the nervous, sensitive, hardworking clubwoman.

Miss Dora, the eccentric, unpredictable, waspish old woman.

Annie held her breath. Lucy could help them. She felt so sure of it. If only she would—

Lucy tucked the shears under her arm, slipped off her gardening gloves. Then she clasped her hands together to hide their trembling. Tears glistened in her eyes as she shook her head. "No." Her voice was as faint as the whistle of wind in a cavern. "No!"

Max ordered veal marsala. Annie debated between corned beef on rye and a chili hamburger and picked the latter.

"There has been some mild concern of late about cholesterol," he said conversationally.

"I think I'll have chocolate fudge pie for dessert."

"How about adding a dollop of whipped cream?"

"Good idea."

He sighed. "You are almost Victorian in your pigginess."

"If I could go back in time, for culinary pleasures, it would be difficult to pick between a Christmas dinner in Victorian England and a wedding feast in ancient Rome."

"Does this mean you are going to develop a matronly figure in your old age?"

"Gee, I don't know. Stick around and find out."

"And have a lot of fun along the way."

"I'll shake on that," and she stuck out a hand. She pumped his hand hard for an instant, then paused and the pleasure seeped out of her face, replaced by worry and discouragement. "Dammit, Lucy knows who wrote that letter. Don't you think? Why else would she always get in such a swivet when we ask her about it?"

Max put down his fork, looking about as stricken as Lucy had.

She mumbled past a mouthful of chili hamburger. "What's wrong?"

"God, do you suppose Gail wrote it?"

Annie stopped chewing to stare at him. "What makes you think that?"

"Lucy's crazy about Gail—and she's looked like hell ever since Corinne got bumped off."

She put her burger down on the plate. "That makes just enough sense to be true." She squinted in concentration. "No, no, wait a minute. That doesn't jibe, because Gail's panicked about Bobby."

"Is she?" Max said coolly.

"Sure she is. She ran to us to see if we could help. She's acted like a heroine tied to the rails every time Bobby is mentioned."

"Look at it this way," Max suggested. "If she's a double murderess, that lavender blue persona of hers has to be more than a little contrived. There may be a hell of a lot more to her than just a pretty face."

Annie looked at him admiringly. "Beneath that Jack Armstrong exterior lurks a Stephen King imagination. I'm impressed."

He smiled modestly.

They ate in silence for a moment, then, as Annie swallowed her last fat-laden bite, she said purposefully, "Okay, we've got first-class analytical brains. Right?"

"Of course."

"So let's think. Why was the letter written?"

"One, to embarrass Corinne," Max suggested. "Or, two, to warn her. You know, something on the order of those street corner signs: repent while you have time."

"Or, three," Annie offered, "it might have been designed to stir up trouble between Corinne and the not-so-well-disguised suspects in the Moneypot plot so that the water would be well-muddied when Corinne was murdered. Or, four, to implicate me."

Max pounced on the last two. "But they would presuppose that murder was intended when the letter was first written."

Annie sighed heavily. "Maybe we don't have first-class brains."

The waiter removed their plates, and Max ordered two beers.

Annie reached for the dessert menu, murmuring, "Fudge pie."

"Nobody would mix beer and fudge pie." But his tone wasn't altogether certain.

Annie reluctantly put down the dessert menu. "Actually, I'm full. Another time."

Max returned to the letter. "If we knew the real reason it was written, it would be a hell of a lot easier to pick out the writer."

She propped her chin on her hand. "Sure. Reason one is motivated by anger. Reason two is more ambivalent. The writer is mad but willing to give her another chance. But reasons three and four—"

He nodded. "Yeah. The die is cast."

Max pulled an envelope from his pocket and listed their suspects.

Annie nodded at the first name. "Okay. Let's take Leighton. He married Corinne and lost the career he wanted. No kids. Not much to care about in his life, so he started to go to seed. Drank too much. But always a gentleman. Then he meets this attractive young woman, who cares about him as a person, not as the financial underpinning of a big house."

"If he wrote it, it would have to be Reason Three."

"Because he wasn't really mad at Corinne, was he? He was disillusioned, and maybe a little bitter. But not mad. And he wouldn't expect that letter to change her, certainly not in any way that could benefit him. Her pride would never allow her to agree to a divorce. So his only motive to write the letter would be to provide a handful of suspects in her murder."

"Which it should have accomplished—except the police chief suffers from xenophobia." Max put a checkmark by Leighton's name.

"Is Leighton that kind of man?" Annie wondered doubtfully. "Devious and crafty? He seems so aboveboard, so likable—"

"Such a gentleman," Max parroted sarcastically.

"Well, he is!"

"Yeah. But he's a man, too. And he'd fallen in love. What was it worth to him?"

"I don't know." She looked at Max for a moment. What was his love worth to her? Everything. Anything. Yes, maybe she had to reconsider Leighton's motives.

"As for Gail, I hate to say it, but I sure can see her writing the letter."

Annie nodded reluctantly. Gail was weak, but she had the cunning and stubbornness of the weak. She would fight for what mattered to her, with any weapon she could find. "She could have written it to strike back at her aunt."

"Or she could have figured that a letter like that would go a long way to spread the wealth in a murder investigation."

"That's too Machiavellian for her," Annie objected.

"How about Bobby? He could have gotten Gail's key to the Society."

Annie shook her head vehemently.

"Sure he could have," Max insisted.

"Oh, I know that. But he wouldn't have written that letter. He's too direct. Too masculine."

Max's brows drew down in a dark frown. "I seem to notice a pattern to your objections. Apparently, good-looking men are exempted from suspicion."

"Don't be silly. I can't help it if Leighton and Bobby are attractive."

"How about Sanford?"

"He isn't attractive, but that's not the reason I can see him doing the letter. Actually, he's a natural. He acted furious when I read the letter, but that could be a cover." She remembered his angry face in his office, and his cold laughter. *I could have strangled her.* She shivered. "He's kind of scary."

"How about Roscoe?"

"No way. He's much too *careful* to do something like that. I mean, he is a lawyer. He'd figure out the letter could be traced to the Society. He'd think it was a crazy idea."

"Something no lawyer would dream of doing. Right?"

"Oh." She considered it. "He might have done it because he'd figure nobody would expect him to do it. That would be doubly clever."

"He's a very clever fellow."

"How about Jessica?" she asked.

"Jessica would act out of pure anger, if she knew how Corinne were upsetting Roscoe."

"The same would go for Edith. And believe me, Edith would have loved to sandbag Corinne. As would have Sybil." Her mouth twisted dryly. "But I doubt if Sybil can write her name. And the same goes for Tim."

"Oh, I think you underestimate Sybil," Max began.

Annie almost rose to the bait, until she saw the mischievous pleasure in his dark blue eyes. She folded her lips firmly shut.

Max made a star by the last name. "Of course, Lucy's an excellent suspect. She has keys and lives right next door to the Prichard House."

"She certainly could have managed it," Annie agreed, "but what happens when we try on the motives? Did she have any reason to be angry with Corinne? All we've picked up is an old story about Gail's father. Seems a little weak to me." She finished her beer, thought briefly about fudge pie, and turned her hands up in defeat. "I still think it's Miss Dora. Or maybe it's like *Murder On The Orient Express*. The Board members all got together at three in the morning and wrote the damned thing together."

Every time Annie saw one of the people on their list that evening during the final Mystery Night program, she wondered: Did you write the letter? Kill Corinne? And Idell?

The Mystery Night crowd was sparse. Only fifty-seven showed up, although the evening had been a sell-out like all the others. Both detectives and Mystery Night suspects showed a marked lack of enthusiasm and a tendency to look over their collective shoulders, except, of course, for the indefatigable Mrs. Brawley, who cornered Annie in the Suspect Interrogation Tent.

"Was the footprint at The Scene of the Crime traced to Nigel Davies?"

Annie looked at her blankly, her mind still juggling the names and faces of the Board members. "Footprint. Oh yes, it matches the shoes he was wearing after tea."

Mrs. Brawley's fox-sharp nose twitched. "After tea. Then he *lied* in his statement." With a whoop, she turned and lunged across the room to the Investigation table. "A search warrant against Nigel Davies. At once!"

The warrant revealed: A note from Susannah Greatheart to Matilda Snooperton, angrily demanding that she release Nigel from a loveless engagement.

Information in hand, Mrs. Brawley scooted across the tent to Roscoe Merrill.

"Your footprint places you at The Scene of the Crime!"

Roscoe went through his lines accurately but without verve, his mind clearly elsewhere.

"I dispute your assumption."

"It is admitted," Mrs. Brawley pressed, "that you wore these shoes *after* tea. Therefore, your presence at the site where Miss Snooperton died cannot be denied. Further, in your room, the search revealed a letter from Miss Greatheart to Miss Snooperton. How could it have come into your possession if you did not take it from Miss Snooperton, dead or alive?"

Roscoe skirted the attack. "I did not take it from Miss Snooperton. I found it in the area where she was killed. It must have dropped from her hand. But I did not see her to speak to."

A careful, lawyerlike response. Annie would have smiled, if murder were a topic for smiles. At this moment, it was not.

At nine o'clock, she looked up to see Chief Wells standing near the main entrance to the Suspect Interrogation Tent. He motioned for her to join him.

"Last night, did you leave here between nine and ten?"

"Is that when you think Idell was killed?"

"Just answer my question."

She fought down the impulse to back away from his bulky, dominating figure.

"I went down to the Inn once. Most everybody took at least one break during that time," and she waved her hand at the suspects, all of whom were watching avidly. She talked too quickly, trying to crack through the glower that seemed a permanent part of his face. "I was with Jessica Merrill. She can tell you. We walked down there and back together."

"You could've gone back."

"Anyone could have," she retorted angrily.

He stumped off then, moving heavily to each Mystery Night suspect. Was he asking about their movements—or hers?

Lucy frowned in concentration and looked as if she were conscientiously struggling to remember. There were dark shadows under her eyes. The bright patch of lipstick on her mouth and the round circles of rouge on her cheeks had aged her decades. She had tried to dress for her role, a silk dress with a gold-and-red flowered pattern and crisp short white gloves. The overall effect was garish.

Roscoe's face was as bland as that of a poker player with a big pot, but the wariness in his shrewd eyes made it clear he was answering carefully. He looked comfortable and assured in his dinner jacket, a man of means, innocent of anything more damning than a regretted romantic interlude.

Jessica smiled and replied briskly. Only the quick slant of her glance toward Annie revealed uneasiness. She wore a silk dress with interlocking shafts of crimson, purple, and cobalt blue, which emphasized her slim grace.

Max glanced once toward Annie, then shook his head sharply and spoke persuasively.

Dr. Sanford smiled lazily. He didn't seem

discomfited by Wells's questions. He was his customary arrogant, confident self.

Edith's huge green eyes flicked nervously from the chief to Annie and back again. She smoothed back a vagrant red-gold curl and answered in monosyllables.

Any one of them could have stepped into Idell's office from the Inn grounds and accepted an offer of sherry. She looked up at Prichard House. The bottom floors were dark, but light streamed from both front and back on the second floor. More than likely, Leighton and Gail were at home and had been at home last evening. Either of them could have walked through the shadows of Swamp Fox Inn and a final visit with Idell. And Bobby Frazier had come by the tent, looking for Gail. As for Sybil and Tim, it would have been simple enough to reach Idell. And Miss Dora was omnipresent.

Whose face had been the last seen by Idell Gordon?

21

ANNIE PUT DOWN her coffee cup with a click and craned her head to peer through the pillars supporting the patio to the garden outside the Inn. Popping up, she told Max, "I'll be right back."

Bobby Frazier bent in a half-crouch, photographing the door to Idell's office. When he lowered the camera, Annie approached.

"Won't you join us for some coffee?"

He looked tired this morning, and he'd nicked his chin shaving. He had the air of a man struggling with an inner crisis, his brown eyes abstracted, his mouth drawn in a grim line. Now, he stared at her, his face neither friendly nor hostile. Then he shrugged. "Yeah. I'll have a cup."

She led him back to their table. He and Max shook hands, exchanging curt greetings.

As he pulled out a chair and it scraped noisily against the flagstones, Frazier looked around the empty patio. "Got it to yourselves this morning." He dropped his camera bag beside the chair.

"They checked out in droves yesterday," Annie explained, then added, as she sipped the pale yellow coffee, "Wish we could have. But tonight's the last night." And how much fun would the Denouement Ball be, under the circumstances?

She tried for a light tone. "How do you like being tied with me as Wells's favorite suspect?"

"Oh, yeah." He wasn't interested.

Annie looked at him sharply. That was funny. He'd tried every way he knew to make it look as though he had no interest in Gail, and, ergo, had no motive. So why did he shrug away Wells's suspicions as unimportant?

But Bobby seemed preoccupied with his own thoughts. He picked a pencil from his shirt pocket and tapped it in an uneven rhythm on the table, but, obviously, he wasn't even aware of his action. "Have you heard about the autopsy report?" he asked abruptly. But he didn't wait for an answer, and his voice was grim as he summed it up for them.

Idell Gordon had a meat pie, orange sherbet, and coffee for dinner, eating alone in her apartment on the second floor. Analysis of the foodstuffs was negative, but the laboratory report found a heavy concentration of cyanide of potassium in the dried wine residue in the sherry glass and in her stomach. Idell Gordon had died of acute cyanide poisoning. Her fingerprints alone were on the wine glass. The remaining sherry in the decanter contained cyanide of potassium. The crystal top of the decanter yielded smudged prints identified as those of Idell Gordon.

"Cyanide." Annie had just picked up her coffee cup. She put it down again. "Oh, my God."

"Yeah." The pencil beat a frenzied tattoo. "They figure she invited somebody to have a glass of sherry while she put the bite on them. She must've decided she could get more than the $5,000 from Leighton."

"Oh, hell yes," Max exclaimed. "That makes all kinds of sense. Idell went after the murderer and threatened to tell Wells unless she were paid off."

"Money's all she ever talked about," Annie agreed. "Money and what a tough time she was having meeting her expenses." She pictured that fat face, the spriggy orange hair and protuberant, greedy brown eyes. "Blackmail."

Only this time, Idell's reach had far exceeded her grasp. "She must have contacted the murderer, made an appointment for Wednesday night."

"But the murderer brought cyanide, not money," Max concluded grimly.

Bobby jammed the pencil so hard against the tabletop that it snapped, then he stared down at it in surprise. "Stupid bitch. And I should have known. I should have taken Wells by the scruff of his goddamned neck and insisted he talk to her."

"Why? You had no reason to guess she was onto the murderer."

"She called me Wednesday, asking about the reward, how it was going to be handled, what a person would have to do to get it. I rattled it off, then I came down on her, asked what she knew. She backed off, said she was just curious, one of her guests had asked her. I thought that was phony, but I was busy, had a deadline, so I said oh sure, give us a call anytime. But I should have kept after her."

"You didn't go to meet her?"

There was an instant of stiff silence. Bobby stared at Annie. "No." He spoke carefully and distinctly. "I did not meet her."

"I didn't mean—" She flushed and started over. "I saw you at the Mystery Night, and since it's just next door..."

"I was looking for Gail."

Max poured fresh coffee for all of them. "Did you find her?"

"Yes. We had a nice talk." He sounded like a high school principal describing a Kiwanis luncheon, but the muscles in his jaw were rigid.

303

Annie squashed a desire to tell him to come off it. She realized more and more that she lacked the finesse needed to inveigle answers from sullen, angry, or frightened people. If only she had the suavity of John Appleby or the unassuming, quiet manner of Father Bredder.

Max, however, excelled in finesse. He propped his elbows on the table and smiled with the blandness of Lord Peter Wimsey. "Is Gail doing okay? What did she have to say?"

"Oh, she thanked me for the stories in the *Courier*, said they were well done. I thanked her. You know, we became acquainted when I did a series on the programs and outreach of the Prichard Museum. She's a very knowledgeable curator, and she's done an outstanding job with limited resources."

Oh, my God, Annie thought. Next he'd list her degrees and publications. She'd had enough.

"When did you fall in love with her?"

His head jerked up; he glared at Annie. "You've got it all wrong. We're friends, that's all."

"Then why did you tell her it didn't matter whether she had any money, that you were going to keep on seeing her no matter what her aunt did?"

"As friends," he reiterated stubbornly. "That's all."

Understanding exploded in her mind, like Fourth of July fireworks. "So Gail didn't have any reason to kill her aunt. Is that what you're saying?"

"Right. It's absurd to even think so. It's laughable, a gentle girl like Gail." But he wasn't laughing, and Annie knew that a frightful scene lurked in the dark corridors of his mind: Gail and Corinne, a quarrel, a burst of white-hot anger, Corinne face-down on the path, Gail standing there, a mallet in her hand.

Behind the tough newsman facade, fear for Gail ate at him. He tried to hide behind bluster. "Any idea Wells has about Gail, it's crap. That's all. Just crap."

As much to distract him as anything else, she said, "I guess they're sure about the autopsy report?"

Frazier looked at her blankly.

"Was it really cyanide that killed Idell?"

If possible, Frazier looked even grimmer. "Yeah. Cyanide of potassium."

"That ought to clear Gail. How could she possibly have access to cyanide of potassium?"

Bobby looked like a man who had opened a door and walked into hell. He didn't seem to be aware of their presence for a long, agonizing moment. Finally, he said dully, "That's a good point." He managed a travesty of a smile. "Of course, nobody with any brains would even consider Gail."

Except Bobby, obviously.

He drank some coffee, put down the empty cup. "Well, I'd better get back to the newsroom." He jerked his head toward the grounds. "Now that I've got a picture of the Death Door." He gave a mirthless laugh. "If you see Gail—Never mind. See you later."

As he strode away, Max sighed. "Poor devil."

"He thinks she did it."

"Yeah."

Annie looked at Max, unaccustomedly somber across the table. He looked tanned and fit, his thick blond hair cut short, his dark blue eyes alert and thoughtful. All as usual, except for the furrow of worry on his brow.

"Dammit," he said, "maybe you should go back to Broward's Rock."

This was so unexpected that she stared at him, momentarily speechless. "Why?"

"Cyanide is nothing to fool with. How do we know the murderer won't sprinkle it everywhere?"

She poked the half-eaten spongy croissant. "It might add a little flavor to this."

"For God's sake, Annie, be serious."

This was such a turnabout that she couldn't repress a grin.

In a moment, he broke into a reluctant smile. "Okay. I know. You *are* serious. Your virtue and your defect."

"I don't know who wrote that damned letter. Or who pinched some cyanide. Or who murdered Corinne and Idell. I'm perfectly safe."

That diverted him. He jammed a hand through his hair. "That's what we need to work on. Where could Gail get cyanide?"

"Bobby obviously has a very clear idea where she might have obtained the poison." And she concluded thoughtfully, "If he knows where Gail could have found cyanide of potassium, that means he knows how to get it, too."

Gail led the way up the magnificent staircase. It rose for three stories, the banisters carved at top and bottom, the railing a gleaming mahogany, the ornate fretwork glistening white. Her room was on the top floor, a bedroom and sitting room that overlooked the front gardens. A group of garden club women snapped pictures of the sweeping azaleas, with occasional furtive snaps aimed at the cane that hid the pond where Corinne died. The sitting room was papered with a mid-eighteenth century Chinese wallpaper with orange-tiled pagodas and tan mud-brick walls. Annie and Max sat on a Chippendale loveseat. It had delicate Chinese fretwork and was upholstered in tan and cream satin. Annie looked for reflections of Gail in the lovely, almost period-perfect room. An open copy of the April *Vogue* lay face down on the woven wicker coffee table. A modern black rocker with a Clemson crest sat beside the fireplace. A collection of miniature pottery dogs decorated half the Adam mantel. Portrait photographs sat at each end, one of Corinne, and the other of a man Annie felt certain must be Cameron, Gail's father. It was the same strikingly handsome face, auburn hair, sky-blue eyes, but there was an air of resignation in his face and perhaps a touch of weakness in his mouth. A chairside booktable held an extensive collection of art books, along with three booklets from the Prichard Museum. The top one pictured a magnificent silver punch-bowl. The cover blurb advertised historic reproductions.

Gail stood in the center of the sitting room, her feet wide apart as if braced against a storm. She wore a print dress in khaki and peony, jungle flowers bright against the tan background. The vivid colors of the dress underscored the waxen shade of her face and the dark smudges beneath her eyes.

"I can't believe it. Why would anyone kill Idell?"

Max spread his arm behind Annie on the sofa top. "The police think she tried to blackmail the letter writer. She'd talked to Bobby Frazier about the award being offered by Leighton. She definitely had money in mind."

Gail's hands curled into tight balls. "She called Bobby?"

"Yes. But when he pressed her about what she knew, she backed off, claimed she was asking for a guest."

She looked at them doubtfully. "That's not likely, is it?"

"No." Annie put it bluntly. "What's likely is that she thought she could get more money somewhere else. Instead, she got cyanide in her sherry."

"Cyanide? Is that what killed her?" Gail sounded interested, but not threatened.

Annie had it down pat by now. "Cyanide of potassium."

Horror dawned slowly on Gail's face. If Bobby Frazier could have seen it, Annie

thought, surely he would have realized her inno-
cence.

Then a slimy thought wriggled in the
recesses of Annie's mind. If Gail were a
double murderer, once out of anger, the
second time from fear, she would have given
thought to the moment when cyanide of
potassium would first be mentioned to her.

"Cyanide of potassium." She whirled away,
walked to the window.

"Do you know where anyone could find it?"

Gail was silent for so long that Annie
thought she didn't intend to answer. Finally,
she turned and faced them, her arms folded
tightly at her waist. "It doesn't mean anything.
It's used for lots of things."

"At the Museum," Max suggested.

Her blue eyes troubled, she turned to him.
"Yes." She almost managed to sound con-
versational. "I believe there is some at the
Museum. Tim uses it in electroplating." At their
silence, she continued, "You know, in making
historical reproductions of things like candlesticks and punch bowls and tankards. We
have an extensive line of reproductions that
we make and sell through the Museum to raise
money."

Annie darted a look at Max. He was so
busy suffering for Gail that he didn't say a word.
Annie didn't believe in festering sores. A
lanced boil heals.

"How did Bobby know about it?"

She swallowed jerkily. "It was last fall,
when he did a series of articles on the Museum
and its programs. He did a special Sunday fea-

ture on Tim and all of his talents, as a painter and engraver—and in electroplating." She rubbed her temple as if it ached. "Tim is truly an outstandingly talented person. I believe it was that article that caught the attention of the New York gallery." A touch of color seeped back into her face. "You see, everyone read about it. I heard so many comments, and we received a spurt of letters from people eager to know all about our line of reproductions."

"Did the article include the information about the use of cyanide of potassium in electroplating?"

"I don't suppose in so many words," she admitted reluctantly. "But anyone who knows anything at all about the process would know. So anyone who read that article would realize we had cyanide of potassium at the Museum. That's obvious."

It was a good deal more obvious that at least three of the people who were intimately associated with Corinne Webster knew about the cyanide of potassium: Gail Prichard, Bobby Frazier, and Tim Bond.

But she was cheering with every word. "So, of course, it doesn't mean a thing that Bobby wrote those articles. Anyone could have known." Then her eyes darkened with pain. "Besides, Bobby didn't have a motive. When I talked to you the other day, I gave you the wrong impression about Bobby and me. We're just friends. Nothing more than that."

"Oh, for God's sake!" Annie exploded. "Don't be such a fool."

She flushed. "I don't know what you mean."

"I mean any idiot—including Chief Wells—can see that Bobby's besotted with you. I don't mean he killed your aunt, but you can't be dumb enough to believe he doesn't care about you."

"He told me it didn't mean anything." Tears brimmed in her eyes. "He said—"

"Of course, he did. The boy's trying to protect you. He's doing his damnedest to keep Chief Wells from even looking your way. You'd have to be blind not to see it."

Gail's strained face reflected a series of emotions—shock, uncertainty, then burgeoning hope.

As the Porsche lunged away from the curb, Max shook his head chidingly.

"Well," Annie said defensively, "I hate stupidity."

"Sometimes, it's better for things not to be quite so clear-cut."

"Do you think he's fooling Wells?"

"No. But he was fooling Gail."

"So what's good about that?"

"It kept her from worrying about him, didn't it?"

They arrived at the Museum right on the heels of Chief Wells.

He disposed of his chewing tobacco in a silver spittoon, then turned his watery blue eyes on them.

311

"Aren't you people out of town yet?"

"I didn't know I was free to go. Besides, we have the ball completing the mystery event tonight."

"I know where to find you if I want you," he growled. "What're you here for?"

Max jerked his head toward the basement stairs. "We heard about the cyanide, too."

"Yeah, the cyanide." His eyes lingered on Annie for a long moment. "Since you're so curious, you can come on downstairs, little lady."

Said the spider to the fly, Annie thought. But they followed him down the steeply pitched stairs to the basement. The hollow echo of hammering led them to Tim, still crating his paintings. He looked at the Chief, and beyond him at Annie and Max, with no enthusiasm. "Look, I've told you everything I did on Monday, and I don't see why I have to go through it again. And I don't know anything about the old lady at the Inn." Sweat trickled down his face and stained his paint-spattered work shirt. His chestnut curls lay limply on his shoulders.

Wells ignored his objections. "Where's the poison?"

Tim led the way to the end of the corridor and a warped yellow door. The poster on it warned POISON. Tim unlocked the door and a heavy, sour smell of chemicals wafted out. He turned on the light. The trays and vats needed for electroplating were neatly arranged on a table against the back wall. A shelf to the right of the table held a number of bottles.

Wells found what he sought on the third shelf from the bottom, a large green stoppered bottled labeled CYANIDE OF POTASSIUM.

"Jesus Christ, there's enough poison in that to kill every living soul in Chastain!" His heavy head swiveled toward the door. "That goddamn lock's a joke."

Bond looked at him in disgust. "We don't feed it to anybody, Chief."

"It killed Idell Gordon," the Chief rasped.

If Tim Bond were acting, he exhibited considerable talent. His eyes went blank with shock, his bony jaw dropped. He took a step back, then said, "Hey, what the hell. Somebody's trying to frame me." His paint-stained hands clenched convulsively. "Listen, I don't know what the hell's going on, but nobody's going to lay this on me."

But Annie abruptly realized the Chief wasn't watching Tim. Instead, those probing, hostile eyes were pinned on her.

"Tell me something, little lady."

She tensed.

"Sybil told me you and your feller came down here and badgered Tim the other day. That's right enough, isn't it?"

"Is it badgering to ask a man who has a damn good motive where he was when the murder was committed?"

But Wells was intent upon his own train of thought. "Now, when you came down here, you couldn't help but see this here yellow door with a POISON sign. Now, could you?"

22

NNIE DUMPED THE envelopes out on her bed, then stared at them in dismay. How could there be so many? She looked at her watch. Almost four o'clock. Where had the day gone? But she knew. It had fled as they fought their way through the clogged streets (Friday featured a Fried Chicken Cook-Off, a China Painting Exhibition, and the finals in the Chastain Speedboat Classic), seeking more information about Idell Gordon, cyanide of potassium, and the whereabouts of all the suspects between 9 and 10 P.M. Wednesday evening. She'd had two more acerbic run-ins with Chief Wells and made another abortive visit to Miss Dora's shuttered home. Now she had only a few hours before the Denouement Ball began—and she'd damned well better have a denouement in hand, or she would be attacked by a band of enraged mystery buffs. And the prizes for the five best costumes— she rummaged frantically in the bottom of the clue box, then heaved a sigh of relief. There they were, five certificates, ranging in value from $5 to $25, good toward any purchase at Death on Demand. So, all she had to do was figure out which team, if any, had named the murderer of the Sticky Wicket Mystery.

If more than one had come up with the right answer, then it would come down to which team turned its answer in first. The mystery winners and costume winners were to be announced at the stroke of midnight.

She stacked the envelopes by day and felt the beginnings of panic. Could she possibly read and digest all these answers in time? It had all seemed so reasonable when she and Max planned it. But they hadn't counted on two real murders.

Max tapped on the door and poked his head in. "Let's go down to the *Courier* and see what we can pick up."

She flapped her hands distractedly. "Tonight. I haven't checked the entries. No time. Go ahead."

He leaned against the doorjamb and chuckled.

She turned on him with slitted eyes. "Can't you see?" She pointed at the four untidy stacks of envelopes. "I've got to read all of those."

"Oh hell, just throw them up in the air and pick a winner."

She glared at him, horrified. "Do you honestly think Mrs. Brawley wouldn't catch me?"

"I guess you're right. But relax, love, you're a speed reader." Kissing her lightly on the cheek, he departed.

It didn't take as long as she expected. For one thing, only two or three teams each evening came up with the right name. Of those, a Monday night team, No. 2, had the right answer for the right reasons, and the time on the envelope was 8-04-36. When she read the name of the team captain, she didn't know whether to laugh or to cry. There was a winner from last night, ringing in at 8-04-37. The Team Captain was—she stared at the list of team members for a long time, then took her pen and carefully altered the time to 8-04-36.

How about that. A tie.

At six-fifteen, she changed into her costume for the Denouement Ball. Max, too, was dressed for his part when he knocked on her door. They grinned at each other.

"That the twain never met was a grave error on the part of the Stratemeyer Syndicate," she said.

He was a marvelously handsome and clean-cut Joe Hardy as he nodded in agreement. "Right on, Nancy. But it might have hacked Ned Nickerson."

They slipped away to Confederate House for an early dinner. As they climbed gray wooden steps to the refurbished barn that overlooked the river, Annie clutched his argyle sweatered arm and pointed to the placard.

"Before the occupation of the area by Federal troops in 1863, work began here on earthwork fortifications. The last remnants of Ft. McReady were washed away in the hurricane of 1893."

Annie peered into a thicket of southern red cedars. "That woman is haunting me."

"I'd say she's the least of your worries."

They settled at a wooden planked table on a gray porch, and Max unloaded the latest.

"Bobby said Wells had his men print practically every square inch of Idell's office, and he's having the lab check any latent prints against yours, his, Gail's, and Tim's. If he finds a match—"

"There I never was. So maybe he'll finally give up on me." She studied the fake parchment menu. Should she go for Daufuskie crabs or duck, oyster and sausage gumbo? "How about the others?"

"They all claim they've never set foot in Idell's office."

Then Max dampened even her appetite.

"One grim note. Apparently, a hell of a lot of cyanide of potassium is missing from that bottle."

What a difference a day made. Whether it was simply the number of hours that had elapsed since Idell's murder or whether the Mystery Night participants were willing to risk all to discover the identity of the Sticky Wicket murderer, the night's turnout was excellent and the mood upbeat. The variety of dress for the ball amazed her. She spotted two Inspector Maigrets, four Hercule Poirots, a sharp-visaged Dick Tracy, and a prim Miss Silver complete with knitting needles, fluffy pink wool, and a brooch on her bosom.

Annie wandered among the tents, eavesdropping.

"Asey Mayo" confided to "Inspector Roderick Alleyn," "This is more fun than *The Mystery of Edwin Drood*."

"Oh, that *was* fun," "Miss Pinkerton" replied. "But my all time stage favorite is *Arsenic and Old Lace*. It's always funny."

In the distance, sheet lightning flickered. They'd been so fortunate with the weather all week. April, of course, was a spring month, and heavy storms rare. Gentle rains were not. She crossed her fingers. If they could just make it to shortly after midnight, it could rain as much as it pleased. She felt uneasy, and was uncertain whether to attribute it to the ominous weather or to the evening.

The mystery enthusiasts were having a wonderful time. The Sticky Wicket cast members were not. They had all dutifully come and mingled with the guests, but their generally stiff and distrait appearances singled them out. Although they knew Wells's suspicions were targeted on Annie and Bobby, they were like horses sensing a coyote's presence. Wells had talked to all of them, once or more. They all knew he had charted their movements to the Inn on Wednesday night. It put an edge to their voices and wariness in their eyes.

Rumors abounded.

Edith insisted to Annie that she'd heard Leighton had been arrested.

Roscoe said that was all wrong, a warrant was being charged out against Bobby.

Max disappeared for awhile and returned with the news that the lights were still burning in the forensic lab at the police station.

Even Sybil and Tim showed up, and Tim said loudly that he didn't know what the hell was going on, but Bobby Frazier'd gone into detail with him about the chemicals he used in electroplating.

It was just short of midnight when Annie looked down from the speaker's stand at a black-clad figure leaning on a silverheaded cane, staring with a death's-head face at the Sticky Wicket suspects as they gathered for the finale. Annie's hand closed on her sheaf of papers. Miss Dora! She took a step toward the stairs, then St. Michael's bell tolled midnight. As lightning blazed in the east, the old woman turned and melded into the deep shadows beneath a live oak tree. Annie hesitated, then faced the audience. Her heart was pounding. The band played a drum tattoo. "Ladies and gentlemen, this is the moment you've all been waiting for."

A vigorous burst of handclapping and cheers was almost lost in the roll of thunder.

"And I believe we just may make it under the wire before the storm breaks. But it is my pleasure first," Annie cried, "to announce the winners of the costume contest."

Max was leading a pleased and excited line of participants to the stage.

"Our fifth place winner is—" She waved her hand and glanced at the card in her hand. "Mrs. Harrison Frankfurt of Savannah, who came tonight as the inimitable Miss Maude Silver, complete with a shawl and brooch."

Mrs. Frankfurt came on stage.

"Our fourth place winner is Mr. Michael Forbes of Charleston, who you will undoubtedly recognize as the greatest sleuth of all time, Sherlock Holmes."

Forbes was tall enough and lean enough to look the part of the master detective in his deerstalker hat and Inverness cape. He waved his Meerschaum pipe and bowed to the cheering crowd.

"Our third place winner is Jeremiah Winston of Hilton Head Island. Let's give him a hand for his portrayal of Sam Spade." Winston slouched on stage in a loose tweed overcoat. A hand-rolled cigarette dangled from his lip.

"Our second place winner is Mr. Bill Brown of Atlanta." A little man with a truly egg-shaped head bounded up the steps. He wore spats, a European-cut suit of the 1920s, and he twirled a sleek drooping mustache with pride. "Ladies and gentlemen, I give you Monsieur Hercule Poirot.

"And, finally, our first place winner, America's favorite detective, Miss Marigold Rembrandt, as portrayed by her creator, America's most popular mystery writer, Emma Clyde."

Cheers, stomping feet, and thunderous applause erupted.

Annie passed out the Death on Demand certificates, shook everybody's hand, allowed Emma to kiss her on both cheeks, and turned back to the mike.

The costume winners filed down, and the Mystery Night suspects mounted the platform.

Annie saw Bobby Frazier standing in front of the platform, notebook in hand. His face was somber, and he needed a shave, which made him look almost unsavory.

"Before we reveal the perpetrator of our

Sticky Wicket murder, I want to introduce our suspects to you in their own right, so that you may thank them for the splendid efforts they've made this week to provide you with a challenging mystery and a pleasant evening.

"Lord Algernon has been played by my good friend and coconspirator, Max Darling.

"Lady Alicia is Mrs. Jessica Merrill, who has worked very hard for the Historical Preservation Society of Chastain.

"Roscoe Merrill, a member of the Society Board and a Chastain lawyer, has played the role of Nigel Davies.

"I'm sure many of you recognized Edith Ferrier, another active clubwoman in Chastain, as Susannah Greatheart.

"And Dr. Robert Sanford has served most capably as the dastardly Reginald Hoxton.

"Finally, Miss Lucy Haines, a very active member of the Society, is Agnes, Lady Alicia's maid.

"A round of applause for our players, please."

Gail stood on the side of the platform opposite Bobby. She was clapping for the suspects, but her eyes were on Bobby. Annie wondered if the damned fools had talked honestly to each other yet.

"Now, for the real story behind the Sticky Wicket Mystery." She paused dramatically, but her eyes skimmed the crowd for Miss Dora.

"These are the clues which should have led you to the correct solution:

"The broken piece of gold link from a necklace which was found in Reginald Hoxton's trouser pocket.

"The telltale mound of wood shavings on the workbench in the toolshed.

"The smudge of putty in Reginald Hoxton's pants pocket.

"The discovery of real rubies secreted in a croquet ball.

"The imitation necklace discovered in Susannah Greatheart's lingerie.

"The attempts of Lady Alicia's maid to scatter suspicion among the guests.

"Lord Algernon's partiality for a pretty face, other than that of his wife.

"What happened at the Gemtree Court on this fateful Saturday? We have a group of guests with some rather dark secrets. Reginald Hoxton is known about London as a man who plays cards too well and too often. Lady Alicia owes him 3,400 pounds, and he is pressing her for payment.

"Miss Matilda Snooperton is a rather unattractive lady, with a penchant for blackmail and illicit liaisons. She has managed to snare a rather unworldly University don, Nigel Davies, but at the same time she is carrying on an affair with Lord Algernon, who has wearied of it. He tells her Saturday that they are through and the best he will do is give her a ticket to Venice.

"Miss Susannah Greatheart is enamored of Nigel Davies and very bitter over his involvement with the insidious Miss Snooperton. She is quite pretty and rather naive and doesn't realize that Lord Algernon has taken a fancy to her.

"Agnes, the maid, is fiercely loyal to her mistress and quite eager to pass on to the police any information she has that would compromise the other guests.

"Lady Alicia professes to have no interest in Miss Snooperton, terms her a dear girl, but she is quite snide about Susannah Greatheart.

"So who did the dastardly deed?"

"Hoxton," a voice rumbled.

"Susannah Greatheart! She's a thief."

"Daves, that's the ticket!"

The Mystery Night participants exploded in chatter. It took Annie a couple of minutes to quiet them down.

"Here is what actually happened. Saturday morning Miss Snooperton sees Lady Alicia in a clandestine meeting at the gazebo with Mr. Hoxton. Lady Alicia gives him her ruby necklace, which is famous throughout England. Miss Snooperton threatens to tell Lord Algernon unless Lady Alicia pays her a substantial sum. Of course, our gambling Lady Alicia is strapped, or she wouldn't have agreed to give the necklace to Hoxton in the first place. She tells Miss Snooperton to meet her at the arbor after tea. They meet, Lady Alicia snatches up a croquet mallet, and that is the end of Miss Snooperton's career in extortion. Lady Alicia's motive, of course, is twofold. Lord Algernon mustn't learn that the necklace has gone to Hoxton, and she is furious over Algernon's involvement with

Miss Snooperton. To pay off Hoxton without discovery, she had recently had a copy made of the necklace. However, now she knows there will be a murder investigation. She decides to confuse the issue by pretending that her necklace has been stolen, in hopes the murder will be linked to the robbery. In the excitement after she announces the robbery, she takes Hoxton aside and tells him that she returned to her room, found her copy gone, and had no choice but to reveal it had been stolen.

"Hoxton, of course, is thrown into a panic. Of all the weekends for someone to rob Lady Alicia! He must hide the real necklace before he is accused of stealing it. However, he is resourceful. Under the guise of searching for the missing Miss Snooperton, he dashes down to his car, gets the car tool, uses it to prize open the lock to the toolshed, drills a hole in one of the croquet balls, and takes the rubies, which he has ripped from their settings, and hides them in the ball, which he closes up with putty. He paints over the spot and hides the ball in the boot of his car.

"Lady Alicia, meanwhile, hides the fake necklace and the murder weapon in Miss Greatheart's room, because she is jealous of Lord Algernon's attraction to her.

"The detectives who correctly identified Lady Alicia as the murderer did so because they realized that only Lady Alicia or Lord Algernon could have arranged for the creation of the fake necklace. Of the two, who needed money? Lady Alicia. The detectives realized, too, that Lady Alicia's maid would know her mistress had removed the necklace for a period of time. They also observed Agnes's frantic efforts to direct suspicion away from her mistress. The successful detectives considered and discarded the idea of two crimes (a fake robbery and an unrelated murder) occurring independently on the same day and concluded the perpetrator was indeed Lady Alicia."

The garden exploded with noise. Annie knew there would be some diehards who would protest, but her strategy was to sweep them right along.

"I know you are all excited to learn who our successful detectives are. I am delighted to tell you that we have a Monday night team as a winner."

Cheers and moans.

"Team No. 2 from Monday night, will you please file up on stage. Look who our mystery captain is! Come right on up here, Marigold Rembrandt—or should I say Emma Clyde?"

Another familiar face, heavy with disappointment, stood near the platform.

"But that's not all." Annie had to shout to be heard. "We have another winning team, which tied for the honor, turning in its solution at the same time last night. Team No. 6!"

Annie would never regret that changed time.

Mrs. Brawley charged up the steps, caught Annie's hands and raised them high, like a prize fighter in triumph.

"Our second winning team is captained

by one of Broward's Rock champion mystery readers, Mrs. Henrietta Brawley."

The band began to play, the winning mystery participants cheered, and the crowd yelled, whistled, and stomped.

Annie grinned. She looked at the cheering mass of spectators, then her face stiffened.

Chief Wells was shouldering through the crowd toward the platform, and there was no mistaking the grim jut of his jaw.

23

THE CROWD THICKENED at the base of the platform as mystery buffs moved toward the steps, eager to congratulate the winners. Annie lost sight of the Chief for a moment, then saw him bulling his way through a clot of contentious losers. The druggist from Broward's Rock was shaking his head in disgust. Wells stepped around him and reached out to clap Bobby Frazier on the shoulder, and she heard snatches of his low-voiced command, "...arresting you...murders of Corinne Webster and Idell Gordon. I wish to inform you of your rights..."

Those near enough to hear stood still to listen, but most of the Mystery Night participants continued to press noisily toward the platform. Lightning flickered on the horizon.

From her vantage point, Annie saw Bobby's head jerk back, but he made no move to escape Wells's grasp. His eyes searched the crowd. She looked, too.

Gail stood at the other end of the platform, caught up in a milling stream of people. She stood on tiptoe, her eyes wide, her face stricken. She struggled to push her way past the crowd, and she began to scream.

"No, he didn't do it. He didn't!"

Bobby started toward her, but Wells yanked his arm. Bobby gave one last despairing look, then walked with Wells to the circular drive where a police car waited.

Stymied by the surging crowd, Gail turned and ran toward the platform steps. She stumbled up them in her haste and darted to Annie. As she yanked the microphone away, her voice, high and strident, boomed across the night. "I killed my aunt! I killed Corinne Webster and Idell Gordon. I did it!"

Lucy huddled on a chair beside Gail's bed, clinging to the girl's hand. The convulsive sobs were beginning to ease.

John Sanford closed his bag and motioned for Annie to come out into the hall.

He rubbed a hand against the stubble on his chin. He looked tired and thin and irritated. "The girl's about to snap. That shot will take hold pretty soon. For Christ's sake, what got into her? What a damn fool thing to do! I've known that kid since she was born. She couldn't kill a cat. Frazier probably did it. A guy like him would never pass up a chance to marry millions." He took a deep breath. "Look, I've got surgery in the morning. I need to get home, get some sleep, but I want you to take this." He opened his bag and lifted out a couple of tablet samples of Valium. "See that Lucy takes these and goes to bed. She's about ready to collapse."

After he left, she eased open the door and stepped back inside Gail's room. The girl's breathing had slowed. Despite her efforts to stay awake, her eyelids kept flickering shut.

Annie walked across the room and stood beside Lucy, who never even looked up, her gaze locked on Gail's pale face. Sanford was right. Lucy needed help, too. She hunched in the chair like an aged crow in bright garb, her red and gold silk dress a shocking contrast to her grieving face.

Annie gently touched her shoulder.

Lucy slowly looked up, her eyes full of distress. "This is so hideous, so dreadful. To see Gail scream and cry..." Tears slipped down her cheeks, staining the silk of her dress, falling as gently and steadily as the spring rain against the windows.

"Shh now. She's asleep. It will be better tomorrow."

Lucy lifted the flaccid hand, held it to her cheek. "She loves him terribly. Oh, God. What are we going to do?"

Annie felt incredibly weary. The delicate Dresden clock on the bedside table chimed twice. Two A.M.

"We can't do anything more tonight. Max is seeing about a lawyer for him, but I'm afraid it pretty well tore it when he confessed, too, after Gail did. Wells got it down. And that seems to me pretty much all they'll need since they found a pencil with his fingerprints on it in Idell's office."

"A pencil?"

"Wells thinks it fell out of his shirt pocket. He always carried a couple of extra pencils there."

Lucy lifted her chin. "He could have gone by Idell's office that night just to talk to her, to see what she knew, then decided to keep quiet when she was found dead."

"He says he went by to talk to her about the reward—and what she thought she knew. That's when he says he dumped cyanide in the sherry, too."

It was almost three by the time Annie got Lucy settled at her house, though she refused the Valium. Returning to the Inn through the steady rain, Annie felt like she'd been flattened by a bulldozer. Max wasn't in his room. Was he still at the jail, or was he trying to explain to a bewildered lawyer the ins and outs of a complicated case: Two dead women, two confessed murderers, one in jail, one ignored.

She sat down in the lumpy chair next to the window. The shutters hadn't been closed for the night. The tan-colored Society building looked insubstantial in the rain. That was where it all started. No, not really. It had begun years ago, when Corinne Prichard Webster began her imperious course through life. That was the beginning, Corinne's arrogance, Corinne's absolute determination to control. But the end of her life had been determined in that quiet building. And the end of Idell Gordon's life had been determined the night she looked out her window and saw someone she knew leaving the Society late at night.

Who had she seen?

Annie jolted upright.

Not Bobby, for God's sake.

Idell was a born gossip. Her mouth never stopped clacking. She talked whether she had anything to say or not. The appearance of Bobby Frazier coming out of the Society Building late at night would have been startling. She certainly would have mentioned it to someone. That meant—Annie pressed her fingers hard against her temples. She was tired, so damn tired, but she knew she was close to a revelation. It meant the person Idell saw that night was someone she knew whose late night appearance at the Society was surprising but not shocking.

A Board member.

She jumped up, began to pace, then gradually her eagerness flagged. Okay, a Board member. They'd been there before: Lucy, Sanford, Gail, Roscoe, Edith, Sybil, Miss Dora. Even the appearance of Leighton would not have surprised Idell. He could have been running an errand for Corinne.

So all she'd done, in her own mind at least, was clear Bobby. And probably Tim.

Damn, damn, damn. It was impossible, a mess. They'd never get it right. And she was too tired to take another step or think another thought. Suddenly, she had an overpowering desire to lie down and sink fathoms deep into sleep. The bed was covered with Mystery Night materials, dumped without any attempt at order as Max hurried to get to the police station and Annie to the Prichard House. Wearily, she began to move the boxes. At least the Sticky Wicket murder was history now. Too bad the clues to Corinne's murder couldn't be tabulated as neatly. Physical clues like snapping red flags. But, actually, actions pointed toward the murderer, too, because murder arose from actions: Lord Algernon's repeated involvement with other women, his wife's jealousy, her avid dependence upon gambling, her desperate efforts to extricate herself from debt, all leading up to the final moment when she struck down her tormentor. And the obvious and pathetic attempts of her loyal maid to—

Annie stood in the middle of the room, clutching a poster container.

Actions.

Images flooded Annie's mind, Corinne's imperious will to rule, the abiding anger resulting from love denied, the conspiratorial eagerness of Idell Gordon to talk, talk, talk, the location of the pond, the telltale placard describing the superstitions of the Low Country, Miss Dora's desperate assertion of

Annie's guilt, the croquet mallet with her own fingerprints, a few smudged, Idell's certainty that more money could be had for silence, her offer of sherry to her murderer.

And Annie knew with certainty who had murdered Corinne Webster and Idell Gordon.

She walked back to the chair, dropped into it, and absently put the poster container atop the air conditioner. She knew, and she took no pleasure in knowing.

But Bobby was in jail, and Bobby could be convicted of murder. Would a jury understand his confession, understand it was a last, desperate, foolish attempt to protect the girl he loved?

Only one thing could save Bobby Frazier.

She jumped up, began to pace. Once, she reached out and touched the phone, ready to call Chief Wells.

But he would never believe her.

She continued to pace.

One action she could take. It would be a gamble. It could have no effect, or it could result in another death.

She didn't want to do it. It was a fateful step. But, finally, she reached out and picked up the telephone and dialed.

It was answered after one ring.

"Yes."

"You killed Corinne. And Idell."

Silence. Annie could hear her own heart hammering.

"How did you know?"

As Annie spoke, her own voice was equally

weary. She listed her reasons, then said, "You know, only one thing will save Bobby Frazier—your confession."

There was no answer. Perhaps the lightest of sighs, then the connection was broken.

Annie wedged a straight chair beneath the doorknob. She moved the rest of the materials from the bed and turned off the light. She lay down, but her eyes didn't close for a long, long time as she watched the tiny line of light that seeped beneath the door. It was almost an hour later that she heard Max come into his room. She wanted very much to call to him, but this decision had been hers and hers alone. She would carry it by herself. She listened to the falling rain.

Max carried the last of the boxes into Death on Demand, then he turned and faced Annie.

"What's going on?"

"What do you mean?"

"Love, I've known you when you were up and when you were down. I've made love to you in the moonlight, danced with you until dawn, witnessed table piggery unbounded, admired your intellect, your serve, and your verve—and I've never known you to say less than three thousand words a minute since the day we met. So something is screwy as hell this morning. I know we haven't had breakfast, and we drove our cars separately back to the ferry, but you haven't said anything but uh-hun and hmm since we got back to the store.

You haven't even commented on the strategy the Atlanta lawyer has in mind for Bobby Frazier. So what gives?"

The bell rang as the front door of Death on Demand opened.

She looked past Max up the central aisle of the store.

Bobby Frazier, his eyes red-rimmed, his jaws covered with the stubble of beard, walked toward them.

Tears brimmed in her eyes. "The case is over," she said, and she reached out to grab Max's hand.

"Over? How can it be over?"

But she was watching Bobby.

He held out his hand, palm up. A cream-colored envelope bore Annie's name in a sloping, feminine script.

"I had to lean like hell on Wells to get it for you. But she wrote this to you, and I knew you should get it." His mouth twisted down. "Sometimes it's handy to be a reporter—when you're not in jail. I even threatened him with false arrest. But he had her other note, her confession." He swallowed jerkily. "She's dead. She had some more of the cyanide."

"Dead. Who's dead?" Max demanded.

They spoke at once, Bobby's voice somber, Annie's tear-choked.

"Lucy Haines."

24

LUCY HAINES!" MAX'S voice rose in astonishment. "How did you know? How did you ever guess?"

"Because of the way people acted." She managed a lopsided smile. "You know how your mother tells you actions speak louder than words? By God, they do. They really do. Just think for a moment:

"Who was crazy about Gail, and saw her chance for love and happiness being destroyed by the same person who had destroyed her own years ago?

"Who was distraught with unhappiness after Corinne was murdered?

"Who implied she'd broken off with Cameron, but *everyone* else remembered it the other way—and collective memory is what you call history.

"Who was a part of Chastain, by birth, by breeding, by social position? Who would Miss Dora protect?

"Who lived next door to the pond and could waylay Corinne there after calling for a meeting?

"Who knew all about the Mystery Nights and the croquet mallet?

"Who always wore gloves when dressed—

but didn't have gloves on when arriving at the murder scene? Who helped me get Corinne out of the pond and thereby accounted for her muddied clothes?

"Who would Idell offer sherry to?" A tear slipped down Annie's cheek. Automatically, Max handed her his handkerchief, which she took gratefully. "So I phoned Lucy and told her I knew."

Max gripped her shoulders. "Why didn't you tell me? My God, what a stupid chance to take. What if she'd come after you?"

"I didn't think she would. She was so tired, tired of it all. And Gail meant more to her than anything, even her own safety. I didn't think she would come." Her voice was grave. "But I put a chair underneath the doorknob."

"And waited for dawn." Bobby looked at her admiringly.

"I hated doing it."

"You should have called me." For once there was no life and humor in Max's voice, just puzzlement and pain. She knew it was important for him to understand. She reached out, held his hands. "I knew I could. Believe me, I know I can always call you. But sometimes you have to do things on your own. I had to do this."

He pulled her into his arms, held her tightly for a moment. "All right," he said gruffly, into her hair. "All right." Then, jamming his hand through his thick blond hair, he herded them toward a table. "I don't know about you, Bobby, but Annie and I haven't had any breakfast coffee."

The reporter hesitated, but Annie took his

hand. "Sanford said Gail would sleep 'til afternoon."

They sat at the table nearest the back wall. Max made wonderfully hot and strong Kona coffee, and Bobby told them what he knew.

"She called Wells this morning. Told him to come over, she had information about the murders, that the front door would be unlocked. She left two sealed letters. In the one to the chief, she said she killed Corinne and Idell. That was all."

Annie looked down at her letter. The penmanship looped gracefully, *Miss Annie Laurance,* in the center of the pale lavender envelope. Taking a deep breath, she picked it up, opened it.

Dear Annie,

I wanted you to know that I decided before you phoned that my only recourse was to inform Harry Wells of the truth. Please do not feel that you precipitated my death. That would grieve me, just as I am grieved over the course of events this past week.

I know this must sound odd to you and self-serving, but I am grieved and remorseful. I did not intend to follow this path.

[There was a splotch of ink, a word scratched out.]

But in this last watch of my night, I must be absolutely honest. I don't know exactly what was in my heart.

When I wrote the letter, and Idell did see me leave the Society building late that night of March 19, I am afraid I was pleased with myself. I was going to make Corinne suffer. But did I then intend to take her life? I would like to think not. To be truthful, I don't know.

I hated Corinne. She lied to Cameron, convinced him I was interested in him for his wealth, and he went away and met and married someone else. Yes, I hated Corinne for that.

And I hated the way she treated those around her, poor Leighton and Edith who tried so hard and talented Tim. Everyone who came within her orbit was drawn close and destroyed.

But, most of all, I hated what she was doing to Gail. Gail is so like her father, trusting and open and generous. I wouldn't have chosen Bobby Frazier for her, but then, that's where Corinne and I differed. I loved Gail, and I would not try to choose for her.

You were right in what you said. It should have occurred to everyone that I lived closest to the pond. I was on my way early to help out with the gala, and I came upon Gail and Bobby quarreling. I could see Corinne's hand, see her succeeding again, as she had succeeded against me. I went back to the house. I was so angry, I paced up and down, up and down. Finally, I called Corinne and argued with her. She was furious. She told me it was none of my concern and that her decision was irrevocable. I didn't know that Gail and Bobby had talked again, and they were going to continue to see each other, no matter what Corinne did. I don't know if I would have acted differently if I had known. But I didn't know, and I asked Corinne to meet me at the pond.

Perhaps that reveals the truth of the matter, for why did I choose the pond? I could have gone to Prichard House; she could have come here. But in my mind I knew that the Mystery Night clues would be in place—and the croquet mallet.

We met, and we quarreled, and she turned to leave, imperious as always. I snatched up the mallet and struck her down.

When it was done, I threw the mallet into the water, then I leaned over Corinne. She was still breathing. It was dreadful and I hate remembering it, but I pulled her into the water—and left her to drown. My gloves, and you were clever to see that I must have been wearing them, were wet. I pulled them off and wadded them up and threw them into the center of the pond. My shoes and dress were wet, too, but I waited by the gate, knowing someone would soon find her and I could dash into the pond. Of course, I heard your screams when you found Corinne, and I came.

As for Idell, she called and said she was going to try for Leighton's reward, unless I could do better than the $5,000. She suggested $10,000. I told her I would bring some money during the Mystery Night program. That afternoon, I went to the Museum. The back door is never locked during working hours, and I slipped down the stairs to the basement. I've been on the Museum Board for years, and I knew all about the electroplating—and the cyanide of potassium. I took some with me in a plastic medicine vial. During the Mystery Night, I walked up to the Inn and went to the office door. Idell and I visited. She wasn't worried. After all, the desk clerk would hear if she called out. We each had a glass of sherry. I told her I thought it was excellent and shouldn't we have another to celebrate our agreement. I was wearing gloves. I got up and stood between her and the decanter and emptied the vial into it, then poured each of us a fresh glass, and watched while she drank hers. It was very quick. I felt sick then. I emptied my second glass into the decanter, then took the glass with me, wrapped up in a paper from her desk. That night, after the mystery program was over, I threw it into the pond.

The clock has just struck five. I've listened to that clock all my life and the deep bell has always meant *'All is well.'* Now it is tolling the end. Please try to explain to Gail that I never meant for her to be hurt, and forgive me for the unhappiness I have caused.

Lucy Haines

The phone rang. With a searching glance at Annie's face, Max reached out and answered.

"Death on Demand." Then his voice relaxed. "Oh sure, Barbie, I'll be down in a little while. Anything new?"

Bobby finished his coffee, and pushed back his chair.

Max whooped on the phone. "Great. Yeah. Bring it down. Right now. No, no, don't open it."

Annie and Bobby looked at him curiously.

Max looked enormously pleased.

Bobby pushed his chair up to the table, then turned to study the watercolors. "I didn't really get a chance to see these during the Mystery Nights."

The front door bell sang, and Barbie came cheerfully down the aisle. "Hi, Annie. Hi, Max. Glad to see you guys back. Been having fun?" She peered at them more closely. "Gee, you look beat." Turning to Max, she thrust a small parcel into his hands. "Here's the package from London."

"Thanks, Barbie. I'll be down in a little while."

She smiled and left.

He took Annie by the arm and steered her up the central aisle to the diagonal shelving that held all the Agatha Christies.

He held out the parcel. "A little something for you."

Max did love a dramatic production. It was probably a first edition of one of her favorites, *Cat Among the Pigeons* or *The Hollow*.

She found some scissors at the main desk and carefully slit open the package. Reaching inside, she felt her first twinge of puzzlement. Not a book. Odd, that felt like a frame—

She pulled it out and lifted it to look. There was clear glass on both sides. Sandwiched between the plates of glass was a single sheet of extremely thin paper, the aerogram used in England during World War II. The writing was small, to conserve space.

7 May 1943
Highgate

My dearest Max,

I am involved in such an absurd project, and I don't quite know how it came about. Stephen Glanville is to blame. He's bullied me into setting a detective story in Ancient Egypt! I resisted at first, but now I am quite into it and...

The letter continued with a reference to the shortage of eggs and news of friends in the theater, a discussion of Iago's character, and how Rosalind, expecting her first child, was feeling.

Annie read it through in a rush, looked up at Max, eyes wide, read it again, then flung herself into his arms.

"Max, Max, Max! Where ever did you get it? How did you possibly find a letter from Agatha Christie to her husband during the War? Oh, my God, she was writing *Death Comes As The End*. How did you do it?"

He smiled cherubically. "I just called around, nudged some people. You like it?"

"Like it? Like it!" She held the framed letter to the light, trying to decide where it would fit best on the shelf. Then she turned to him, "Max, you're wonderful."

He nodded complacently.

"What can I ever do—" She stopped short, looked at him in growing understanding.

He knew when to attack. "Actually, you know, I've been thinking about September."

She nodded in complete understanding.

"And I think you're right about a wedding here on Broward's Rock."

She was speechless.

"Of course," he held up an admonishing finger, "I thought up an innovation or two."

"Oh?"

"Yes, a lovely, simple wedding at St. Mary's-By-The-Sea, then I'd like to plan the rest of it." He smiled his best, most Maxish smile.

"It's the latest thing." His voice was at its smoothest, most persuasive. "You know, you've read all about it in the *New York Times,* the three-day wedding. We'll invite everybody, at my expense, of course, to the Island. We'll have a bachelor's golf game on Friday, and you can plan a tennis tournament for the bridesmaids, and a dinner that night at the club, then the wedding Saturday morning, and perhaps a regatta in the afternoon. On Sunday, we can—"

She looked at the precious framed letter and then at Max. Was she a pigheaded, stiff-necked, class-conscious spoilsport? Perhaps it was time to fish or cut bait. If she married Max, she married his millions. After all, marriage was for better or worse.

She was turning to step into his arms, when Bobby called out, "Hey, Annie!"

She gave Max a just-a-minute look and turned toward the coffee area. "Yes?"

"How much are these paintings? Gee, I'd love to buy them. I collect hard-boileds."

"Do you know them all?"

"Sure." He pointed to the paintings in order. "The first picture is Sam Spade in *The Maltese Falcon,* the second is Philip Marlowe in *The Big Sleep,* the third is Lew Archer in *The Moving Target,* the fourth is Travis McGee in *The Dreadful Lemon Sky,* and the last one's Spenser in *The Godwulf Manuscript.*" He grinned. "Do you suppose we'll ever find out Spenser's first name?"

CAROLYN G. HART is the author of the Death on Demand mysteries featuring Annie Darling, including *Something Wicked,* for which she won an Agatha and an Anthony; *Honeymoon with Murder,* which won an Anthony; and *A Little Class on Murder,* which won a Macavity. She is also the author of the Henrie O mysteries. She lives in Oklahoma City with her husband, Phil.